praise for if you rescue me

"This book got me at page one and never let go. Jerusha is an amazing storyteller..."

– JULIE ARDUINI, AUTHOR OF *SURRENDERING TIME SERIES*

"...hits the ground running and never lets up 'til it ends... I was drawn in from the first and held on for dear life, ending with a smile on my face, and a warm glow in my heart."

– BETTY THOMASON OWENS, AWARD-WINNING AUTHOR OF *ANNABELLE'S RUTH*

"Jerusha Agen finds the heart of a wayward child and delves inside the issues of abandonment in this awesome story of redemption."

– FAY LAMB, AUTHOR OF *STORMS IN SERENITY*

"To say [If You Rescue Me] held my attention is an understatement. Not only is it a wonderful romance, it is also a beautiful story of a Redeemer who loves and cares for the least and the dirtiest, and reaches down to save the lost from the filth and hopelessness of sin."

– READER REVIEW

If You Rescue Me

books by jerusha agen

SISTERS REDEEMED SERIES

If You Dance with Me

If You Light My Way

If You Rescue Me

GUARDIANS UNLEASHED SERIES

Rising Danger (Prequel)

Hidden Danger

Covert Danger (2022)

Unseen Danger (2023)

Falling Danger (2023)

Untitled Book Five (2024)

If You Rescue Me

JERUSHA AGEN

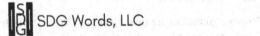

© 2022 by Jerusha Agen

Published by SDG Words, LLC
www.JerushaAgen.com

Previously published as *This Redeemer* (Write Integrity Press)

All rights reserved. No part of this publication may be reproduced, stored in a retrieval system, or transmitted in any form or by any means—for example, electronic, photocopy, recording—without the prior written permission of the publisher. The only exception is brief quotations in printed reviews.

Library of Congress Control Number: 2022904488

ISBN 978-1-956683-13-4

Scripture quotations are from The ESV® Bible (The Holy Bible, English Standard Version®), copyright © 2001 by Crossway, a publishing ministry of Good News Publishers. Used by permission. All rights reserved.

This book is a work of fiction. Names, characters, places, and incidents are the product of the author's imagination or are used fictitiously. Any resemblance to actual events, locales, or persons, living or dead, is coincidental.

acknowledgments

My first thanks for this book has to go to Lt. Patrick Shrift, my brother in Christ and number one police source, without whom this novel would never have been possible. Thank you for your enthusiasm about this idea from the start and your tireless effort to make sure I had all the law enforcement information I needed to not only create the story, but to make it an accurate representation of a police officer's work, challenges, and character.

In addition, I owe a debt of gratitude to Sgt. Derrick Brown who showed infinite patience and kindness in giving me a behind-the-scenes experience of police work while answering my multitude of questions. Thanks to Sgt. Karl Lau, also, who took the time and interest to join in the effort of educating me about the police world.

While I owe a special thanks to these police officers for their help with this novel, I also want to thank them and all police officers for their sacrificial and heroic dedication to protecting and serving me and the people of all communities across our nation. You truly make a difference.

Thanks also to Angelique Daley for proofreading this and all the relaunched *Sisters Redeemed* novels. Your sharp eye for errors has been a blessing.

To all the survivors, may you find true freedom in the Redeemer, Jesus Christ

Soli Deo Gloria

one

*"For You are our Father,
though Abraham does not know us,
and Israel does not acknowledge us;
You, O Lord, are our Father,
our Redeemer from of old is Your name."*
– Isaiah 63:16

CHARLOTTE DAVIS CLOSED HER EYES. *Breathe.*

The tromp of footsteps on the stairs matched the pounding of her heart.

Tommy slammed into the apartment, smacking the door against the wall as he stumbled into the room. Patches of sweat darkened his T-shirt around his arms.

Charlotte pretended to concentrate on the bowl that sat in front of Phoebe at the table. Her hand shook as she poured cereal into the bowl. She smoothed her hand over Phoebe's damp hair. Even little kids sweated in this heat wave.

Tommy teetered farther inside and put his hand on the back

of the torn armchair to steady himself as his tilted cowboy hat finally fell off his head. "Not enough," he slurred.

Charlotte swallowed. Normal drunk was bad enough. This was really, really drunk.

"We didn't get enough." He squinted at her through red eyes.

"Is there any left?"

He grunted a laugh. "We didn't get nothin'. How's there gonna be some left?"

"Our rent is due."

He coughed and leaned harder on the armchair.

"Our rent, Tommy." Her throat constricted, warning signals blaring in her brain. *Don't push him.* She didn't know what else to do. "For this apartment. We're going to get kicked out if we don't make the payment. And there isn't any food left. What are we going to eat?"

He shook his head, drops of sweat falling off his forehead. "I'm...so...sick...of your naggin'." He punched out each word one at a time as he lifted his head to glare at her. "All you do is complain. I gotta do everything. I get the money to keep a roof over your head. You and your dumb kid, you just sit around all day." He shoved away from the armchair and stomped in her direction.

She instinctively moved to stand behind a chair, but he walked past her and went to the refrigerator. He swung open the door and looked inside.

He slammed it shut, making her start. "Where's the beer?" He opened the empty cabinets, smacking the doors so hard she thought they'd pop off the hinges.

"Where's the beer?" he yelled as he swung to face her.

Phoebe started whimpering and covered her face with her hands.

"You drank it all." Charlotte didn't meet his eyes.

Tommy shrieked, his full cheeks flushing bright red. "I told you to get me some."

He hadn't, but Charlotte couldn't say that. "I didn't have any money." Maybe that would work.

He cussed and jerked open the bottom cabinets. "Can't believe a word that comes outta your mouth. No wonder your momma hated you."

Don't listen. Just get through. Charlotte tuned out the insults Tommy kept shooting at her and looked at Phoebe instead.

Phoebe still covered her eyes, whimpering non-stop.

Charlotte was too far away to reach her, and who knew what Tommy would do if she tried to go to Phoebe now.

What was he looking for?

"Where's the money?" Tommy stood up straight, puffing a little.

Her breath left her body. How did he know? She'd been so careful. "What money?" She forced herself not to bite her lip.

That's your tell, Momma always said.

Tommy stalked toward her, hot anger spitting from his eyes. "You don't con me!"

She scurried around the table and faced him as she backed away.

"You con them other people. You don't con me. You got it?"

Her leg bumped the armchair behind her, and she scooted around it, putting the chair between herself and Tommy. "I got it." She softened her voice to pleading submission. "Really, I didn't mean to con you, Tommy. It's me, you know? Tommy? Baby?"

He stopped on the other side of the chair. The flash that had briefly given life to his dull green eyes vanished. "I know you keep extra cash somewhere. Where is it?"

They needed that. It was her only hope now that he kept getting worse. "I know you're hurting, Tommy. We've all had it rough. I know you don't really want to live like this."

3

His mouth twisted. "What are you talkin' about?" He let out a grunt. "Will you shut up that kid!" Not a question.

Phoebe swayed back and forth as she whimpered.

"It's okay, baby girl." That wasn't going to be enough.

"You shut her up, or I will."

The curl of Tommy's lips sent a surge of fear through Charlotte's veins.

She risked coming out from behind the chair to go to her daughter. Charlotte stood beside Phoebe as she put her arms around the little girl and held Phoebe's head against her. "Shhh, baby girl," Charlotte whispered. "You have to stop."

"Gimme the money."

Charlotte tried not to jump at Tommy's voice, suddenly so near. She stared at the top of Phoebe's head.

If he drank that up now, they wouldn't have anything. She had to save the money for them. He'd see that when he slept it off. "There isn't any."

He grabbed her arm and launched her away from Phoebe, crashing her into a chair that toppled, spearing her back and neck as she fell against it.

Tommy jerked toward Phoebe. "I told you to shut up!" He smacked her little face.

She shrieked, a sound that stabbed Charlotte more painfully than any chair.

Charlotte scrambled to her feet and hurried back to the table. She forced herself between them, shoving her hand into Tommy's chest. "It's in the freezer, Tommy!" she shouted up at him. "The money's in the freezer!"

He grabbed her arms, squeezing hard as his red eyes burned a hole in her. "I oughtta kill you right now."

She held her breath and stared at the crazed fury in his eyes. Did he mean it this time?

He let her go.

She didn't dare move as he went to the freezer and took out

the wad of cash. He shoved the bills in his back jeans pocket and headed for the door.

He stopped, turned back, and pointed at her. "You're lucky I don't kill you."

She closed her eyes as the door slammed shut behind him. *Breathe. Keep breathing.* They had survived.

Phoebe's sobbing broke through Charlotte's relief. The trembling started, turning Charlotte's knees wobbly as she lifted Phoebe into her arms.

Phoebe's long limbs hung to Charlotte's knees, but the girl was so skinny Charlotte had no more trouble carrying her now than when she was five.

"He's gone, baby girl," Charlotte whispered in her daughter's ear as Phoebe squeezed her neck. "Momma's here." But what good would that do the next time?

Sobs racked Phoebe's body as Charlotte held her close, Charlotte's own hands trembling on Phoebe's back. The blow to her baby girl's face stung like a stab in Charlotte's heart. She was used to taking what she got, but Tommy had never laid a hand on Phoebe. No one had.

And no one was going to again.

Charlotte clenched her jaw. She had to get Phoebe out, away from here, away from Tommy. The wild idea started Charlotte's heart fluttering. How? Where could they go?

Something green on the floor caught her eye.

"I have to put you down, baby girl." Charlotte kissed Phoebe's wet cheek. "Just for a second." She gently set Phoebe in the armchair then went to see if the green thing was what she thought.

The money. Must have fallen out of Tommy's pocket when he left.

Charlotte winced at the pain in her bruised back as she bent to pick up the thick wad of bills—the most money she'd ever had in her life. Maybe it would be enough to get them somewhere safer. But she'd have to figure out a way to get more money wherever they went. Too bad she hadn't thought more about this before. She could have planned for it.

You get out, Charlie. Momma's raspy voice echoed in Charlotte's memory. *You get away from that man and go to your daddy. I found him.*

A dying woman's confession. Or was it supposed to be a gift? Charlotte hadn't seen it that way when her mother pressed the paper with some guy's name and address on it into Charlotte's hand.

Charlotte hadn't known her daddy was lost. Just dead. Finding out he was alive didn't help anything. Just meant he had left her and Momma alone all those years, letting them rot. He never cared about his own daughter enough to take her out of the pigsty she lived in and get her away from her no-good momma. Charlotte had almost thrown the paper away, but she had stuffed it in the back of her underwear drawer instead.

"I'll be right back, baby girl." Charlotte brushed her hand over Phoebe's hair and headed for the bedroom. She dug for the paper, letting out a breath when she felt its crumpled edge. She took it out and stared at the name and address, scratched out by Momma's shaky hand.

Charlotte bit her lip. She should have just enough money to get there by bus. She hoped.

The daddy she never knew was the last person in the world she wanted to see, but she had to do it for Phoebe. Tommy didn't know a thing about Charlotte's daddy being alive, so it was the one place he'd never think to look. If she was smart about how they got there, maybe he wouldn't be able to follow them. Maybe.

Phoebe's sobs drifted into the bedroom.

Charlotte didn't have any choice. She opened another drawer and grabbed Phoebe's two outfits, stuffing them in a shopping bag. She just had to hope her deadbeat daddy would be their ticket out.

~

WAS this what freedom looked like? Charlotte held Phoebe's hand in hers as they stared at the fancy house, surrounded by the most perfect yard she'd ever seen up close.

The soft green grass, not crunchy and brown like Texas grass, was trimmed exactly to the edge of the clean brick path that led to the front door. The bushes that lined the house were neatly shaped, like somebody had threatened them with a beating if they dared put a leaf out of place. A cool breeze drifted under the large trees in the yard, chilling Charlotte's shoulders, left bare by her knit tank top.

Or maybe this place was giving her a chill. The one-story house wasn't huge like mansions she'd seen on TV, but the brick walls, arched windows, and grand entrance were unlike any place she'd been in. If she played it right, they were about to get inside this one.

She gave Phoebe's hand a squeeze as she started forward, a bitter taste seeping into her mouth. So this was how the man who abandoned her lived. The contrast between this place and the crummy apartments her mother had kept her in made Charlotte sick.

Charlotte stopped in front of the large, wooden door. Just meant this guy had more to lose. He'd be quick to pay her whatever she wanted to get out of his life fast.

And he could definitely afford to pay.

Charlotte took a deep breath and pressed the doorbell button.

A chime sounded in the house, drifting to where Charlotte waited.

"It'll be okay, baby girl," she whispered, hoping it was true.

The door pulled slowly open, and a man looked at her with brown eyes so like hers she thought she might have been staring in a mirror. "Can I help you?"

She opened her mouth to speak but closed it again.

His nose was just like hers, his chin, the too-tall forehead.

"Miss? Are you all right?" He had the nerve to ask her that.

"Are you Marcus Sanders?" The answer was obvious, but she wanted to hear him admit it.

"Yes."

"I'm your daughter."

two

"Let no one deceive himself. If anyone among you thinks that he is wise in this age, let him become a fool that he may become wise."
– 1 Corinthians 3:18

SERGEANT GABRIEL KELLY unbuckled his seatbelt as he came up on the block of the disturbance call. He didn't need anything to slow him down for this one. Domestic violence calls were unpredictable enough without adding suspicious vehicles to the mix.

Car G-14 waited just ahead, parked next to the curb. Officer Pete Reed stood next to the squad with his rookie partner, Jim Malloy.

The two officers turned in Gabe's direction as he slowly pulled up, his gaze moving from them to scan the empty street, the sunlit yard in front of the poorly-tended gray house they staged by, the rose bushes lining the next lawn—the last piece of grass between them and the little yellow house he knew all too well.

Gabe tugged at the neck of the body armor under his shirt and got out of the car as Pete approached. "What have you got, Pete?"

Pete nodded to the red sedan parked up the street. "Car matches the description and plate numbers of the getaway vehicle at the robbery on Taylor twenty minutes ago. It's stolen."

"You were here for the DV?"

Pete nodded. "Neighbor phoned it in. Said a woman was screaming. Not a peep since we got here."

Gabe looked at the side of the quiet little yellow house he could glimpse from this hidden vantage point. "Peggy Greer's place."

"Think it's her brother again?" Pete wiped his hand across the beads of sweat on his forehead.

"Probably, but that wouldn't explain the car. He doesn't have robbery on his record." Gabe tried not to think about the heat building inside his own navy blue, polyester uniform shirt, layered over body armor. At least Pennsylvania summers weren't nearly as hot as he had been used to in Texas.

"How do you want to handle it?"

"Let's—"

A woman's scream cut through the thick air. Something crashed in the yellow house, loud enough to carry the distance.

"We're going in." Gabe drew his gun and nodded to Pete. "Cover the back." Gabe glanced at the rookie. "Jim, you're with me."

Gabe darted across the first yard at an angle and gripped his lapel mic. "Four Adam 224, Dispatch. We're making entry."

"Two twenty-four, 10-4." The woman's voice crackled over the radio.

Gabe stayed low as he moved and glanced behind to be sure Jim was doing the same.

He was, gripping the patrol rifle as he followed Gabe. Probably the first time the kid had to carry the rifle. Hopefully, he wouldn't have to use it.

Another scream prompted Gabe to pick up the pace as he followed the line of bushes for concealment in the second yard.

Pete split off and disappeared from view, moving quickly to the back of the house.

Gabe and Jim reached the front wall and ducked under a shaded window on the way to taking their positions by the door. His weapon ready, Gabe pressed his back against the chipped siding and made eye contact with Jim.

The rookie nodded.

"Police!" Gabe kicked the door open. He swept the gun with his gaze across the room.

Peggy Greer sprawled on the floor, leaning against a toppled armchair, a broken table and crushed glass around her. Blood seeped from a cut on her leg. Her lip was bloodied, her cheeks wet with tears.

Gabe clenched his jaw. "Where is he, Peggy?"

"The window..." She choked out the words between shaky sobs. "He just went out the window. In the bedroom."

"Does he have a weapon?"

She managed to nod. "A gun."

Gabe glanced at Jim. "Stay with her." Gabe moved quickly to the bedroom, thankful he'd been to the house before and knew the layout. There was no guarantee Pete would catch Peggy's brother if he went out the side instead of the back. And he was armed this time.

Gabe covered the kitchen and bathroom doorways with his gun as he went, trying to get to the bedroom as fast as he could without being suckered. He reached the bedroom doorway and peered in, gun ready.

Nothing but an open window.

Peggy screamed from the living room. Not the desperate scream of before, but a lower-pitched, angry yell.

Gabe ran back the way he came, heart pounding. *What in the world?*

Jim cried out as Gabe reached the living room.

Peggy hung on Jim's back, her hand clutching the knife she had plunged into his shoulder.

Jim's rifle lay on the floor in front of him.

With Jim between Gabe and the woman, shooting was out. Gabe holstered his gun as he rushed behind the crazed woman and yanked her off, pulling her to the floor while she kicked and yelled. He cuffed her as fast as he could subdue her flailing arms and turned to Jim.

The rookie slumped to the floor, the knife still in his shoulder as he leaned against the same chair where they had found the battered woman.

"Hang in there, Jim. You'll be fine." Gabe grabbed his lapel mic as he picked up the rifle and checked that the safety was on. "Four Adam 224, Dispatch."

An eternity seemed to pass before the response. "Two twenty-four."

"Officer down with stab wound to upper torso and severe bleeding. Still conscious. Send EMS. Also need EMS for injured suspect." He answered dispatch's responding questions on autopilot, watching the woman on the floor.

She was subdued now that she was cuffed, simpering and crying like she had the last three times he had come to this house after her older brother worked her over. The poor woman had tried so hard to pretend she had been hurt some other way, to make excuses for the brother who beat her so mercilessly. Didn't make sense. Never did.

"Five Adam 212." Pete's voice came over the radio. "Suspect in custody."

At least Pete had done his job. One more bad guy off the street.

Jim moaned.

Gabe knelt next to the rookie. "Help's on the way, buddy."

Blood seeped from the gash around the knife.

Gabe fished in his pocket for latex gloves. He'd have to do what he could to stop the bleeding before the ambulance got there.

Pain clenched his chest as if he were the one who'd been stabbed. He'd led a rookie into a trap he didn't see because of pity and concern. That kind of mistake was unforgivable. Maybe he should've called in two officers down.

THE GUY'S look was priceless. If he didn't deserve it so much, Charlotte could almost feel bad for this Marcus Sanders.

His eyes stayed as wide as saucers after she announced she was his daughter, and he opened and closed his mouth like a fish. At least he had let her step inside with Phoebe.

"I was thinking." A woman's elegant voice called from another room, followed by a long-legged blonde. "What do you think of caramel next—" Her arched brows delicately lifted above large, blue eyes as she paused, her gaze on Charlotte and Phoebe. "I'm sorry." She smiled, showing perfect white teeth. "I thought it was a delivery."

Marcus cleared his throat. Twice. "Honey, this is ... uh ..."

He shifted his gaze away from the blonde to look at Charlotte instead. "Charlotte, this," he gestured to the blonde, "is my eldest...I mean my daughter, Nye." His cheeks turned red as radishes.

Sure. Charlotte just bet he had a daughter who was a supermodel. So Daddy had a girlfriend on the side. Judging from the big bump on her otherwise stick-width frame, it looked like he'd knocked her up, too. Getting dough from this jerk might be easier than she thought.

"Nye, Charlotte is..." He stared at Charlotte, clearly still without a clue what to call her in front of his girlfriend who looked younger than the real daughter who'd just showed up.

Good grief. The guy was the worst liar she'd ever seen. "An old friend," Charlotte filled in for him. Might as well show she was willing to help him out...for a price.

"Nice to meet you." The supermodel held out her manicured hand, but Charlotte grabbed Phoebe's little hand and held it instead.

"Well," her smile left her eyes, but held at the white teeth, "I should probably get going."

"No." Marcus blinked as if he surprised himself with the quick reaction. "Will you stay for a bit, honey? I have to talk to Charlotte privately, but I'd like it if you stayed."

The girlfriend touched her slim fingers to his sleeve. "Sure. I need to clean up a few more things in the kitchen anyway."

The kitchen? Charlotte fought the urge to roll her eyes. She thought the affair with the beautiful maid only happened on TV.

Marcus looked everywhere but at Charlotte after the supermodel left the room. At least he had the decency to feel somewhat ashamed, or at least awkward. He probably didn't know what decency was. Rich people like him loved to look down their noses at people like her and Tommy, judging them for how they lived, but this guy was ten times worse.

He had left his own daughter and never cared if she was alive or dead. Now he was playing around with some supermodel, probably while his unsuspecting wife was out shopping for more beautiful things for their beautiful house.

Charlotte blinked back the moisture that sprang to her eyes. This loser was not going to see any sadness from her. "Look, I can see you have a nice setup here for yourself." She'd just get the pitch over with and get out. "I don't need to ruin it. I just need some help to get back on the road."

Phoebe whimpered and tugged on Charlotte's hand.

Charlotte looked down to see the little girl sag like she was about to sit on the floor. "Can we sit down somewhere?" They'd do better to beat it fast, but Phoebe was awfully tired. "We came a long way."

"We—" His voice caught. He cleared his throat again. "We can go to my study."

Charlotte kept a hold on Phoebe's hand as they cautiously followed him through a dark room with a huge pool table and ended up in another room with a fireplace, desk, and manly, oversized sofa and armchairs. The guy was richer than she'd thought.

He watched them as Charlotte led Phoebe to the sofa, where the little girl sat down, keeping herself rigid at the edge of the cushion, despite her exhaustion. Two days of riding a bus and hitching might've worn her out, but it hadn't killed her survival instinct.

People didn't think Phoebe was bright, but Charlotte knew the girl could sense they weren't welcome here just as much as Charlotte could.

"What's your little girl's name?" Marcus gazed at Phoebe with a hint of softness around his eyes.

Was that kindness or something else? Who knew how far this guy's problems went. She stepped in front of Phoebe, blocking his view of her. "Phoebe."

His eyes jerked to her face.

She had his attention now. "Same as my momma's name. Phoebe Davis." She watched the words hit their mark.

"Impossible." His eyes took on the empty stare of someone who had drifted years away. "I don't have any other daughters."

"So you don't remember her?" That figured. He probably had a dozen girlfriends he didn't remember.

"No, I...I do remember her. I just...I knew her for such a short time. I..." He sank into an armchair like he'd fall down if the chair wasn't there.

"I was born thirty-three years ago on July twenty-eighth, if you want to know. Nine months earlier was October. My mother went to Texas U same as you."

He stared at nothing beyond him. Was he in shock?

"Is there anything else you want to know? I can give you whatever facts you need to be convinced."

"Dear Lord...It can't be." His eyes shined like they were wet.

Was he that shocked she had found him? That she'd showed up now? She was threatening to crash his whole life. That would be hard to swallow.

She crossed her arms. "If you're worried about your family finding out, I won't have to tell them. For a price. All I want is enough money to pay for a hotel or apartment somewhere for my kid."

The moisture threatened to spill from his eyes as he continued to stare at the wall.

"Just for tonight." She couldn't believe she was taking pity on this man after all he'd done, but she would back off a little for the moment. She could come back tomorrow and get more, enough for them to get set up somewhere Tommy wouldn't find them.

The guy didn't react. Like he wasn't even hearing her anymore.

She grabbed Phoebe's hand and pulled her up, turning to face the man again. "Do you have enough for that, at least?"

He finally looked at Charlotte, his eyes moving over her face as if he was trying to analyze every feature.

"We just need enough to stay overnight."

"Okay." He rose from the chair. His fingers shook as he pulled a wallet out of his pocket and gave her two hundred dollars in cash.

He was way richer than she'd thought.

She hid her surprise as she took the money and shoved it in her pocket. Getting more shouldn't be hard at all. "This will be enough for now, but you'll have to give me more if you want me to leave without telling anyone." She turned away and started to lead Phoebe from the room. "I'll be back tomorrow."

When she reached the next room with the pool table, there was a noise. She paused. Had he called to her? She could almost imagine he had asked her to wait.

Charlotte shook her head and continued forward, trying to banish the little-girl dream for the daddy she had needed.

STAY WITH HER. Gabe slid his palms over his face as if that could erase his frustration or the memory of his words to Jim. Why had he left the rookie alone with that woman?

Lieutenant MacDonald pushed through the doors of the hallway and headed across the ER waiting room.

Gabe stood to his feet, searching the lieutenant's neutral expression to determine Jim's fate.

The lieutenant stopped in front of Gabe as his lips pressed together in a half-smile. "He's going to make it."

Gabe let out the breath he didn't know he'd been holding.

"He hadn't lost too much blood thanks to you."

Gabe shook his head. "He doesn't have any reason to thank me."

The lieutenant met Gabe's gaze with understanding in his eyes. "He will be out of commission for a while. The doctor said it could take six months of therapy for him to get that arm working again. I guess the knife hit the wrong place."

Gabe winced, remembering the knife protruding from Jim's shoulder as he'd lain against the chair, his mouth twisted in pain.

The lieutenant put his hand on Gabe's all-too-healthy shoulder. "I know you feel responsible. As his superior officer, you have a reason to. But your tactics were sound. It wasn't your fault."

"And here I thought you might say 'I told you so.'" Gabe gave the lieutenant a sardonic smile that he couldn't keep up for more than a second. "We both know the truth, L.T. You were the one who told me a hundred times in training to stop assuming the best about people."

"The truth is," his gaze was as firm as his tone, "Jim never should have turned his back on that woman. It was a rookie mistake, and he'd be the first to say he made it."

"I thought she was a victim, too. I wouldn't have left him alone with her otherwise. And if that robbery suspect hadn't been fleeing at the same time..."

"And if and if..." The lieutenant lowered his hand but kept his eyes on Gabe. "Don't do that to yourself, Gabe. The Monday morning crowd will second guess you enough as it is. The fact is, you made the same call most of us would have in that scenario. You had a history with her, and you had a fleeing suspect. It just turned out to be the wrong call this time."

"Thanks." The frustration curdling in Gabe's stomach hadn't faded a bit, but the lieutenant didn't give that kind of support to everyone.

"And don't worry about the review."

Gabe hadn't even thought about it. Now his stomach had another reason to churn, with nerves this time.

"You'll come out just fine." The lieutenant looked at his watch. "Jim's wife is in the room with him now. I thought you might want to be the one to drive her home?"

Gabe nodded.

"I'd like to give you a day or two off, but you know how thin we're stretched."

"That's fine. I'd rather get back at it."

"Good call. I'll see you tomorrow."

"Right." Gabe didn't watch the lieutenant leave. Instead, he stared at the doors to the hallway where Jim lay, his wife probably holding his hand, maybe crying. *Thank You, Lord, that it wasn't worse.*

At least Jim would still be able to use his arm...eventually. He could have been killed. And it would have been Gabe's fault.

Despite what the lieutenant said, Gabe couldn't shake the guilt. If only he hadn't been so distracted and so sure Peggy wasn't dangerous.

Gabe sank down in the chair and rested his head in his hands. Momma had sure done a good job teaching her boy to treat women well. Too good. Seemed like he was still trying to protect and cherish every one of them, as if they were all her—sweet, victimized women just trying to break free.

Momma hadn't met women like the ones on these streets. Even she wouldn't have trusted them. Today was the last time he would.

three

> "For nothing is hidden except to made manifest; nor is anything secret except to come to light."
> – Mark 4:22

THE DOOR swung open before Charlotte's knuckles touched the wood.

Marcus stood in the opening, his face pale, eyes rimmed in red. Probably not from booze.

Charlotte glanced down at Phoebe beside her and tried to squash the unexpected twinge of guilt. The guy had left her alone for thirty-three years. He didn't deserve her pity.

"Come in. Please." He moved to the side and stuck out his hand like they were some grand guests instead of family crashers.

Charlotte held tight to Phoebe's hand as they passed him into the house.

"I'm sorry about yesterday." He still wore expensive-looking formal clothes, a tie over his dress shirt and everything, but he didn't look so polished anymore. He was crumpled and worn.

He smoothed a hand over his brown hair, a little darker than hers. "I was so shocked...I just didn't know how to react. When you were born...well—would you like to sit down? I'm sorry. Come over here." He led them to the sofas that were in the open room by the entry.

Charlotte sat next to Phoebe this time, both of them perched near the edge of the cushions while Charlotte kept a hold of Phoebe's hand.

Marcus went to a chair farther away but seemed to change his mind and walked closer instead, sitting on the fancy glass coffee table in front of them. He met Charlotte's gaze. "The time you were born coincides with...when I knew your mother. I can't deny you're my daughter. Just looking at you, I know it's true."

He glanced away, squeezing one of his hands in the other. "I just wish I had known." His voice caught. He pressed his lips together for a second then turned his gaze to her again. "I am so sorry. So sorry that I never knew about you."

She blinked at him as his voice grew thick, like he could barely get the words past the emotion.

"I never would have left you, Charlotte. I would have been in your life."

A lump moved up her throat and lodged there.

One tear dropped down his cheek as his eyes bored into hers.

Had he really not known about her? It would be like her mother to never have told him. Very like her to make Charlotte suffer more. Maybe he hadn't even lied about the chick at the house yesterday. Maybe she really was his other daughter.

Charlotte cleared her throat, trying to get rid of the lump. Even if it was true he hadn't known about her, there was no way he'd want anything to do with her now. He had his own family.

One look at his rich house and his clothes told her he wouldn't want anything to do with a loser like her.

A clang burst from the other room, making Charlotte start and drop Phoebe's hand.

"It's just my wife. Caroline. I think she's fixing lunch."

His wife. That should be fun. "Did you tell her?"

"I did."

"Bet that went over well." Her tone signaled she was actually betting the opposite.

"It's a shock for all of us."

"All of you?"

"I have two daughters. Nye, whom you met, and Oriana."

"Oh." He'd told them that fast? The guy was either brave or stupid. Either way, there was no hope now for getting a payoff to keep quiet. She could still press him for money to make up for the years of neglect. He seemed to feel guilty right now.

Her gaze fell on his hands, resting on his knees. They were manly, strong-looking hands, the skin a little weathered and freckled with age. They were just like the ones she used to imagine pushing her on a swing, handing her an ice cream cone, or holding her hand.

She bit her lip and stood. "Come on, Phoebe."

He looked up at her. "Where are you going?"

"Away." She headed for the door.

"Would you stay here?"

She stopped.

"With us?"

She slowly turned. Had she heard him right?

His expression looked sincere as he stood by the table. "Please, I'd love to have you here. I want my family to meet you, and I want to get to know you." He walked closer to her. "I just found out about you. I can't let you go so soon."

Could it be true? She wanted to believe he hadn't known,

that he wanted to love her now. But stuff like that didn't happen in real life. Not in hers, anyway.

She reached to take Phoebe's hand and leave, but the waiting hand wasn't there. She jerked her gaze to the living room.

Phoebe still sat on the sofa, watching Charlotte and Marcus.

Charlotte stared at her daughter. Phoebe always followed, always clinging. Did she want to stay? Maybe Phoebe knew they didn't have the money to go anywhere else.

Charlotte chewed on her lip as thoughts battled in her mind. Tommy would never think to look for them here, would he? But could she stay in a house filled with people who didn't want her there? That situation would be no different than anywhere else. At least here, no one would try to kill them. At least, she didn't think so.

Marcus held out his hand to her, that familiar hand from her little-girl dreams. "Please?" He smiled gently.

Looking at the hopeful lift of his eyebrows, she could believe, just for an instant, that he really did want her there.

He could be faking. He might turn out to be mean and hate her.

She nodded, not ready to take his hand. Whichever way things panned out, at least she'd finally find out what it was like to have a daddy.

"ABOUT TIME YOU SHOWED UP."

Gabe turned to see Oriana approach with Sunny from the entrance to the Christian Community Center. Gabe shook his head. Despite her blindness, Oriana always knew who he was without a word from him.

He smiled down at the beautiful golden retriever at her side.

"I know what you're both hoping for." Oriana faked a sigh.

"Okay." She bent to unhook Sunny's harness and let the wiggling dog go to Gabe.

Gabe crouched down to meet him. "Hey, Sunny. How's my boy?" He ruffled the golden's soft fur as the dog wagged his whole body.

"Sometimes I think God gave me Sunny more for everyone else than for me, the way he loves to cheer people up."

Gabe looked up at Oriana's infectious smile. "The rest of us need it more." He gave Sunny a pat on his side and stood.

"Glad to hear you admit it. Even I can tell you've been carrying a rain cloud with you everywhere you go lately."

"And just how can you tell that?"

"Barometric pressure." Her smile stretched bigger as Gabe laughed. "I've been wondering what happened to that laugh."

"You've probably also been wondering about these donations." He turned to the stack of boxes he had set on the faded blacktop of the small parking lot. "Want to show me where they go?"

"Where are they from?"

"Church."

"Oh, that'll be the books and toys." She slipped Sunny's harness on him again as she spoke. "Follow me." She and Sunny gracefully turned together and led the way into the building as Gabe picked up a box and followed. "So the kids are still asking about you…if you're coming back to coach basketball."

Good thing she couldn't see the frown that settled on his face. "That's nice of them. I've meant to come by more often, but things are pretty busy at work lately." The words were true, but he doubted Oriana would buy them. "I just don't have the time for the kind of investment they need for basketball these days." Gabe followed her into the activity room where he lowered the box to the floor.

"Are you sure the time is what you're worried about?"

He didn't know how to answer that…honestly.

A rare frown tilted her mouth this time. "I know it was hard when you found Cebe hanging out with those dealers. But I'm sure you must have encountered worse. You're a police officer."

"You're right. I have." He was looking at an example. Oriana's sightless brown eyes stared at him as a reminder of the evil people were capable of. And that was all the fault of a kid she had tried to help. No wonder this job had started to get to him then. Not really the job itself, but the breed of people he had to deal with on the job.

"I know I'm famous for sticking my nose where it doesn't belong," her brow furrowed, "but something's been different with you lately. You've changed. We've all noticed. I'm mostly worried about the kids who have noticed." She tightened her grip on the strap that connected to Sunny's harness. "They aren't all like Cebe. Some are still here and learning about Jesus, about hope for a better life."

"And that's great, Oriana." Gabe's stomach clenched at the thought that he could be distressing her. "I completely support what you're doing. If I didn't, I wouldn't still be here."

"Oh, I know that, Gabe." Her fingers relaxed on the harness. "And I hope I haven't scared you off now."

"Nah, no worries." He waved her concern away with a hand, even though she couldn't see the gesture. "I love your whole family too much to get scared away from y'all that easily."

A strange look he couldn't identify crossed her face. Worry?

Whatever the expression meant, she replaced it quickly with one of her bright smiles. "Speaking of family, Mom keeps hoping you're going to bring a young lady to our Sunday brunch one of these times. She won't stop talking about all the young women who are interested in you at church."

Gabe sighed. Thanks to Peggy Greer, he was even more turned off by women than kids right now, present company excluded. "I hope Caroline doesn't get set on the idea of matching me up with someone. If she's hoping I'll get married someday, she's going to be sorely disappointed."

Oriana's brow furrowed. "I think I said the wrong thing again."

A pang of guilt made Gabe cringe. He was eternally grateful to the Sanders for bringing him into their family since they'd learned he didn't have one of his own. Getting irritated wasn't the way to show it. "I'm sorry, Oriana. That was uncalled for."

"No, I'm sorry I was being a busybody. I hope you know I don't care if you ever have a girlfriend or not. But I do wish you'd reconsider working with the kids. I never saw, figuratively speaking, of course," she added with a wink, "anyone win the kids' trust as quickly as you did."

They won his, too. That was the problem.

"Not all the kids will turn out like Cebe, and even he isn't necessarily lost forever." Oriana smiled again. "You never know what God will do."

Gabe wished he had her faith, but it was too dangerous in his line of work. Thinking like that had landed a young rookie in the ER and cut Gabe's heart more than once. He just couldn't set himself up for that kind of fall again.

CHARLOTTE FOLLOWED Caroline down the hallway, Phoebe holding on to the hem of Charlotte's tank top as they went.

Dressed in a smart red suit that showed off her slim figure, Marcus's wife carried herself like a queen as she moved through the house to give them the grand tour. She looked like an older version of the pregnant daughter with the strange name. In this family, even the grandma made Charlotte look bad.

They stopped at a bathroom that was cleaner and bigger than any Charlotte had used before.

"There are extra towels in there." Caroline pointed at closed closet doors. "As well as soap and shampoo." She looked at Phoebe. "Saturday was always bath night for our girls. We liked the family to be fresh and clean for church."

Charlotte smoothed her hand over Phoebe's oily hair. "I was going to give her a bath tonight anyway." Whatever made things easier.

Caroline smiled, a smile that didn't quite reach her cool blue eyes. "Last is your room." She stepped out of the bathroom and went a few feet to the door across the small hallway. "I hope you two don't mind sharing." She stepped inside the bedroom and turned on the light. "Our previous home had much more space for guests, but we downsized when Marcus retired."

Charlotte's gaze roamed the room and swung over the huge double bed. This house was plenty big and rich, but Caroline looked like the kind of lady who'd cost a lot to keep happy.

"We have an air mattress we can bring in." Caroline narrowed her eyes as she looked at the room. "I'll have to ask Marcus where he put it."

"No, it's fine."

Caroline arched an eyebrow.

"We can share this bed."

"If you're sure."

Charlotte nodded, hoping this was the end of the tour. Caroline obviously wasn't happy about them being there, though she was trying to cover it with smiles and politeness. If Charlotte were in Caroline's position, she wouldn't have bothered with all that, Southern rules or not. Maybe Caroline had already blown up at Marcus when he told her the news and was going to leave him soon. She'd be crazy not to.

Of course, Charlotte had never left Tommy even when she found out about his flings. But Queen Caroline didn't look like the kind of woman who'd have to put up with that.

"Well, I'll leave you to get settled then." Caroline gave her another forced smile. "If you need anything at all, let us know. Our room is at the end of the hall."

Was Caroline really letting Marcus sleep in the same room with her? Charlotte would have put money on the guess that Marcus had at least been sent to the basement.

"I'll see you in the morning. The girls are so looking forward to meeting you and Phoebe tomorrow."

Charlotte just bet they were.

"We leave at seven thirty."

Charlotte's jaw dropped. "In the morning?"

"Yes. Marcus teaches a class, and I go to the women's study, so we like to get there early."

Caroline widened her smile, as if that would make seven thirty a.m. sound bearable. "You're welcome to join my class."

"I don't get up that early." And she was not going to start now. Definitely not for church.

"Oh." Caroline's pristine smile wobbled a bit. "I think I'll just skip my class this week then." The white teeth flashed again. "That way we'll be able to ride together at nine thirty. That will get us there in time for the service."

Maybe this chick was smarter than she looked. Smart enough not to trust Charlotte alone in the house.

Charlotte nodded.

"Good night, then. Good night, Phoebe." Caroline cast her smile on Phoebe before she left the room.

Charlotte shut the door and let out a deep sigh. She turned to survey the room again. Was she dreaming that they were going to stay in such a clean, big room?

The huge bed alone was the most inviting thing she thought she'd ever seen. The bedspread was even the pretty pink color she loved but had never gotten to have in the apartment because Tommy hated it.

The thought of Tommy made her glance out the window.

The leaves of the bush outside brushed the glass with the gentle breeze.

Calm down. She tried to breathe evenly. He couldn't have found them. At least not yet. Not this fast. Fear squeezed her heart. He would find her. Only a matter of time until he did. She wouldn't be able to leave him so easily.

Phoebe tugged on Charlotte's tank top.

Charlotte looked down to see Phoebe staring at the room.

"Home?" Phoebe asked in the sweet, tiny voice Charlotte hardly ever got to hear.

"No, baby girl. Not home." Charlotte crouched down behind Phoebe and wrapped her arms around her little girl. "When we find one," Charlotte murmured against Phoebe's hair, "we won't have to be scared anymore."

CHARLOTTE'S EYES POPPED OPEN, her heart racing. Why?

Phoebe moaned as she lay beside Charlotte in the bed.

Oh. That was why. Charlotte's heart rate slowed...until someone knocked on the door.

Tommy?

"Charlotte. It's Marcus."

She still tensed. Was he riled about the noise?

"Are you all right? I heard moaning." His voice was quiet, calm, almost like he was really concerned.

"Yeah, fine. Phoebe was just having a nightmare." Not really, but a nightmare made more sense than trying to explain Phoebe's moaning fits. She had already had three that week, but Charlotte should have known there'd be more with all the stress. And a moaning fit always came after a shower or bath.

Charlotte had tried to make the shower as brief as possible, but the fear of the water had still filled Phoebe's eyes and her trembling body as the spray poured on her.

Phoebe sat up and pulled her legs to her chest. She started rocking back and forth, her eyes wide open as she moaned.

This was going to be a bad one. How could Charlotte keep her quiet here? She reached for Phoebe and pulled her close, holding her shaking body as she had done so many times on the hard staircase outside the apartment in Dallas, hoping they wouldn't wake Tommy.

Now in a fancy bed, Charlotte covered her daughter's trembling hands, icy cold as usual, hoping they wouldn't get kicked out of this place.

"Can I help somehow?"

Marcus's voice startled Charlotte. He hadn't left? "I could warm some milk, if you think that would help."

She'd think he would rather throw it at her. Or at least his wife would.

Phoebe shook against Charlotte's chest.

She pressed a hand to the little girl's damp hair. Maybe milk wasn't such a bad idea. The one time she had bought some before Tommy got his hands on the cash, Phoebe had loved it. "Yeah. Might be good."

Charlotte released Phoebe temporarily to get out of the bed and go around to where she could lift the little girl in her arms. She went to the door, Phoebe's long legs dangling as Charlotte managed to pull the knob.

Marcus stood there looking bleary-eyed, wearing a loose dark robe over silk pajamas.

He better not have any funny business in mind, hanging around her at night like this. He'd have a fight on his hands.

She might be short, but she was strong and had surprised more than one louse who tried to take more than she wanted to give. She was about to shoot him a warning glare, but he turned away and shuffled down the hallway.

She hefted Phoebe higher and followed him, watching the

stooped shoulders and tired walk she hadn't noticed earlier in the day. He was older than she thought.

They passed through the darkened living room, where a blanket and sheet lay on the sofa. "Sleeping out here?" She nodded to the evidence when he paused to look at her.

He continued to the kitchen, where he turned on the light, making them all squint as their eyes adjusted. "We're just taking a little time to get over the shock. That's all."

Was he blaming her? It was his fault.

"Yeah." Charlotte wasn't going to take the rap for his fall. "I bet she thought you'd never cheated on her before."

"I didn't cheat on her." He paused then sighed. "Well, that's not quite true." He went to the small breakfast table and pulled out a chair.

She thought he was going to sit down, but he swept his hand toward it instead, like she was supposed to take it. She went to the chair and carefully sat down, letting Phoebe's legs dangle on each side of her lap as the little girl continued to moan, more softly now.

"I wasn't married when I met your mother. Caroline and I were dating, though, so it was still cheating in that sense." He got out a pan as he talked and filled it with milk from the fridge. "We were in college, and Caroline was studying abroad in London for a semester. I met your mother at a bar one night and..." He put the lid back on the milk and returned it to the fridge, his cheeks turning red as brick. "You know the rest."

He took a few steps to stand at the table, facing Charlotte as he braced his hands on the back of a chair. "I wasn't a Christian at the time, and I made a lot of mistakes that I later realized were pretty awful."

What was he talking about? She knew a pack of church-going Christian folks, and they were the worst kind of people. Didn't mean a thing where she came from. But if he was actually sorry, it'd be good for her. If he turned out to just be a religious nut or something, she'd get out of there fast.

"Is she really okay?" He looked at Phoebe, his forehead marked with deep lines as she kept moaning.

"She will be." Charlotte stroked Phoebe's blond hair. "She does this a lot. She's just scared."

"She looks cold." He watched her for another second then walked out of the room.

Charlotte barely had time to wonder where he'd got to before he returned, carrying the blanket from the sofa.

He gently draped the soft afghan over Phoebe as she shook in Charlotte's arms.

Charlotte moved her hands to hold the blanket in place, pretending to be busy with that while she tried to figure out the strange man. Charlotte barged into his life, ruined his marriage, and even tried to blackmail him, but he was as cool as a cucumber so far. A very nice cucumber.

A knot twisted in her stomach. What was his game? He had invited them into his home. Maybe putting her where he could keep an eye on her? Or did he have something worse in mind?

Her eyes narrowed as she watched him stir the milk on the stove. Nobody was that nice for nothing. She'd have to get her guard back up with this one, or she might end up being the sucker who got taken for a ride.

four

> "... they may indeed see but not perceive,
> and may indeed hear but not understand,
> lest they should turn and be forgiven."
> – Mark 4:12

CHARLOTTE YAWNED AGAIN and tried to force her heavy eyelids open.

The gray-haired preacher had to have been talking for at least an hour. He peered through his glasses at the people who somehow managed to stay awake for all this talk. "Paul doesn't beat around the bush here." He pointed to the open book on the stand thing in front of him. "He says very clearly, 'Do not be deceived: neither the sexually immoral, nor idolaters, nor adulterers, nor men who practice homosexuality, nor thieves, nor the greedy, nor drunkards, nor revilers, nor swindlers will inherit the kingdom of God.'"

Well, that covered just about everybody. Charlotte swallowed another yawn, careful not to move enough to disturb Phoebe, who slept with her head nestled in Charlotte's side. Why would anyone even want to inherit the kingdom of God? Wouldn't do any good in the real world.

She blew out a sigh and let her gaze wander over the rows of benches next to them. She still hadn't been able to pick out Marcus's other daughter, though she'd been told the daughter would be there.

Charlotte caught plenty of stares from people on the benches.

They quickly looked away when she spotted them. Had they heard about her already? Maybe they were just making up their own stories to explain who she was. From what she'd heard, churches had the worst gossips.

She moved her gaze a little farther back, stopping on a hot guy who watched the preacher. He reminded her of some actor. What was the name?

Of course. The supermodel daughter was sitting right next to him. They were obviously made for each other. The blonde gave Charlotte a tense, close-lipped smile that didn't reach her eyes—the perfect copy of her mother's usual expression for Charlotte.

Charlotte didn't need to have finished high school to read the signs when she had arrived at the church with Caroline and Marcus, and Caroline had made sure to sit on the far side of her husband, separating herself from Charlotte and Phoebe on his other side.

Maybe Caroline and the blonde daughter would pay Charlotte to leave. She would need the money if she and Phoebe were going to make it without Tommy.

Spotting the other daughter should be easy—just look for the unhappy face. But the other faces Charlotte skimmed were all smiling.

A black lady nodded at the minister with an "Amen."

Charlotte turned to the preacher to hear what he had said to make everyone so happy, but she was only in time to see him close his eyes and start praying.

She glanced around. All the people, except a few kids here and there, closed their eyes. Did that many people really believe this stuff?

Marcus and Caroline had their eyes closed and so did the supermodel and the hot guy with her. Maybe church was as much a way of life in Pennsylvania as it was in Texas. She still bet going to church didn't make a squat of difference in these folks' lives any more than it did with Texans.

Momma always said the Bible Belt was only good for givin' a lickin.' Charlotte wasn't in the Bible Belt now, but she had a feeling she might get a bad lickin' at their family brunch today.

"Amen," the preacher finally said.

There was a light touch on Charlotte's hand.

She looked to see Marcus give her a small smile. The warmth in his eyes made her want to smile back, but Caroline watched from over his shoulder, a frown pulling at her pink, lipstick-lined mouth.

Maybe Marcus had meant something different than just kindness by the smile. Whatever he meant by it, Charlotte was sure his smile was the only thing even close to kindness she was going to get today.

THIS WAS SO AWKWARD. In all the months of going to the Sanders' house for their Sunday brunch since last Christmas, Gabe had never once felt out of place. They had welcomed him into their family like a long-lost son and given him no reason to feel like an intruder. But now the long-lost daughter had shown up.

A real long-lost daughter, according to Marcus.

The petite woman sat across from Gabe now, cleaning the

last bit of food from her plate. There was no denying her obvious resemblance to Marcus. She looked more like him than the two daughters Gabe already knew. She had the same, rounded nose, though it was smaller and cuter on her, along with the same rounded chin. Long lashes shielded the huge brown eyes he had only caught glimpses of as she darted her gaze away from anyone who looked at her.

She put her fork down on the table and just stared at the empty plate in front of her, though her rigid posture told him she was clearly alert and listening to the conversation. The awkwardness apparently hadn't ruined her appetite.

The woman's little girl still picked at her food, which her mom had cut into small pieces for her. The pretty, delicate girl picked up the portions with her fingers instead of the fork, quietly putting them in her mouth and chewing about twenty times before she swallowed.

Gabe had time to count. No one seemed to know what to say beyond empty small talk. He could track on one hand the times he had been at a loss for words in his life, but this was one of them. He wasn't even sure who to look at.

Marcus Sanders had cheated on his wife? He had a child he didn't even know about? Or maybe he hadn't wanted to know.

Never in a million years would Gabe have tagged Marcus as a deadbeat dad. The idea was unbelievable. Marcus was a fine Christian man. Gabe was sure of it. Or was he wrong about that, too?

Gabe looked at Marcus, surprised to meet his watching gaze.

Guilt hung on the brows that lowered over Marcus's eyes. Or was it apology?

"So, Charlotte," Oriana tried again with a smile, "what do you think of the weather here so far? Everyone's complaining about how hot it is, but I bet you're used to much worse in Texas."

Leave it to Oriana to find a way to be genuinely warm even

in this situation. Her effort seemed to be wasted on Charlotte, since she still stared at Oriana with a mixture of fascination and mistrust, as if she had never seen a blind person before.

At least Oriana was trying. Cullen kept a calming hand over Nye's on the table as she kept quiet, and Caroline hadn't touched her food at all, though she had nervously chatted with Gabe a couple times.

Oriana's husband, Nicanor, was the only one besides Oriana who seemed unaffected. He just listened to Oriana talk with a half-smile. The guy never said anything anyway, so the situation wasn't cramping his style.

"Gabe really helped in that way."

Oriana's mention of his name made Gabe pay attention to what she was saying to Charlotte. "It's so important that the kids at the center get to interact positively with police officers."

Gabe couldn't stop the tug of the smile on his face. Oriana was sure persistent, using this moment as a way of giving him another hint that he should get back to working with the kids at CCC.

Then he saw Charlotte.

Her gaze dropped immediately when he glanced at her, but not before he caught the widening of her eyes. He knew that look well—the fear on the streets for the police uniform. The fear of just the title, the idea of a police officer. His smile flipped downward as his eyes narrowed. Just who was she, and what was she up to?

"Well, Gabe." Marcus's smile was strained. "Do you have time for a little pool before your shift?"

"Sounds fun. I have a couple hours yet." Joining Marcus and Nye's husband, Cullen, for pool in the study after the Sunday brunch was traditional, but Marcus still politely gave an invitation every time. "Have to take advantage of Russell not being here to make me look bad."

Cullen chuckled at the teasing reference to his grandfather.

"He tells me he's practicing at Mom's, but I'm hoping she'll keep him too busy for that. I don't want to think about how good he'd get if that's all he did for a whole summer."

"Your granddad is plenty good enough as it is." Marcus smiled at Cullen before he stood and swung his gaze to Charlotte. "Charlotte, would you like to join us?"

She looked at Marcus with her eyes narrowed slightly, as if he had just asked her something dirty. Maybe she had a problem playing with only men. Gabe had been told Oriana played a mean game of pool, but that was before the blindness.

Charlotte shook her head.

"Surprise," Oriana announced. "Nicanor and I don't have anywhere to run off to today."

"Well, that is a surprise." Caroline gave Oriana the first real smile Gabe had seen on her face all day.

Gabe knew they all approved of the reasons Oriana usually made a quick exit after brunch, since she only left to go to CCC or one of her speaking engagements about the center and her drug awareness initiative. But she was always missed.

"It's important to be here today." Oriana smiled at Charlotte. "I want to spend some time getting to know my new sister."

Marcus bestowed a grateful smile on Oriana, showing that Gabe wasn't the only one who was touched by her open-heartedness.

Caroline didn't manage to look quite as pleased as she rose from her chair. "I have some coffee in the kitchen. We can sit at the breakfast table and chat a while."

Charlotte stayed where she was, looking down and not saying a word while the decisions were made and the other daughters' husbands pulled out their wives' chairs.

Where are your manners, boy? Gabe could hear Momma's scolding in his ear.

He dropped his napkin next to his plate and went around the

end of the table to reach Charlotte. He touched the back of her chair.

She jerked and swung her head around to see him, her eyes wide.

"Sorry." He pulled his hands off the chair and took a step back, needing to slow his own startled pulse.

She scrambled to her feet, keeping her gaze averted as she grabbed her daughter's hand and pulled the girl at a fast clip to the kitchen.

Gabe watched the doorway where she had disappeared. He should be more concerned about what the woman was really doing here, but instead that dumb, unteachable part of his heart wanted to follow her and make sure she was okay. To make things right. To protect her.

He knew the look that had flashed across her face when he'd startled her. He'd seen it on the faces of hundreds of victims. He'd also seen it on the faces of people he mistakenly thought were only victims.

He blew out a breath to release the tension he felt like he'd been holding for the last hour. Good thing he had to leave soon for work. Maybe a night on the job would remind him to toughen up again.

Cullen was already setting up for the break by the time Gabe reached the rec room. Only about a minute into the silence that followed Gabe's entrance, Marcus cleared his throat.

"I know you both probably have questions about Charlotte and this situation." Marcus put one hand into the pocket of his slacks while he clutched an upright cue with his other hand. "You might even have some...negative feelings toward me about it. I'd understand if you did. But I want you both to please ask me anything you want. Tell me what you're thinking."

Cullen straightened instead of taking the break.

"Please." Marcus stared intently at them. "I think of you

both as my sons. I want to have things out in the open and right between us."

"Are you sure she's your daughter?" A natural question for Cullen, the lawyer, to ask.

"Yes."

"Does she have evidence?" Gabe had to ask the good cop's question, too.

"She has all the evidence she needs. It all fits." He paused. "I want you to know that I wasn't married to Caroline when I met Charlotte's mother. I was dating Caroline at the time, however, and I never told her about it. Charlotte's mother and what happened with her are a part of a past that has haunted me through the years, never so horribly as right now. I became a Christian about a year later, and Caroline a year after that. I never went back to the lifestyle I had before Christ changed me."

Marcus leaned his cue against the wall and turned to face them again, unshed tears glimmering in his eyes. "I know I'm forgiven, but...at times like this, I don't see how it could be. I've done some terrible things. And this one..." He clasped his hands together, as if for a strangled prayer. "I never knew the extent of the consequences. I never knew I had a daughter and left her alone out there somewhere." Marcus sniffed and wiped at a drop that spilled over.

"We've all needed our share of forgiveness." Cullen looked at Marcus with the compassion Gabe should have felt. "Thank the Lord that His forgiveness is sufficient for the worst of sins, even when we don't realize how much wrong we've really done."

Marcus nodded. "Amen." He glanced at Gabe and Cullen. "You're here to play pool, not listen to me blubber. Go ahead and break, Cullen."

Gabe should have said something, but the words lodged in his throat. The image of a little girl, alone and lost, longing for a daddy, overcame any pity he might have had for Marcus. Gabe's memory of pressing his own six-year-old face to the screen of the porch door, watching for Daddy to return, blocked out Marcus's tears.

Gabe thought he knew Marcus and the Sanders family. Was there really no one who could be trusted in this life?

CHARLOTTE'S HAND shook as she set the coffee mug on the table. She glanced at the women who sat around her, hoping none of them noticed how nervous she was. The knot that had tied up her stomach when they all came for brunch was still there, but at least she could breathe a little easier now that the giant cop was out of the room.

The black guy was even bigger than the enforcers she'd seen in Dallas. He had set her nerves on edge the second she first saw him, and when they said he was a cop, she knew his size wasn't the only reason for the added twist in her gut.

She'd always had a nose for cops. But she still never would've guessed he was one. Somebody's heavy maybe, but not a cop.

"So, Phoebe," Oriana smiled from across the small table, "how old are you?"

"She's ten." Charlotte tried to divert the attention away by answering quickly.

Phoebe wouldn't like all these people staring at her. Not that Charlotte liked their attention on her any better.

Caroline raised her eyebrows. "I thought she was seven. She's so small."

Was that a criticism? Charlotte was short, too, so what did they expect from her daughter?

Charlotte quietly and slowly released a breath. She should be able to relax now that the cop was gone, but instead she felt like she was in the lineup at Miss America.

The obvious fact that Charlotte was the ugly duckling in the room wasn't lost on her. If Nye was the blonde supermodel, Oriana was her perfect brown-haired counterpart. A little curvier than Nye, Oriana was still tall and thin with smooth skin that looked perfect even without makeup.

Well, Charlotte didn't have a beautiful mother to take after like they did. Momma always said she took after her daddy more, anyway. Turned out she was right for once. Funny that Charlotte had ended up looking so much more like Marcus than the two daughters he knew about.

Oriana did also have brown eyes and hair, but her hair, though short, was thick and shiny instead of thin and mousey colored like Charlotte's.

Even little Phoebe looked more like she belonged with this group of women than Charlotte. Phoebe was at least pretty. Her freshly washed hair, blond like her worthless daddy's, shone like sunshine, masking her eyes when she tilted her head to stare at the dog.

Oriana's guide dog fit the beauty requirements of this family as he lay on the floor, his smooth fur rising and falling with his panting while he watched the women at the table.

"I think Phoebe wants to pet Sunny." Nye smiled at Phoebe.

Oriana beamed. "You can pet him if you'd like to, Phoebe. He's not working right now."

Phoebe slid off her chair and went to Sunny.

Charlotte watched carefully, but the dog just licked Phoebe's hand once as soon as she was close and then panted happily when Phoebe sat beside him on the floor, stroking his side.

"Don't worry. He's great with kids." Did Oriana always smile? Or was she just putting on a friendly show for Charlotte? The act was a little over the top.

At least Oriana's blindness made her not quite as perfect as she looked. How would Caroline have handled her daughter being born blind? Or becoming blind later? Probably not too well. Caroline was obviously the kind of woman who would demand perfection from everyone.

"I'm impressed, Phoebe." Oriana somehow knew just where to turn her head to face Phoebe. "You're so polite and quiet. You could teach some of my kids at the center how to behave with others. Did your mother teach you good manners?"

Phoebe kept looking at the dog's face, running her hand along his furry side with long, even strokes.

"She can't talk very much," Charlotte finally said.

"Can't?" Oriana turned to Charlotte, lines crossing her forehead.

Oops. Shouldn't have said that. Charlotte shrugged. "She doesn't have to talk. I know what she needs."

"Why doesn't she talk?"

Great. Now Caroline was interested. Probably judging along with everyone else.

"She talks some." Charlotte didn't meet their condemning gazes. She was not a bad mother, no matter what they thought.

Nye eventually broke the awkward silence. "What grade is Phoebe in at school?"

Nye's calm, polite tone smoothed Charlotte's raised hackles a bit, but the question presented another problem. "Second grade," Charlotte spit out, knowing she had to sound sure and confident to sell the lie.

"Second?" Caroline raised her eyebrows again. "Isn't she too old for second grade?"

Charlotte swallowed. Stupid mistake. But how was Charlotte to know? She hadn't sent Phoebe to school since kindergarten, where the other kids picked on Phoebe, and the teachers said she was retarded, too slow to learn.

Charlotte set her jaw. "There's nothing wrong with Phoebe." These women could judge her all they wanted, but not Phoebe.

"Of course not." Oriana shined her smile on Phoebe. "She's special. I can tell."

Phoebe risked a quick look at Oriana, though she kept her little head tucked as she continued to pet the dog.

A surge of pride flowed to Charlotte's chest. Phoebe understood a lot more than people thought. But she was also too young to know that people were not always what they seemed.

Charlotte's job was to protect her daughter. Even Oriana could just be faking kindness to get rid of them sooner. Kindness, especially in a situation like this, was never for real, never for free.

"I just had a thought." Oriana's eagerness seemed to put brightness on the faces of Caroline and Nye as they watched her. "Could you bring Phoebe to the center tomorrow, Charlotte? The kids and I are getting ready for a big Fourth of July bash this week, and we could really use more help making the decorations. Do you think Phoebe would like that?"

Charlotte watched Phoebe, still petting the dog. Were they even going to be there tomorrow?

Charlotte hadn't decided what to do or known what would happen. She wasn't even sure she'd make it through this coffee without getting kicked out. These people had to tire of their act soon. She knew they hated her underneath the smiles.

"You are staying for a while, right?" Oriana bit her lip.

Funny. That's what Charlotte always did. Were they more alike than she thought? Like sisters?

"I certainly hope you're planning to stay." Caroline looked at Charlotte. "Marcus would be so disappointed if you didn't." There was something very commanding in Caroline's words.

Charlotte wondered what the blonde model thought, but Nye just kept her lips pressed into a tight-lipped smile and watched Phoebe.

Charlotte couldn't do this anymore. She couldn't take the scrutiny—everyone looking at Phoebe and asking questions. If they spent much time around Phoebe, would they have more questions? Would they see she hadn't been educated right?

That she was different? They'd start to think Charlotte wasn't a good mother. She had seen that thought already in their eyes.

Panic shot up her throat. She jumped up and grabbed Phoebe away from the dog. She searched for something to say. "Time for Phoebe's nap." Charlotte pulled her daughter out of the room, glad the women didn't know that Phoebe didn't take naps.

Phoebe started to whimper as they reached the living room.

The panic followed Charlotte. They should leave. This was a bad idea.

She looked at the front door in the entryway. Tommy could be on his way there now. He could already be there.

She bit her lip while Phoebe continued to whimper. They were out of money and had nowhere to go, no place Charlotte could take a kid. And she wasn't going to leave Phoebe behind.

The hair on the back of her neck stood up. She wasn't alone.

She jerked her gaze to the sofa.

Oriana's husband, Nick-something, sat with a book open on his lap. He was so quiet she hadn't even seen him when she entered. Was he reading a Bible? The book looked like the Bible she had seen on the coffee table earlier. That would be weird. The guy was young and gave off hot Latin dancer vibes without a whiff of religious stuffiness.

He looked up and met her stare, his blue eyes probing and intense. What was he looking for?

She turned away and pulled whimpering Phoebe toward the entry area. They needed to get out of here. She stopped and stared at the door. What if Tommy was out there?

"Is everything okay?"

Charlotte jumped at the deep rumble behind her. It wasn't the Nick guy. Instead, Charlotte had to tilt her head back to see the face of the giant black cop. Busted.

He suddenly crouched down, shrinking to half his previous height in front of Phoebe.

The whimpering stopped. Phoebe stared at the cop's much larger face.

"Hey." His tone was gentle and soft as he met Phoebe's stare. "Things aren't that bad, are they?"

He had no idea. Charlotte closed her mouth, which had fallen open when he crouched down. She crossed her arms. Typical guy. Pat the girl's hand and all must be okay.

He stood and reached into the pocket of his dress pants.

Charlotte tensed. What was he doing?

He dropped down again and slowly extended his huge hand toward Phoebe—a hand that held a red lollipop. "I was saving this for later, but...I think it's meant for you instead."

Phoebe stared at him for a couple seconds. Then she took the lollipop.

He smiled. "It's cherry flavored."

He stood and turned to Charlotte with a smile that transformed his grim face. The show of white teeth was downright cute against his dark skin, especially with the twinkle it added to his eyes.

A nice cop? Impossible. Almost as impossible as the warmth that coursed through her body under that smile. Probably just nerves. But the feeling disappeared when his smile faded as he looked down at her.

Suspicion appeared in his eyes again. He probably saw right through her. "Were you leaving?"

How did he know? Was he going to stop her?

"Um...no." She shook her head and grabbed Phoebe's free hand to take her away from the door. She looked back to see Gabe reach for the door handle.

"See you, Nicanor," he called over his shoulder as he opened the door and walked onto the shaded path outside.

Charlotte let out a breath when the door shut behind him. She turned around only to see Nicanor watching her with those intense eyes.

Charlotte took Phoebe with her and headed for the bedroom. There were too many people in this house. But if she was going to keep them from getting more suspicious of her than they already were, she'd have to play along better. She wouldn't hope for them to like her. No one but Tommy ever had. Still, she had to at least get them to relax around her and not see her as the chick who was there to ruin their lives.

She'd start with Oriana. The blind woman was so determined to be friendly that she'd be the easiest one to play. Oriana might have a con of her own going on, being so sickeningly sweet all the time, but she was the best shot right now for getting Caroline to let Charlotte stay long enough to get a plan together.

Besides, Phoebe loved Oriana's dog. Charlotte hadn't found anyone or anything Phoebe had connected with so much before...except for that cop. Weird. Phoebe was terrified of men, but she had looked right at him instead of ducking away or totally zoning out.

Charlotte reached the bedroom and led Phoebe inside, releasing her hand. Charlotte closed the door and leaned against it, tilting her head to stare up at the white ceiling like its bumpy surface could help them. If a cop was this family's best friend, she and Phoebe were in worse trouble than she thought.

Phoebe tugged on the hem of Charlotte's tank top.

Charlotte looked down at her beautiful girl.

Phoebe held out the wet lollipop. "Want?"

Charlotte smiled through the moisture blurring her view. "No, baby girl."

Phoebe shoved the lollipop back into her mouth as Charlotte dropped to her level.

She pulled Phoebe into a tight hug, fighting to hold back her tears. She had to find a way to get enough money for them to run farther. Soon. They weren't safe here with all these questions and a cop breathing down their necks. But would they be safe anywhere?

You're mine, baby.

Charlotte shut her eyes, trying to squeeze out the memory of Tommy's words.

I ain't never lettin' you go.

Charlotte shivered as she held Phoebe.

The little girl wrapped her arms around Charlotte and rested her chin on Charlotte's shoulder.

How had Charlotte ended up with such a precious girl? A fiery power flamed in her chest and surged through her veins. She would take care of Phoebe. She would find a way to give her a real home, a safe place where she didn't need to be afraid anymore. She'd do it or die trying.

five

> *"The chimes of time ring out the news*
> *Another day is through*
> *Someone slipped and fell,*
> *Was that someone you?"*
> – Carl Stuart Hamblen, "It Is No Secret (What God Can Do)"

GABE MUST BE DESPERATE. He stood on the sidewalk, the hot sun beating down on his dark uniform shirt as he watched Pete question an elderly man who claimed his wallet was stolen on the bus. Gabe's assistance was completely unnecessary, even though Pete's new temporary partner was another rookie.

In a way, stopping to assist was needed just to save Gabe's sanity. He hadn't been able to focus on his mundane paperwork at the office, and he'd thought hitting the street might help. But things were slow—few calls to distract him from thinking about the internal investigation and the unsettling revelations about the Sanders.

Maybe things would pick up when the early part of the evening was over. Gabe loved how the night shift could go from dead to crazy instantly, and he hoped that would be the case tonight.

The investigation was really getting on his nerves. He'd probably be cleared, but the knowledge didn't stop the swirling in the pit of his stomach. Maybe because he knew they shouldn't clear him. The incident replayed over and over again in his head. Why had he trusted Peggy? He should have known, should have picked up on her body language, her facial expression...something.

"Just slow down, and try to relax." Pete's words sounded like they were aimed at Gabe, but he realized as he came out of his reverie that Pete was still talking to the alleged victim. "Try to remember what happened as clearly as you can."

The few strands of white hair that lay across the top of the man's head exposed his pink scalp as he sat on the bench, peering up at them through glasses. "A young fella, I'm sure it was a man, pushed right into me. Just pushed right into me when all I was trying to do was get off the bus. I knew he put his hand in my pocket right away, because I felt it. You can feel it, you know. Like this." He reached into the pocket of his blazer.

"Hold it." Gabe's hand jerked to his holstered weapon. "Leave your hands where we can see them."

Pete glanced at Gabe out of the corner of his eye.

Pete was right. Gabe's voice had been uncharacteristically sharp, and his reaction a little extreme. Gabe sighed inwardly. Maybe he was learning his lesson after all.

"Can you describe the man who shoved you?" Pete's tone was unusually soft, probably trying to make up for Gabe's *bad cop* impersonation.

"He had dark hair. Young. A big man. But not nearly as big as the officer here." The elderly man gestured with an arthritic hand toward Gabe but kept his head down as if not daring to meet Gabe's eyes.

Gabe stepped away, giving space for the guy to relax and for himself to chill. "Nothing here to see, folks." He motioned for the small cluster of onlookers to move on. As they dispersed, Gabe went to his squad. Now he was stalking around scaring old men. But for all he knew, that old guy could be a psycho killer about to jump them all.

Gabe got into the car and shook his head. Being more on his guard might be a good thing, but he didn't like it. Could he really live his life suspecting absolutely everyone? To have no innocent people to protect from the dangerous ones?

And would he have to suspect the Sanders, too? They were his only family now, but Marcus had sure turned out to have some surprises.

Granted, they were all in the past. Even Gabe had stuff in his past he wasn't proud of. Nothing like leaving a kid without a father, though. That was the kind of thing people he dealt with on the job did, the kind of thing people like his dad did.

Kids who got abandoned like that didn't often do well, and just a few minutes of observing Charlotte told him she wasn't any different. He hoped she wasn't going to be more trouble to the Sanders than just dropping the lost daughter bombshell.

Gabe tilted the screen of his MDT computer so he could see it without glare from the sunlight and typed in Charlotte Davis. He added the birth year Marcus had mentioned and ran the query.

Nothing. Not even a parking ticket, though he doubted she had a car. Her torn jeans and faded tank top had looked as worn as if she didn't own more than two outfits.

How about the mother? Gabe entered Phoebe Davis and waited for the second it took for the information to come up on the screen.

Two counts of retail theft and probation. Not a promising family history for the mysterious Charlotte.

The image of her face filled his vision, those long eye lashes framing the huge brown eyes that seemed to plead with him, asking him for help.

Gabe punched a key to clear the search on the MDT and put the car in gear.

Yeah. And she was probably as innocent as that girl who'd stabbed Jim in the back.

CHARLOTTE LOOKED up at the sign above the door one more time: *CHRISTIAN COMMUNITY CENTER.*

This should be the place, but it sure didn't look like anything up to the Sanders' fancy standards. Still, she didn't think Caroline would have dropped them off at the wrong location.

Phoebe gripped the hem of Charlotte's tank top as Charlotte pushed into the heavy metal door that creaked loudly when she opened it. They walked into a dim, cold hallway with a hard floor.

Charlotte jerked when the door clanged shut behind them. What was this place? An old office building? A factory? All she knew for sure was it looked as old as the apartment buildings she'd lived in. The place was cleaner, like someone had made an effort to scrub away years of dirt and did what they could to patch holes in the walls.

Phoebe stared at the pictures on those walls as they went down the hallway. They were colorful, unrecognizable drawings obviously done by kids, but they did a lot to make the cold building less scary.

The laughter and chatter of children drifted to Charlotte from a room off the hall. She paused at the open doorway and looked inside while Phoebe ducked behind her. Twenty or more kids were standing or sitting at round tables as two old ladies helped them with whatever they were doing. From the glue bottles on the tables and stacks of colored paper, Charlotte guessed they were working on a craft of some sort.

No Oriana. Charlotte turned away from the room just as Phoebe was starting to peer around her jeans at the other kids.

There seemed to be a deep voice carrying from somewhere farther down the hallway.

As she passed under a handmade sign that read, GOD BLESS AMERICA, a low-pitched rumble came from the next doorway.

"I probably should've just skipped the brunch."

Gabe.

"I felt badly about making things more awkward." Who was he talking to?

Charlotte slowed to a stop when she could see inside the room at an angle. Looked like a kitchen.

"Oh, you shouldn't have felt awkward. We were glad to have you there." Sounded like Oriana. Sure enough, Oriana stepped into Charlotte's view.

Charlotte tensed, then relaxed when she remembered Oriana couldn't see her.

"You're like our brother now so, of course, we wanted you there." Oriana smiled, probably at Gabe, which would put him near the open doorway. "You're one of the family now, like it or not, so you might as well get used to our expanding numbers." She laughed.

She could laugh about it? The woman really was crazy.

"Doesn't it bother you?" Gabe's tone was way more serious.

Charlotte held her breath to hear Oriana's answer.

"At this point, I'm much more worried about what Charlotte and Phoebe are going through." Was she serious? Of course, she did manage to sneak around the real question by saying that instead.

The pull on Charlotte's tank top released, and Phoebe passed her into the kitchen, making a beeline for Oriana's dog, who sat next to his owner with a harness on.

Charlotte stared as if watching a dream. Phoebe never let go of her in public.

"Phoebe?" Oriana turned her head toward Phoebe as she slid to the floor by the dog. How'd she know who it was?

"Phoebe is petting Sunny," Gabe told Oriana. "Is that okay?"

"Sure. I don't think this one time will confuse him. He knows Phoebe is special." Oriana turned her smile in Charlotte's direction, as if knowing she was there.

Charlotte stepped into the room and squeaked out an awkward, "Hi."

Gabe stood just to the side of the door, much closer than she had expected. Wow, he was big. Muscles bulged beneath the light material of his blue T-shirt.

She sidestepped away from him, wondering why her cheeks flushed with heat.

"Charlotte! I'm so happy you came." Oriana beamed a brighter smile than before and came toward Charlotte, her hands stretched out in front of her.

Charlotte reluctantly took hold of Oriana's hands as she came closer. Oriana quickly released Charlotte's hands and changed the gesture into a hug.

Moisture pricked at Charlotte's eyes, unconnected to any thought or feeling. She didn't like hugs. And this woman had to be more than crazy to be hugging Charlotte already.

Charlotte pulled back as soon as she could without offending Oriana. She searched for something to say. "Phoebe sure likes your dog."

Oriana's sightless eyes sparkled. "I think it's mutual."

Charlotte glanced at Gabe, who just watched them with the cop face he had when he didn't smile.

The hard line of his mouth suddenly broke, revealing that

softening smile. "Hey." His voice was deep enough to shake the ground she stood on.

She swallowed, hoping to find her voice. "Hey," she eventually managed.

"Phoebe," Oriana turned to face Phoebe, who still sat on the floor by Sunny, "we have something really fun you can do with the other kids today. Do you like stars?" Phoebe just watched Sunny and stroked his fur.

"Does Phoebe ever talk, Charlotte?"

Charlotte tensed. Questions again. "Not to strangers." The stranger thing usually worked.

"Well, I hope we won't be strangers soon."

"Oriana." Nicanor's heavily accented voice came from the doorway where he stood, his hand propped against the frame like he'd been there a while. Judging from Gabe and Oriana's startled jerks toward the door, they hadn't heard him come in either. "I'm leaving now." His blue eyes bored into Charlotte with that unreadable expression.

At least he was leaving. She couldn't handle two suspicious men at the same time. They looked as different from each other as night and day, but both seemed to know too much.

"I'll walk you out." Oriana went to Nicanor and slipped her arm through his. She tilted her head in Gabe's direction. "Gabe, would you mind showing Phoebe and Charlotte where the other kids are working on the stars? I'll be right back."

"Sure, no problem."

"Sunny, stay with Phoebe." The dog shifted his brown eyes to watch Oriana like he understood what she was saying.

Charlotte's heart rate sped up as Oriana and Nicanor disappeared, leaving her alone with Gabe.

Her gaze bounced from the yellow refrigerator to the old yellow countertops to the white oven—anywhere but the cop who could scare all her secrets out or knock her senseless with one shake.

"Well," he rumbled, "shall we?"

Charlotte chanced a glance and saw his long arm lift as he gestured toward the doorway. She nodded and opened her mouth to call Phoebe—

"Come on, Phoebe." Gabe beat Charlotte to it. "We're going to show you how to make the most beautiful stars you've ever seen."

Phoebe looked directly at Gabe with a clear, focused gaze Charlotte had only seen a handful of times. The little girl got to her feet and walked toward him like Charlotte wasn't in the room anymore.

Gabe started to lead the way through the doorway but paused when Phoebe slipped her hand into his. He smiled down at her then kept walking, like he knew making a big deal would ruin it.

Charlotte slowly followed them, her mind making a very big deal out of what she'd just seen as Sunny jogged past her to catch up. Phoebe had never, absolutely never, taken the hand of a stranger before. She wouldn't even touch them or let them touch her. There was something very strange about this cop she was following back up the long hallway.

He turned into the first room they had seen earlier, and Charlotte followed, still blinking to see if she could awake from the sight of her little girl holding on to this giant black man like he was her daddy. There was no way he could remind her of her blond-haired, blue-eyed father, especially since the jerk had left the second he'd found out that Phoebe wasn't like other kids.

Phoebe shifted herself partially behind Gabe, peering around his leg at the noisy kids who were still scattered all over the room, mostly at the tables.

Sunny paused by her side, his tail wagging.

"It's okay, Phoebe." Gabe gently put his huge hand behind Phoebe's head as he turned so that she was at his side instead of hiding behind him. "These kids are nice."

Yeah, right. Charlotte had yet to meet a nice kid where Phoebe was concerned.

"And see that lady over there?" Gabe pointed to an old woman who helped a kid at the farthest table. "That's Mrs. Peters. She's a very special lady who loves little girls and can show you how to make your very own stars."

Mrs. Peters glanced up and waved as she made her way over to them. "Who might this be?" She peered at Phoebe from under dyed red hair that looked like it had been permed a thousand times.

"This is Phoebe, Mrs. Peters." Gabe looked back and forth between the woman and Phoebe. "I told her you know how to make stars."

"Oh, yes." She put her wrinkled hands together. "Would you like to learn?"

Phoebe looked up at Gabe. Why did she want an okay from him instead of her own mother?

He nodded. "Sounds awfully fun to me."

Phoebe went forward to follow Mrs. Peters but didn't let go of Gabe's hand.

Gabe glanced at Charlotte with a shoulder shrug and a cute little smile that didn't belong on his very masculine face as he let Phoebe pull him to the closest empty chair at a table.

Charlotte stood glued in place. Should she feel threatened? Should she be worried? The flutter in her stomach seemed to tell her she should...or did that have more to do with something else? Like a certain smile.

Footsteps just behind Charlotte saved her from having to answer that question.

Sunny trotted over to greet Oriana as she stopped at Charlotte's side. "Hi, buddy." She ruffled the fur on his neck as she bent to take hold of the harness strap. "Is Phoebe settling in okay?"

Charlotte nodded. Oops.

Oriana couldn't see it.

"Yeah. They're showing her how to make the stars for your decorations, I guess."

"Great. Though the decorations are more the kids' than mine."

"Phoebe's not very good with her hands. She might not be able to do it right."

"Oh, I'm sure she'll do great." Oriana's smile held steady. "We don't ask for perfection here. Speaking of perfection, I could really use your help. Would you mind coming back to the kitchen with me?"

"Um..." Charlotte looked at Phoebe.

Gabe and Mrs. Peters hovered over her daughter as they helped her put glue on a red paper star.

"Phoebe will be absolutely safe with Mrs. Peters." Oriana must be used to dealing with worried parents. She had a pitch ready. "She's our best volunteer. She's been with us from the start of this place, and the kids all love her."

Phoebe hadn't looked for Charlotte once, so she must not be scared. Strange as that was. "Okay. If it doesn't take long."

"I don't think it should. Thank you."

Charlotte followed Oriana and Sunny back into the hallway and to the kitchen.

"Smell the cookies?" Oriana tilted her nose up as they entered the room.

Sugar cookies, Charlotte guessed from the aroma that had filled the room in the time since she had left it.

"They don't smell burnt yet anyway." Oriana wrinkled her nose. "I'd like to decorate the cookies with something patriotic, but I'm afraid decorating cookies is something I still haven't managed to get the knack of again. Yet." She laughed. "I'd probably get most of the frosting on the counter if I tried."

So she had been able to do it before. Did that mean she had been able to see?

Oriana let go of Sunny's harness. "Sunny, down."

The dog obediently slid to the floor, panting with a smile as steady as his owner's.

"So you haven't always been blind?" Probably a rude question, but the words were out of Charlotte's mouth before she could stop them.

Oriana didn't look phased at all as she opened a drawer and took out the longest oven mitts Charlotte had ever seen. "Nope. It happened about...oh, a little over eight months ago, I guess." She laughed. "The only reason I can keep count so well is because Nye found out she was pregnant around the same time. We're all looking forward to having a new member of the family." Her smile finally sagged a little, as if she realized what she had just said.

Just not this way, she was probably thinking.

Oriana pulled on the mitts and stood in front of the oven. She touched both sides of the oven, like she was figuring out where she was. Then she opened the door and reached inside for the top cookie sheet.

Charlotte bit her lip. Should she offer to help?

Oriana pulled out the tray of baked cookies and carefully lifted them to the stovetop. She seemed determined to do everything.

Charlotte wouldn't go anywhere near a hot oven if she couldn't see.

Oriana reached in again and grabbed the other cookie sheet.

"How did it happen?"

Oriana closed the door and tilted her head toward Charlotte.

"I mean, what made you blind?"

"Oh, I was attacked by some gang members and ended up hitting my head on a brick wall. Do these look done to you?" She slipped off her mitt and tapped one of the cookies with a finger like they were having a normal cookie baking conversation.

Maybe the hit on Oriana's head had affected her brain, too. Nobody could be that happy about something like that otherwise. Oriana looked like she was only in her twenties. Young, beautiful, and she was attacked by bangers and robbed of her sight? She really was crazy not to be angry or at least depressed.

There's no way Charlotte could be related to her. Cheerfulness like that did not run through Charlotte's veins.

"I think they're done. Would you mind decorating them? I think the first batch should be cool enough by now. They're over on the counter there by the decorating stuff Mrs. Peters set out." Oriana pointed to the counter along the opposite wall where decorating tips and bags waited next to racks with more cookies.

Charlotte bit her lip as she went over to the equipment. She'd never done anything like this, though as a little girl she used to watch Mrs. Martin, the only nice lady in their neighborhood, decorate cookies and cakes at the bakery before it closed.

Charlotte let her lip go and shrugged. She'd always been good with her hands—the one thing Momma actually liked about her...and used to full advantage. "What do you want on the cookies?"

Oriana turned to face her. "Whatever you think looks good, I guess. We have star shapes and flags, so just be creative. I trust you."

Charlotte narrowed her eyes at Oriana. That had to be the first time anyone had ever said those words to Charlotte. Downright stupid, really. Like asking for it.

She tucked her thin hair behind her ear and turned to her workspace. Maybe it would help that she used to draw a lot as a kid, before she got too busy and too grown up to dream about fairytale animals and people she could bring to life with a pencil or crayons. Or maybe Momma's reaction to the picture Charlotte had drawn on the wall of their house was what made her stop.

Charlotte put a tip at the end of the bag, just like Mrs.

Martin, and scooped a glob of frosting out of the bowl with the spatula to put in the decorating bag. She held the full bag in her hand, twisting the top. The bag felt right against her palm, and in a blink she was a little girl again, clutching her pencil and creating the butterfly she saw in her mind on the scrap of paper she'd found.

A smile crept onto Charlotte's face. Yeah, maybe she could do this.

Only a few minutes later, it seemed, and she finished putting blue frosting on the last cookie. "All done."

Oriana stepped over to the counter, a smile on her face. "Mmm, the smell of frosting. I wish I could see them. I know they're just beautiful. The kids are going to love them so much."

Phoebe. Charlotte's gaze flew to the clock on the wall. Forty-five minutes? How could she have left Phoebe alone that long with strangers?

Charlotte ripped off the apron Oriana had loaned her. "I have to find Phoebe."

"I'm sure she's fine..." Oriana's voice faded as Charlotte rushed from the room and into the hallway.

Charlotte ran to the craft room. Phoebe wasn't there. No one was there, not one single kid. Where was she?

Panic kicked Charlotte's heart rate into high gear as she swung away from the room and headed the other way, past the kitchen to parts of the building she hadn't seen yet. How could she have left Phoebe alone with those people? What was she thinking?

A deep laugh echoed from behind the metal door at the end of the hallway. The cop?

Charlotte pushed against the bar to swing the door open, her eyes widening at the size of the gym in front of her. Charlotte's heart lurched into her throat.

The cop stood by a wall, which was spattered with July Fourth decorations. He held Phoebe in his hands, high above his head as she tried to stick a star on the wall above the others. If he dropped her...

Phoebe hated heights. What was she doing up there? She swung her little hand, trying to slap the star on the wall.

Why was she even letting the guy touch her? She shrieked anytime a man put his hands on her.

The cop's dark arm was twice the width of Phoebe's body as the muscles bulged against his shirt sleeve. He should be able to hold her with all that muscle, right?

Charlotte held her breath.

Phoebe took another wild slap at the wall, but the star slipped from her hand. She looked down at the fluttering star.

Her shriek split the air. She kicked in his hands, struggling, screaming.

Charlotte ran to them as he lowered Phoebe against his chest.

"It's okay, Phoebe. I've got you." His words did nothing, if Phoebe could even hear them with all her shrieks.

She threw her hands wildly around her, smacking his head as he set her on the ground.

"Phoebe. Momma's here." Charlotte crouched down by Phoebe just as the little girl turned into her arms. She clutched Phoebe close and stood, holding the light, long-legged girl against her.

Charlotte glared up at the cop as Phoebe whimpered in her ear. "Just what do you think you were doing?"

He held up his hands, surprise flickering in his dark eyes. "Hey, I'm still trying to figure out what just happened."

"She's afraid of heights! What were you doing holding her up there like that? She could've fallen."

He frowned. "I was careful, and she was perfectly safe. I didn't know she was afraid of heights. She wanted me to lift her up so she could hang the star."

"Did she tell you that?" Charlotte snapped the question at him.

He narrowed his eyes.

A warning bell went off in her brain. What was she doing chewing out the cop? The very big, male cop.

She spun on her heel and walked to the door as quickly as she could without jostling Phoebe too much. They had better get out while they still could.

Charlotte leaned into the bar to open the door and nearly crashed into Oriana on the other side.

Oriana blinked, looking as startled as Charlotte felt. "Charlotte? Is everything okay?"

"No. The cop almost killed my daughter in there." Okay, so she hadn't calmed down enough yet. *Breathe. Breathe.* "I'm going back to the house. Phoebe won't calm down for a long time after something like this."

"Can I help?" Oriana was finally without her smile, lines on her forehead instead. "How about a cookie? Phoebe, would you like a cookie? We have some really yummy ones that your mommy decorated."

Charlotte bit her lip, glancing over her shoulder even though she knew she would have heard the door if the cop had followed her. Sweets were the only things that could distract Phoebe enough to get her to stop crying once she started. "Whatever. We can try a cookie."

She reluctantly followed Oriana to the kitchen, listening for the door to open at any moment and a big, angry cop to come crashing through. What was she thinking trying to bawl him out? Some cops she knew would have already had cuffs on her by now if she'd done that to them.

Charlotte sat on a chair and put Phoebe in her lap as Oriana brought one of the frosted stars over in a napkin, which she handed to Charlotte.

"Phoebe? Here's a cookie for you."

Phoebe turned her head to burrow her face in Charlotte's chest, still crying.

"You'll love it, baby girl." Charlotte stroked Phoebe's smooth hair. "I painted it all pretty just for you. Will you try it, please? For me?"

The whimpering stopped. Phoebe lifted her head slightly, enough to peek at the cookie in Charlotte's hand. After a few seconds, Phoebe reached out her small hand for the cookie and started to nibble on it.

Whatever was squeezing Charlotte's heart loosened its hold as Phoebe ate the cookie, her features relaxing into her normal expression.

"Charlotte, I know it might not be any of my business, but..."

Charlotte froze, bracing herself.

"I've noticed Phoebe is very different from other kids her age. Has she ever been diagnosed with any...condition or anything like that?"

"There's nothing wrong with her." Charlotte stroked Phoebe's hair faster as heat rushed through her body. "She's just quiet. And lots of people are afraid of heights."

The cop stalked into the room, making Charlotte jump.

She hadn't heard the door from the gym. She stared at him, putting her hands on Phoebe's arms to grab her for a quick getaway. Charlotte had yelled at a cop. She had asked for it.

But he looked away from her at the decorated cookies instead. His eyebrows went up. "Who decorated these?"

Oriana's smile reappeared. "Charlotte was nice enough to do it for me."

"Wow." He stared at the cookies. "Oriana, these cookies are beautiful. They look so perfect...like at a bakery, but more artistic."

Oriana turned her head to Charlotte. "You didn't tell me you were an artist."

Charlotte kept her muscles tense, ready for action. Were they conning her?

The cop looked at Charlotte and took a few steps toward her.

She gripped Phoebe's arm.

He stopped. The corners of his eyes softened with the line of his mouth. "I need to apologize. I am so sorry for scaring Phoebe." His gaze drifted to the little girl, who licked frosting from her fingers. "I would never do that on purpose." He looked at Charlotte. "I hope that both of you can forgive me."

Now she'd seen everything. A cop apologizing to her? Maybe he was crazy, too.

"I'd like to make it up to you and Phoebe. Maybe I could buy you lunch?"

Charlotte's mouth went dry as a desert. She swallowed down the sand she could swear coated the inside.

"Isn't Dad taking you to lunch, Charlotte?"

Charlotte nodded, nearly tempted to hug Oriana herself for giving her the easy out. She swallowed again and managed to croak, "Yes." She avoided the cop's eyes. Lunch with a cop? With this cop?

She had to be dreaming the nuttiest dream she'd ever had. She only hoped she wouldn't wake up to see Tommy, spitting mad because she'd left him.

THE SUN BEAT down on Charlotte's shoulders as she finished her lunch outside of a cafe. Her chair was just beyond the shade cast by the large umbrella, but she didn't care. The warmth reminded her of Texas. Not that the place she grew up held anything good other than being familiar. But at least she knew what to expect there.

Here, people were so unpredictable. Take Marcus, who sat across from her in the shade of the umbrella, his eyes crinkling at the corners as they met the sunlight behind her. His gaze held no suspicion, no hate, not even dislike. She didn't want to try to label what she did see there. It couldn't be what her dreams would hope for.

"I feel like there's so much ground to cover." His smile angled sideways. "There's still so much I don't know about you that I want to."

More? He'd already been grilling her for an hour.

At least Phoebe had enjoyed this meal. She had downed the burger right away and now was busy cleaning the rest of the fries off her plate. She hadn't cleared her plate since they'd left Dallas.

"What was your upbringing like?" Marcus stared at Charlotte. "Your childhood?"

How could he ask her about that? "I didn't have a father."

His smile dropped with her answer.

What did he expect? If he wanted to ditch his guilt by getting her to say her life was all lollipops and roses, he was going to be disappointed.

He looked down and touched the beaded moisture on his glass of lemonade with a fingertip. "I've been thinking about Phoebe, your mother, I mean. How is she?"

"She's dead."

His gaze jerked to her face. "I'm sorry...I didn't..." He looked across the street as he sucked in a deep breath and let it out in a sigh. "How did she die?"

"I don't know. Maybe cancer. Or liquor. She wouldn't go to a doc."

His eyes were wet when he looked at her again. "Was she a good mother to you?"

Charlotte could be honest. When she'd first showed up on his doorstep, she had longed to yell out the truth about the mother he had left her alone with—that she was okay when sober and terrible when drunk. That she'd turned her own daughter into a criminal. But Charlotte hadn't expected her deadbeat daddy to be like this...to look at her with such regret in his eyes.

Her throat tightened. She shrugged her shoulders and turned her head away.

"I am so sorry, Charlotte. I'd give anything to go back. Truly, I would."

She glanced at him in time to see the tear drop onto his tan cheek. Why didn't he want her gone? Why didn't he hate her? She would know how to handle that.

Marcus wiped the tear off with his napkin. "Well, you're probably tired of hearing me say I'm sorry." He set the napkin next to his empty plate on the table. "I don't want to say it anymore."

The brown-haired waitress showed up just then, leaving Charlotte with plenty of time to get good and nervous about what Marcus was going to say while the girl left the bill and took away their dishes.

Was this the moment Charlotte had been expecting? The ultimatum of when she had to get out of his house?

He met Charlotte's gaze once the waitress left with the credit card he handed her. "I want to *show* you how sorry I am." He glanced at Phoebe, who stared across the street. "And how much I love you and Phoebe."

Love? Charlotte couldn't have moved if somebody yelled a bomb was about to go off. He was talking love? Only one other person had ever told her he loved her, and she had just left him in Texas.

"I'd like you to stay with us, if you're willing." He held up his hand like he was going to stop her protest, but shock froze her mind. "I know, you'd probably prefer a place of your own, but hear me out. If you would consider staying with us, we could turn my study into a room for you, and Phoebe could have the room you're sharing now. So you'd have plenty of space and your own beds." Excitement hit his eyes, reminding her of the glimmer she'd seen in the eyes of a salesman she'd sweet-talked at a store once.

"Caroline has already been looking for a suitable job opening for you in the area. She's great at that kind of thing."

Charlotte just bet she was. Of course, Caroline wanted Charlotte to stop mooching off them. She probably wanted Charlotte out of the house, too.

Charlotte stifled a sigh. She knew it sounded too good to be true. Caroline would get Charlotte a job and then kick her out, saying that she could afford to live on her own.

But wasn't that what Charlotte wanted anyway? She didn't want to stay with a family she didn't know and who couldn't ever accept her, especially if they found out what she was really like...what she had done.

"How about some ice cream?" Marcus's random question brought Charlotte out of her thoughts to see him nod toward Phoebe.

Her daughter stared across the street at an ice cream stand and the children who walked away from it, licking dripping cones in their hands.

Charlotte had made sure Phoebe got a cone once. Every kid should have a taste of that kind of dream. But Phoebe might have been too little then to remember. Charlotte stroked Phoebe's hair. "Sure."

As soon as the waitress returned the credit card to Marcus, Charlotte and Phoebe walked with him across the street, where he ordered them cones.

Charlotte took Phoebe's bubble gum ice cream from the ice cream guy and handed it to Phoebe.

Her eyes were huge as she reached for the cone with both hands.

Charlotte had to smile at the wonder on her baby girl's face. Charlotte turned back to get her own ice cream.

Marcus held the mint chip cone out to her.

She paused, her gaze on his hand—the weathered, freckled, and manly hand her little girl imagination had dreamed of doing just this, handing her a cone.

Tears sprang to Charlotte's eyes as she grabbed the cone and turned away. She wasn't a little girl anymore. She was a grown woman with a daughter of her own. She bit her lip, trying to hold back the tears.

Why couldn't he have been there before when she really needed him? She sucked in a shaky breath and looked across the street, trying to fix her eyes on anything that could distract her from the ache in her heart.

A man watched them. He was stocky and thick, with long hair sticking out from under a cowboy hat.

Her breath caught.

Tommy.

She spun around. Where was Phoebe? Panic closed Charlotte's throat.

Then she saw them. Marcus and Phoebe had moved a few feet away and sat on a bench by the sidewalk.

Phoebe would follow anyone at a distance, even if she was terrified of them. She had been trained to. But right then, Charlotte would give anything to undo the habit just to know Phoebe was always at her side.

Charlotte checked across the street.

He was gone. Or at least she couldn't see him. Was it Tommy? Couldn't have been. Not here. Not so soon.

But that hat. Could he have followed her after all?

I'll never let you go, baby. His words repeated in her mind.

She shivered, despite the hot sun on her neck.

Something sticky touched her hand. She looked down to see green ice cream running over her fingers.

Her heart still pounding, Charlotte dropped the cone into the trash can next to the ice cream stand and went to get Phoebe.

"We have to go." She put her hand on Phoebe's shoulder since the girl still held her cone with two hands.

Marcus looked up at Charlotte. His forehead wrinkled at whatever he saw on her face. "Is something wrong?"

"No." Charlotte tried to steady her voice. Hopefully he wouldn't see the shaking of the hand that gripped Phoebe's shoulder.

He hadn't protected her when she was a little girl, and now he couldn't...even if she wanted him to.

six

*"I am the one who helps you, declares the Lord;
Your Redeemer is the Holy One of Israel."*
– Isaiah 41:14b

CHARLOTTE DAVIS NEEDED someone to protect her. Gabe gripped the steering wheel of his squad as he tried to mentally prepare for the burglary call he drove to in the darkness, but all his tired mind seemed able to do was conjure up the image of Charlotte's spitfire angry face when she thought her daughter was in danger. Or maybe he was getting most distracted by the memory of her wide eyes when she backed down like a momma bear who'd just realized she was facing a hunter with a rifle.

Gabe sighed. His hope to be distracted by exciting calls wasn't working. Even with plenty of action this night, he still thought too much. What was it about the petite, spirited woman that got under his skin?

She had even gotten him mad when she first lit into him

about endangering Phoebe, but his anger cooled as soon as he saw the fear hit her eyes, and she ran away. When he had found her again in the kitchen, she had clutched Phoebe like she thought he would take her away as she sat poised on the chair, ready to bolt.

Charlotte sure loved her little girl. Gabe didn't often see good mothers like that on the job. If only they were all like Charlotte or his own momma, whose watchful care had saved his life more than once.

Right now, Momma would tell him to pay more attention to what he was doing. A burglary call at 0100 could be full of surprises.

Gabe spotted the liquor store that was the last business before the auto repair garage where the silent alarm had been triggered. He turned off his headlights as he slowed and pulled into the alley next to the dark store. He carefully rolled the squad to the back where Officer Reese Lewis staged.

Lewis stood in the shadows by the marked car, holding a rifle.

Gabe stopped his squad car and used the radio to report his arrival. "Four Adam 224, Dispatch, Code 23."

"Two twenty four, 10-4."

He got out, careful to noiselessly close the door behind him. The silent alarm had gone off only five minutes before, and they had to assume the suspect was still inside until they proved otherwise.

"K-9 team?" Lewis whispered when Gabe got close.

"All tied up. You got me instead."

Lewis snorted a quiet laugh. "How's your nose working tonight?"

"Not too good, but my teeth are sharp." Gabe grinned.

"Let's hope your bite is worse than your bark." Lewis's smile flashed white in the darkness.

"Let's hope we won't have to find out." Gabe sobered as he

scanned the darkness around them. Ambulance sirens sounded in the distance. "Baker and Ferris are on the perimeter if we need them. How many entrances?"

"Two. Johnson's watching the front. The side door we can see from here is the only other exit."

Gabe glanced at the gray door on the windowless side of the garage. Steel from the look of it. "I'll meet Johnson at the front. You get the side."

"You bark. I'll bite, Sarge." Lewis patted his rifle.

Gabe shook his head with a grin, knowing Lewis had no more desire to use his weapon than Gabe did. "Thanks. Call it in, Rin Tin Tin."

Gabe lowered the volume on his radio as he headed toward the garage building, gun gripped in his hand. He reached the wall of the garage and moved along it until he neared the front. He paused by the corner and peered around.

Clear.

"Johnson?" Gabe whispered.

"Here, Sarge." Johnson looked out from the darkened doorway of the liquor store.

Gabe tilted his lapel mic toward his mouth. "Two twenty-four to three thirty-nine."

"Three thirty-nine in position." Lewis's voice came through softly with the volume so low.

"Ten four." Gabe nodded for Johnson to position with him by the front door. "Ready in fifteen." A jagged hole smashed in the glass panel above the doorknob revealed only darkness inside.

GABE QUIETLY TURNED the knob to be sure it was still unlocked as he ticked off the seconds in his head, the adrenaline starting to pump through his veins. At fifteen seconds, he slowly opened the door, crouched low, his weapon raised.

His breathing quickened as he reached just inside the door,

hoping to find a light switch in the usual place on the wall next to the entrance before the suspect took a shot at him. His fingers touched the plastic of the switch, and he flicked it on.

The small room brightened from the overhead light fixture.

He stayed to the edge of the doorway and surveyed the contents of the room—a few chairs by one wall, a small water cooler in the corner, and a counter that stood away from the opposite wall. Nothing looked disturbed, aside from the open door at the other end of the room that may or may not have been left that way by the owner.

Gabe nodded to Johnson and went inside, going to the end of the counter that someone could easily hide behind.

Nothing.

Lights came on in the other room beyond the open doorway. Lewis?

Johnson went to the wall by the door and pressed his back against it.

Gabe slowly approached the doorway, adrenaline rushing to his ears. He took the same position as Johnson, but on the opposite wall, as they looked into the next room to see what they could from their concealed viewpoint.

The door led to the garage portion of the building—a large, open area with a cement floor. A few cars were parked near the walls and two sat in the middle of the space, one with the hood propped open.

Lewis moved with his back along the far wall, checking between the cars as he went, his gun ready.

Gabe and Johnson turned into the room and started to do the same as Lewis on their side of the garage. The surge of adrenaline faded as Gabe came to the disappointing realization that they had missed the suspect.

"We're clear, boys." Gabe holstered his weapon and reached for his lapel mic. "Four Adam 224, Dispatch. Gone on arrival. No description or direction of travel at this time. Will secure the scene for investigators." He glanced at Lewis and Johnson. "Let's look around and see what we've got."

The garage and its contents looked untouched. No engines, tires, or radios missing from the cars.

Gabe returned to the room at the front. The cash register on top of the counter was the next obvious target. He went behind the counter. Sure enough, the cash drawer had a scrape along the top edge as if it had been forced open. He'd leave the final verdict to the detectives.

Funny, whoever it was had closed the drawer again.

"Hey, Sarge." Lewis's voice carried from the garage. "You'll want to see this."

Gabe went to the garage area where Lewis and Johnson stared down at something on the floor near a car.

As Gabe walked closer, he could make out an oil slick that had captured the men's attention. "What's up?"

Lewis pointed down as Gabe stopped next to the puddle.

An oily footprint, clear and undamaged, was next to the slick.

"Looks like somebody wasn't watching his step," Lewis quipped.

"Or hers," Johnson muttered.

Lewis laughed. "Only if she has your shoe size, Johnson."

Gabe stared at the footprint. He had to be imagining things.

"What is it, Sarge?"

"Does that look like a cowboy boot to you?"

Lewis studied the print then shrugged. "How should I know? I'm a Chicago boy, Texas."

"Right." Gabe looked at the long, narrow toe of the print. In all his years in Harper, he hadn't seen anyone wear cowboy boots. Most folks didn't even wear them in Texas anymore. At least not in the big cities.

He shook his head. One woman from Texas shows up, and

he was seeing cowboy boots. Must be more tired than he thought.

Gabe left Lewis and Johnson to wait for the detectives and gladly sank into the seat of his squad. He lifted the lid of the MDT and saw the time on the screen. Only two and a half hours to go.

Two hours later, Gabe was counting the minutes until the end of his shift as he drove the streets, scanning the darkness and shadows for anything unusual. He'd never counted the time before, actually wanting a shift to end. Then again, he'd never felt it was so pointless before either.

He'd just brought in Toddling Teddy, a.k.a. Theodore Walters, who'd earned his nickname for his many public intoxication arrests. The guy was seventy-three years old, and he never learned. He was just wasting on alcohol whatever time he had left and the little money he managed to scrape up. But he seemed to want it that way. He always said he was sorry and ashamed of himself when they released him after he was sober. Then they'd find him again, drunk and yelling or tumbling over garbage cans in his neighborhood. A waste of life and of Gabe's time.

Gabe slowed the squad.

A cool light shined through the shades covering the front windows of Barb Bakes bakery.

Gabe glanced at the time on the MDT screen: 3:37 a.m.

Barb was never there that early.

Gabe pulled up in front of the bakery.

The rear bumper of Barb's dark green car stuck out from the alley next to the bakery where she always parked. Probably fine, but Gabe would never be able to sleep tonight if anything happened to the precinct's favorite doughnut baker.

After calling in his location, Gabe got out of the squad and went to the door.

The oblong face that answered his knock featured thick,

stern eyebrows under short black hair. "You're early today." Barb spun away from the door and headed to her kitchen area in back, apparently expecting him to follow.

Gabe trailed behind her, glad he knew her well enough to catch the pleased glimmer in her eyes before she had turned away. Her grim expression and no-nonsense tone did nothing for customer satisfaction, but a woman who could bake like Barb didn't need smiles to bring in business.

"So are you." Gabe raised his voice to be heard above the timer that blared.

"Have to keep up with demand." Barb went to the oven and used her towel to grab several sheets of cookies and transfer them to the counter.

"So business is good, then?"

"Yep." Barb pressed a button on a huge blender, creating more noise to talk over. "I'm going to have to hire someone soon if I can find anybody good enough. At least someone who can assemble and decorate, even if they can't bake."

"Good idea." Gabe had to stop himself from reaching for one of the chocolate chip cookies on the cooling rack. The smells were out of this world. "You should have company if you're going to work so early. It isn't safe for you to be here alone at this hour."

"Don't worry about me." Barb handed him a cookie from a different tray.

Gabe smiled at her way of saying thank you. He looked at the cookie in his hand. The frosting on top formed a star, very like Charlotte's, but not quite as perfectly shaped.

Oriana had mentioned Charlotte was looking for work.

"I might know someone for the job."

"Send 'em over." Barb didn't look up as she shaped dough for some kind of pastry.

Gabe wondered how Charlotte would respond if he told her about the opportunity. Probably best to do it through Oriana or

Marcus. He didn't know how long Charlotte was even going to be in Harper, but with a job she might stay longer.

For some reason, he found himself hoping she would. Or maybe he just wanted to be helpful. Her eyes told him she needed help.

Why did he have the feeling a job wouldn't be enough?

THE HOUSE WAS quiet when Charlotte led Phoebe through the dining room, heading for the kitchen.

Caroline and Marcus probably got up at six in the morning instead of ten. Hopefully, they would have already left for whatever they did every day, and Charlotte could finally relax. She yawned as she entered the kitchen.

"Good morning."

Charlotte started at the cheerful voice.

Caroline stood by the counter, holding a mug and a glass of orange juice. "You're up. How wonderful." Caroline's bright smile could compete with the sun.

Charlotte wasn't awake enough to face either kind of light.

"You're just in time to see Marcus before he leaves. Would you like coffee? I thought Phoebe would like orange juice? How about some toast to start and then some eggs?"

Charlotte slowly blinked her partially-closed eyes. About all she got out of that spew of questions was that Marcus was leaving.

"You just sit down and relax while I make you and Phoebe some breakfast." Caroline smiled again.

Charlotte would narrow her eyes if she could without shutting them completely. Why was the woman being so especially nice this morning?

"Charlotte." Marcus walked into the kitchen with a mug in his hand. His smile was softer, slower, and more real than Caroline's as he met Charlotte's gaze with the gentle brown eyes that crinkled at the corners.

That smile, she could take.

"I was hoping you would be up before I had to leave. I wanted to tell you the good news myself."

Charlotte let Phoebe pull her to the table and the orange juice, glad for the excuse not to look at him. Good news for who?

"You've got a job."

"Probably," Caroline inserted.

Marcus glanced at his wife then smiled at Charlotte. "I'm sure it will work out. Barbara Stinton over at Barb Bakes, a bakery downtown, needs an assistant to decorate cakes and cookies."

Caroline set a plate with toast on the table and looked at Charlotte. "She said she'll let you interview on the job tomorrow morning."

Phoebe grabbed a slice of toast while Charlotte lost her appetite to the swirling in her stomach. She didn't think they'd find work for her so fast. She couldn't be tied down like that. They had to keep moving or Tommy would find them.

"Gabe told Oriana about the job." Marcus's smile slipped to one side. "Apparently, he's good friends with the owner Barbara, and he recommended you."

"I wasn't planning to stay that long," Charlotte blurted out. Of course, she still didn't have any money or a place to go if she left. But a job from the cop? Just how tight was he with this Barbara woman? She told herself she only cared because she couldn't very well work for a cop's spy.

Her gaze drifted to Marcus's face.

His smile had vanished and the lines on his forehead deepened.

If Charlotte didn't know better, she'd say he looked sad...like he really wanted her to stay. Her heart squeezed with the hope.

She looked at Caroline to stop the dreaming.

The woman's mouth pressed into a grim line. She sure didn't want Charlotte to take the job and stay. "I think we girls need to go shopping today."

Charlotte blinked. She thought she was getting wider awake, but Caroline's random announcement made her wonder if she was still asleep.

Caroline turned to Marcus, who watched her with his eyebrows raised.

At least Charlotte wasn't the only one who thought Caroline was being weird.

"Phoebe needs new clothes, whether or not they're planning to stay."

Caroline got her there. Phoebe did need new stuff. She only had what Charlotte could afford—clothes that were now too small and worn. But the idea of going somewhere alone with Caroline, especially shopping, made Charlotte's stomach churn some more.

"Of course she does." Marcus tried for a smile but didn't seem to have the will for it. "Buy her whatever she wants. Charlotte, I hope you'll let Caroline buy you whatever you might need, too."

Asking him to just give Charlotte his credit card probably wouldn't work. Not with Caroline standing there.

The watchdog smiled at Marcus. "You'll be late getting to the bank, dear, if you don't hurry."

Marcus nodded and set his mug in the sink.

Caroline touched his shoulder. "Don't worry. We'll have a lovely time and be back here when you get home."

Marcus squeezed her hand and a look passed between them that Charlotte couldn't read. He stepped away from the sink and walked toward Charlotte.

She instinctively wanted to take a step back, but she forced herself to stay still.

He stopped in front of her and met her gaze. "I hope you'll reconsider and think about staying with us. Just a little longer." Moisture shined in his eyes.

Charlotte dropped her gaze as a lump rose in her throat.

His hands softly touched her arms and, before she knew what was happening, he was hugging her.

Her arms hung limply. She'd never been hugged by a man who wanted anything nice. Never hugged so gently. So safely.

He pulled back.

Would he be insulted that she hadn't hugged him back?

He didn't seem to be. He looked at Phoebe with the same emotion in his eyes that he had when he had met Charlotte's gaze. Was it love?

She didn't know what love looked like—at least not in a father. Tommy loved her, of course, but that was different.

Charlotte didn't have much time to think about Marcus as Caroline whisked them out to the "perfect little place" in the Bellevue suburb. After an hour of shopping with Caroline, Charlotte felt like she'd been in the Texas sun too long—an ache started at the back of her head as her brain slogged through a confused muddle for no good reason.

Must have been the millions of outfits Caroline had brought to the dressing room for Charlotte to help Phoebe try on. Charlotte had just shrugged at the clothes when Caroline pretended to want her opinion. The outfits for Phoebe weren't what Charlotte would've picked, but Charlotte never knew anything about how to dress right. Momma had always reminded her of that.

Poor little Phoebe was starting to droop by the time Caroline showed up with another stack of clothes, just as Charlotte buttoned up Phoebe's blue dress.

"Oh, Phoebe." Caroline scanned Phoebe with her eyes. "You look so beautiful."

Phoebe pressed the tips of her fingers together and stared

down at her shoes. She was getting too tired. If they didn't quit soon, she'd either fall asleep or have a fit.

Caroline set the stack of clothes on the little bench in the small square dressing room. "Last bunch to try. I promise."

Charlotte glanced at Caroline. She would've thought Caroline would insist on another hour yet. Was it possible the woman was learning to read Phoebe a little bit?

Caroline picked up the top clothing item—a pink sundress. "It's too big."

Caroline glanced at Charlotte. "Oh, not for Phoebe. For you."

Great. Another woman who was going to control her, telling her what to wear and that she was never good enough. Charlotte ground her teeth together. She knew staying was a bad idea. She'd have to come up with a different plan.

Caroline set the dress down on the bench. "I'm sorry, Charlotte."

Charlotte jerked her gaze to Caroline's blue eyes, sure she had misheard.

A frown tugged down Caroline's perfect, lipstick-lined lips. "That was presumptuous of me. I didn't mean to interfere or to indicate any judgment on what you're wearing now." Her eyes softened. "You're lovely."

Charlotte looked down at her grubby, stained tank top and sloppy jeans that were a man's hand-me-downs she had found at a secondhand shop.

Caroline smiled, the first one aimed at Charlotte that actually reached her eyes. "You have a loveliness that's obvious, no matter what you wear."

Charlotte narrowed her eyes. She was a little old for the Disney princess line. What was Caroline after?

Phoebe lowered herself to sit on the floor.

Caroline sighed and turned her gaze from Phoebe to Charlotte. "I really have to apologize again, Charlotte." For wearing Phoebe out?

"I'm sorry for being cold to you at first. It's been...difficult for me, this...situation." She crossed her arms and turned to face the closed curtain. "I knew Marcus had been with other women before we met and before he came to faith. I wasn't perfect either. But I didn't know he had cheated on me when we were dating." Caroline turned back and met Charlotte's gaze. "And I never in my wildest dreams would have imagined that he had another daughter with someone else."

Charlotte looked at Phoebe for an excuse not to see the hurt in Caroline's eyes. It wasn't Charlotte's fault. She hadn't asked to be born and abandoned.

Caroline took in a shaky breath. "Learning about you was a lot to adjust to. I was angry at first, but I know God has a purpose in this."

Charlotte glanced at Caroline.

The pain in her eyes was gone. In its place, there was something different...something calm. So much for Caroline being smart. She couldn't be very bright if she believed in a God Who would let an innocent girl suffer without a father and let Caroline's own family be destroyed like this.

Caroline met Charlotte's gaze. "God has helped me see there's joy to be found in having another daughter."

"I already had a mother." And Charlotte did not need another one.

"Oh, I know." Delicate lines appeared on Caroline's forehead. "I just meant to say that you don't have to leave because of me. You won't feel unwelcome anymore. Marcus dearly wants you and Phoebe to stay, Charlotte. I hope you will."

So that was it. Caroline was saying all this to make Marcus happy. Had he made her do it? Or did she love him that much, even though he had treated her badly? Charlotte dropped her gaze to the pink sundress.

Was it possible she and Caroline had something in common after all? Charlotte knew what it was like to be needed by a man who wasn't always nice. A pang shot through Charlotte's heart. She missed feeling needed.

For the first time since she'd left him, Charlotte wondered if Tommy was okay. He was probably lost without her. He depended on her so much. How was he getting his meals without her there to cook for him? And where was he getting money to buy food without her?

She swallowed the rising guilt in her throat. Maybe she shouldn't have taken that money when she left. He wouldn't be able to get more very well without her. He might get into trouble trying. Maybe she should go back.

His green eyes, filled with fury when she had come to the apartment late once, flashed in her mind. She saw his twisted features, felt the hot pain of slaps across her face. What would he do if she tried to go back now? He might hurt Phoebe this time.

No, she couldn't go back. And she couldn't go farther away until she got money of her own. But she didn't want to get it the old way. She had never wanted to be that kind of person from the very first time Momma made her do it.

Maybe a job was the answer...for now.

"Charlotte? Are you all right? Is something wrong with the dress?" Caroline watched her.

Charlotte lifted her gaze from the sundress. "Tell Marcus I'll take the job."

A smile brightened Caroline's whole face. "Thank you. Marcus will be very happy."

Charlotte hoped so. He'd sure be the only one.

CHARLOTTE SLOWED when she reached the doorway of the bedroom. She had left the door closed when she went to get the glass of milk in her hand, but now the door stood open, and she heard a voice. A man's voice. Alone in there with Phoebe.

Her breath caught as she turned into the room, the milk shaking.

Phoebe lay in the bed, where Charlotte had left her. The girl's head turned toward Marcus, who sat on a chair next to the bed.

Charlotte stood frozen in place. Was she dreaming? The scene was like something out of a movie.

Marcus held a kid's book and was actually reading out loud to Phoebe. "And here's the princess on her pony." He turned the book to show Phoebe a brightly colored picture and smiled at Charlotte. "I hope you don't mind. I used to love reading to my girls."

A shake of her head was all Charlotte could manage with the tightness of her throat. Tears stung her eyes.

What was with her today? Momma always said Charlotte was a crybaby, but she'd never been this bad.

Charlotte went to set the milk on the nightstand by Phoebe's side of the bed as Marcus continued to read.

The little girl didn't seem to know Charlotte was even there. She stared, wide-eyed at Marcus, her mouth partway open.

Great. She'd never go to sleep now. Good thing Charlotte had never told Phoebe stories before, or she'd have had even more sleepless nights with her daughter.

Charlotte went back to the door. She wasn't needed here. She stopped in the hall. Better not to go too far. Phoebe might want her.

Charlotte leaned back against the wall.

Marcus's slightly rough voice drifted into the hallway.

She closed her eyes and there she was—in her little girl dream of a daddy who read to her at night and tucked her into bed, kissing her nose and telling her he loved her. Like a father should. Like what she should have had...what Phoebe should have had. If they stayed, would Marcus be that for Phoebe? Would he keep treating her so nicely, or was this just his way of dealing with a guilt trip that would wear off in a couple days?

If he was going to turn on them, Charlotte should stop him now. Better for Phoebe not to get used to this, to get attached, than to have it all yanked away later. Charlotte should march in there and tell Marcus to stop. She could say Phoebe had to sleep, or that she had to get to bed now because of getting up early for the bakery job. But Charlotte couldn't move.

The warmth of his voice curled around her.

She crossed her arms over her chest, keeping her eyes closed. If this was a dream, she didn't want to wake up.

seven

"For judgment is without mercy to one who has shown no mercy. Mercy triumphs over judgment."
– James 2:13

GABE TAPPED his fingers on the steering wheel as he kept his gaze locked on the black car in front of him.

In this neighborhood, the darkened windows and booming music screamed gangster, probably just like the occupants intended. One thing they likely hadn't wanted was Gabe showing up behind them to run their plates and find out they didn't match the car.

The driver had taken the first right turn possible, another sure sign Gabe was on to something. Gabe never could figure out why people thought that tactic would actually work to lose the police.

As soon as Gabe had hit the lights, the driver had pulled into the parking lot of a twenty-four-hour gas station. Probably dealing with a revoked license or something worse. Whatever it was, the driver expected to have to leave the car for a while, or he would've pulled over on the street instead.

Or this might be a setup.

Gabe looked at the time. Only three minutes had passed while he waited for Pete to show up, but it felt like fifteen. As long as the driver didn't get impatient and try to bolt, the time might help make the car's occupants squirm a little. Could give them more time to work on their story or hiding evidence, too.

It was smarter to wait.

Gabe forced himself to stay in his seat, tapping his fingers on the wheel in time with his self-reminders.

Pete finally pulled his marked car up next to Gabe's squad.

Gabe got out and hid a wince as David Madison emerged from Pete's squad instead of Jim. Nothing against Madison, but the rookie was a painful reminder of what Gabe had done to Jim.

"Drugs, anyone?" Pete shot a meaningful glance at the gangster car.

"Ya think?" Gabe rolled his eyes as he gripped his flashlight.

"Go ahead. We'll cover." Pete led Madison as they approached the car on the passenger side while Gabe went to make contact with the driver.

Gabe's heartbeat calmed slightly when the driver's window rolled down at his approach. Maybe he'd get some cooperation. Gabe held back a cough at the overwhelming pine odor that spewed out the open window. A felony forest if he'd ever smelled one.

"Whadup, officer?" The driver's glassy eyes wandered as incoherently as his mumble. Another man sat in the passenger seat, watching Pete in the side mirror.

The parking lot lamps and Pete's flashlight shining into the car from the passenger side provided enough illumination for Gabe to see the interior without using his own flashlight. Didn't look like there were any other passengers in the back.

Four green tree air fresheners hung from the rearview mirror. Pine might be a refreshing scent in small doses, but this was ridiculous. "Step out of the car, please."

"Sure, officer." The guy tugged the bill of the black cap he wore over a red bandana.

Gabe looked over the car at Pete, whose sidelong glance told Gabe he wasn't alone in his amusement. The driver's politeness was as obvious as the felony forest hanging from the mirror. He was trying to hide something.

To be sure the guy didn't grab for anything else, Gabe shined his flashlight on the driver as he reached for the door handle.

"You, too." Pete kept his light on the passenger. Another red bandana on that guy's head assured Gabe his gut had been correct—these men were gang members. Five years on the Gang Task Force had been enough for Gabe, but the promotion to patrol sergeant unfortunately didn't mean he could totally avoid the same kind of criminals and crimes.

As the driver stood, steadying himself on the car door, Gabe got a whiff of something else. No matter how much these users tried, they still couldn't cover that strong vinegar odor. Heroin.

"Have you been smoking anything?" Gabe looked at the shifty-eyed driver.

The guy was about five-eleven and scrawny. "No, sir."

"No heroin or anything like that?"

He shook his head like it weighed a ton as he managed to fold his arms over his chest.

"So that isn't what I smell?"

No response at all this time.

Gabe could've rolled his eyes at the predictability of this whole scenario. He'd known the car was worth running the moment he'd seen it, and, as usual, he wasn't wrong when he was suspicious.

Only when he wasn't suspicious did he get blindsided.

There was nothing pleasant about always being right when

he suspected people. Sure, his job was easier that way, but he didn't like how it made him feel—being able to size up a person at first glance and having his worst thoughts about people be the right ones.

"Sorry, pal, but I know the smell of smoked heroin too well." If they hadn't used up their stash, Gabe could get these guys on possession. "Go over there by your buddy."

The driver sluggishly walked to where Pete and Madison watched the passenger.

Gabe opened the driver's car door and shined his flashlight over the front seat and floor. Bits of burned aluminum foil from the makeshift pipe they must have used were scattered on the mud-stained floor mats. Gabe swung his light to the back.

A boy sprawled across the backseat, his arm dangling to the floor. Cebe?

Gabe pulled back and jerked open the back door. He felt for a pulse on Cebe's neck, his own heart rapidly hitting his ribcage.

The beating was faint, but still there.

"Madison, call for EMS!" Gabe swung his head out of the car to shout. "Fourteen-year-old male with possible heroin OD." Gabe shined the flashlight on Cebe and put his hand on the boy's shoulder. "Cebe?"

His black eyelashes touched his cheeks as if he were just a normal teenager, sleeping.

Gabe's throat clenched. "Cebe, can you hear me?"

He shook Cebe gently. This was no normal sleep. *Please, Lord.*

Please, Lord what? Gabe's own thoughts mocked him. Save the kid so he could grow up to be an addict or a banger like his buddies who turned him on?

Gabe gripped his flashlight as if it was his lifeline as he waited with Cebe, staring at the boy's chest to make sure it continued to rise with his breathing.

The flashlight's handle was wet with sweat by the time Gabe

returned it to his belt as the ambulance finally drove off with Cebe inside, siren blaring.

He should call Oriana. She'd want to know. She'd probably go to the hospital and love on the kid, just like he was another Dez. She didn't realize that Dez would probably be the only street kid she'd see change like that. If his becoming a Christian had been real at all.

Gabe clenched his teeth together. He used to think like she did, hoping he could bring about change by catching kids before they were hardened criminals. He'd tried to get involved with the youth and show them a better way. He had even thought that joining the Gang Task Force would enable him to eliminate gang activity in the area and thereby help the kids looking for families in the violence of gangs.

But it didn't work. None of what he had tried worked. He had seen too many kids like Cebe to believe in that hope anymore. A visit to the hospital for OD was what had sent Cebe to the center on probation in the first place. If he survived this time, he'd keep doing the same stuff until he killed himself or ended up in prison. Kids like that grew up into repeat felony offenders like the driver and his pal.

Gabe turned to see Madison lower the cuffed suspects into the back of the squad. They were getting arrested this time. But it wouldn't be long enough until they'd be back on the streets, getting more kids hooked.

A low whistle sounded at Gabe's elbow.

Gabe hadn't even heard Pete come over.

"If looks could kill." Pete watched Gabe with a smile playing on his lips, but his eyes held concern.

Gabe took in a breath and tried for a lighter expression. "Thanks for booking them for me."

"You had more important things to do."

Gabe appreciated Pete's tactfulness. He probably suspected what Gabe knew. If Gabe hadn't had Cebe to look after, he might have done something to those losers that he'd regret. Anger still mixed up a nauseating concoction in his stomach. Anyone who'd get a kid high and leave him dying in the backseat had to be insane.

"Was that the kid you knew from CCC?"

Gabe nodded, wishing he could deny it.

"It's not our job to rehabilitate. Just get 'em off the streets and make the city safer for the innocent."

"Yeah." The reminder didn't surprise him. They'd known each other since their start on the force, too long to stand on formality now that Gabe was the superior officer. "The trouble is, I'm not sure how to tell who the innocent people are anymore."

Pete was silent a moment. "I know what you mean. MacDonald would say that's for the courts to decide."

Gabe tried for half a grin. "Sounds good on the poster, doesn't it?"

Pete chuckled. "Yeah." He looked at his watch, tapping the backlight. "Hey, shift is done. How about a sandwich or some eggs at Jean's after the reports?"

"Eh, not today, Pete. I have to drive a friend to work." Gabe wasn't sorry to have an excuse to opt out of the early-morning heartburn at their favorite and only twenty-four-hour diner in the area.

Pete looked at Gabe with narrowed eyes, then smiled. "A lady friend?"

Leave it to a cop to read the scenario like a book. Gabe shrugged. "Her father didn't want her taking the bus at four fifteen in the morning."

"Sure..." Pete drew out the word with a teasing grin. "Sounds more like a cop's concern to me."

"You sound like a cop who needs to get home and sleep." Gabe wasn't about to admit he was the one who had first pointed out that Charlotte shouldn't take the bus alone at that time of the morning or that he had volunteered the idea of driving her to work. It made sense since he got done with his shift just then anyway.

"Well, I hope this woman isn't like the last one you tried to help." Pete grinned. "Better check her for a knife before she gets in the car."

The ribbing was normal—a usual cop joke to make them laugh so they could handle the things that would make other people cry. But this time, Gabe didn't feel like laughing. He just hoped the joke didn't hold an ounce of truth.

A PERSON HAD to be insane to get up this early. Charlotte's legs felt like they were dragging on the floor and her eyelids like someone kept pushing them down. She couldn't believe she had actually managed to drag herself out of bed at 4:00 a.m.

Charlotte put on the light jacket Caroline had insisted they buy for her for the cool mornings and walked to the bed where Phoebe soundly slept.

Her long, pale eyelashes quivered. Maybe she was dreaming.

Here's hoping it was a good one. Charlotte bent over and gently kissed Phoebe's smooth forehead. At least Marcus and Caroline hadn't fought Charlotte on still sharing the room. Phoebe was happier this way. She'd never be able to be on her own, at least not in an unfamiliar place like this.

Charlotte went to the door and turned back one more time.

Her little girl looked like a sleeping angel as she lay under the pink cover.

Charlotte bit her lip. She had never left Phoebe with other people like this. What if something happened to her? What if she panicked when she woke up and saw Charlotte was gone?

Charlotte's lower lip stung with the pressure of her teeth.

She had to do this...for them. They needed the money to get away.

Before she could change her mind, she opened the door and closed it behind her, forcing herself to walk down the hall and make her way through the house to the front door.

Caroline stood in the entryway, wearing a pretty blue robe over pajamas and holding a thermos in her hand. Caroline's eyes weren't open as far as usual, but she still looked better than Charlotte ever did even at a normal time.

"I hope your first day goes very well." Caroline handed Charlotte the thermos. "I thought you might want some coffee."

Tea would be nicer, but Charlotte couldn't believe Caroline was giving her anything. Maybe Charlotte was still sleeping. Caroline being here to see her off and giving her coffee at this unheard of hour made everything so strange, like a dream.

Charlotte looked back toward the direction of the bedroom where Phoebe slept. Was she wrong to trust these people with her baby girl?

Caroline squeezed Charlotte's arm. "Phoebe will be fine." Her smile stretched into a yawn, and she covered her mouth. "Excuse me. Don't worry. Phoebe and I will have a nice morning together, and then she'll have a wonderful time with Oriana at the center."

Charlotte bit her wounded lip and made herself step out the door, feeling like she just tore out part of her heart. The lump growing in her throat lurched higher when she saw Gabe's car parked in the street. She froze.

He sat there behind the wheel, watching her.

She couldn't do it. She couldn't get in a car with a cop. Why had she agreed to go to work this way? She didn't need a ride. She'd been out in the dark a million times in her life, most of them a heap more dangerous than this. But no one had ever cared before. Now she had three people telling her she shouldn't take the bus alone, that she needed an escort to be safe.

Caroline and Marcus had insisted, telling her Gabe knew what he was talking about since he was a police officer. As if that helped. That was the part that made her the most nervous. This was all the cop's idea. She hadn't figured out why yet.

Marcus was clear that he trusted Gabe completely to take care of Charlotte, but she wasn't so sure. If he was a dirty cop, she'd be safer taking the bus. If he was a clean cop—that is, if there was such a thing—she was probably still safer on the bus. What happened if he got suspicious of her and found out the kind of stuff she'd done? Just when the Sanders were accepting her and Phoebe at face value, no more questions asked.

"Are you all right?"

When had he gotten out? Gabe stood by the suddenly little car and held the passenger door open for her.

Her heartbeat sped up. No way out now. She nodded and hurried to get in. At least he wasn't driving a cop car.

Gabe shut the door and went around the front.

Charlotte stared straight ahead when he sat behind the wheel, her nerves wound tight as a rope. Maybe he'd get the message and not try to talk.

He was watching her. She could feel his eyes on her. What was he going to do?

"The seatbelt's by your shoulder there."

Was that all? Breathe. She had to remember to breathe. She grabbed the belt and buckled it around her.

He turned on his signal light before he pulled out into the street.

Charlotte squelched the urge to roll her eyes. She was riding with the perfect cop.

He swung the car into the Sanders' driveway and backed out to turn in the other direction. Once they were on the road, he glanced at her.

"I'd say good morning," his deep voice bounced off the walls of the car, "but I know how annoying that can be when you're not used to getting up this early."

She caught a glimpse of his smile from the corner of her eye. She'd like to see it brighten up his face, but she didn't dare risk turning her head. Safer not to encourage the small talk.

"Or maybe you're an early riser anyway?"

Did she have to answer that? She shook her head, hoping that would be enough.

"I think you'll like working at the bakery. Barb's a great lady. And, man, can she bake." He tossed her another smile. "I think I've put on more than a few pounds from her goodies."

What was with the friendly act? He didn't have anything to gain by it. At least not that she could think of. She gripped the armrest along the door. Was he doing a good cop routine?

"So how do you like Harper so far?"

More questions. She stared ahead at the dark road. Swallowed. "Fine."

"I suppose you might not have seen much of it yet. The area the Sanders live in is one of the nicer spots, though."

She believed it. Money apparently did grow on trees in some places...or for some people.

"Less crime there."

She squeezed the armrest harder.

"Downtown isn't doing too well. There are some plans to revitalize it, but the gang activity makes it hard. Barb's bakery is just on the edge of downtown. It's better than the heart of the city, but not the safest area, so I'm glad this worked out to take you." He turned onto another street. "Hopping on the freeway would get us there, too, but I thought you might like the scenic route."

Now he was playing tour guide? She peeked at him without turning her head much.

His large hands were relaxed and confident on the steering wheel as he handled the car. His features were calm, and his eyes crinkled a little at the corners like he was about to smile again. Just what was he hoping to get out of this tour guide chauffeur routine?

She had to squeeze her lips together to keep from voicing the question. Probably just make him suspicious...or offended and looking for a reason to arrest her.

"There's a small amusement park about a mile down that road." He pointed to a street that split off as they drove through an intersection, the traffic lights blinking yellow.

Nobody but the cop and the baker were crazy enough to be up this early.

"Up here's the performing arts center." He nodded to a large, stone building cast in shadows on the right. "Some pretty good shows come there sometimes. Mostly musicals and dancing, if you like that kind of thing."

Was he saying she didn't look like the type? He was right. Though maybe she would like it if she'd ever been given the chance. Shows like that took money.

He smiled as he pointed out the next landmark—some art museum she didn't care enough to hear about. The smile didn't show any sign of extra meaning.

Was she reading too much into his friendliness and all this effort to keep her safe? No, he was a cop. He had to have some nasty reason for doing all this.

Charlotte looked out the side window. They must be getting closer to downtown. The buildings started to look poorer, rundown. She breathed a little easier as things became more familiar, like what she knew.

"This area always reminds me a little of Dallas. Not exactly, but similar."

Charlotte turned to him without meaning to. "You're from Dallas?"

"Yes, ma'am." His rumble gained a southern drawl as he laid it on thick. "Born and bred."

No way. No one had mentioned it before.

He grinned. "Though I stopped wearing cowboy boots when I was a kid."

Her heart jumped. Why say cowboy boots? Tommy wore cowboy boots religiously. Always had. No, she was being silly. The cop couldn't know. The idea that she could come all this way and meet a fellow Texan, especially from Dallas, seemed unbelievable.

He turned the wheel to take a different street. "I hear you're from Dallas, too."

Her eyes narrowed. Was he making this up? Did he know Tommy? Or even her? She had to find out.

She cleared her throat. "What brought you to Pennsylvania?" He wouldn't think anything of that question, would he? Should be normal. More small talk.

He glanced at her, like he was surprised she'd asked. "Boy, I haven't thought about that for a while. I guess I wanted to see other parts of the country. My momma had passed on by the time I graduated from the police academy, and I didn't have any other family left. I was free to go wherever I wanted, so when this job opened up, I took it."

She let out a long breath, hoping he didn't hear it. He wasn't a cop in Texas. The good news must have softened her up a little, because she actually felt bad when she realized what he'd said. His momma was dead, and he didn't have any family. She'd never thought of sharing anything in common with a cop before.

She watched his dark profile. "I'm sorry about your momma."

He looked at her, taking his eyes off the road for a second. "Thank you." He faced forward again. "Here we are." He slowed the car and pulled next to the curb.

The little building by the dark sidewalk had two doors. Over one was a big sign: *BARB BAKES*.

A flutter started up in Charlotte's stomach. She hadn't had a job for two years, and before that she'd never been able to keep one. Maybe this time, it'd be different.

She heard a door open and looked to see Gabe getting out of the car. Where was he going? Before she could move, he was at her door and pulled it open.

She stared out the opening. He had to be kidding. She thought he had only opened her door at the house because he got tired of waiting for her to get in.

This guy was a better conman than any she'd known in Dallas. Being a cop, a girl might actually fall for the door-opening routine instead of seeing right through it. But she couldn't exactly call him on it, though she still couldn't figure out what he wanted with the nice guy act.

She got out of the car while avoiding his gaze. Not hard, since he towered above her. She started toward the building but paused when he reached the door first and knocked. She looked up at him.

"Thought I'd introduce you to Barb." He tried the doorknob when there was no response. The door opened when he turned the knob. "After you."

She walked through, trying not to think about what he was up to. Forget just cops—no man was that sweet unless he wanted something.

"Barb," he called, looking past the long bakery case to a doorway that heat radiated out of.

Charlotte inhaled the smells. Bread and cake must already be baking.

A middle-aged woman a little taller than Charlotte came out, wiping her hands on a white towel. She looked like a hawk, staring at Charlotte over a long, sharp nose.

"Barb," Gabe smiled between them, "this is Charlotte. Charlotte, Barb."

"You can call me Barbara." She flipped the towel over her shoulder and crossed her arms. "I hear you can decorate."

Charlotte nodded, her throat constricting under the woman's pointed gaze.

"Ever worked in a bakery before?"

"Yes."

Gabe glanced at her with his eyebrows raised.

Did he know she was lying? She had watched Mrs. Martin decorate in a bakery. That should count.

He smiled, no hint of suspicion in his dark eyes. "I'll leave you two ladies to get acquainted then." He took a few steps like he was going to pass Charlotte on his way to the door, but he paused next to her. "Don't worry." He lowered his voice to a loud whisper. "Her bark is worse than her bite."

He tossed a boyish grin at Barbara that sent a strange jolt to Charlotte's heart. He could be a charmer if he put his mind to it. He and the baker must be tight, though it didn't look like they were anything more than friends. She was too old for him anyway.

Gabe's smile turned warmer as he looked down at Charlotte. "I'm glad to hear you're going to stay."

He was gone before she could think of what to say...or think. What was with the people in this town? Was the cop even trusting her already?

She should be glad. They'd be easy to fool if she needed to, and they wouldn't ask too many questions. But the rock that settled in her stomach felt a lot more like guilt than relief. Or was it just plain fear? These people couldn't be for real. They had to be pretending to like her and trust her because they wanted something in return. She was afraid to find out what that something was.

Charlotte followed Barbara to the back of the bakery as she tried not to listen to the little voice in her head, the voice that said she was more afraid they didn't want anything at all.

eight

*"Let the groans of the prisoners come before You;
according to your great power, preserve those doomed to die!"*
– Psalm 79:11

"TAKE A COOKIE WITH YOU."

Charlotte turned back as Barbara took a tray of decorated cookies out of the case.

"You've earned it." There was no sign of a smile on Barbara's long face, but what she said was a lot higher praise than Charlotte thought she'd ever get from the woman.

She took one of the flower cookies. They had turned out especially well.

"See you tomorrow." Barbara put the tray back in the case without looking at Charlotte again.

Charlotte went to the door, wishing she had a bag to save the cookie for Phoebe. Maybe Gabe was right about Barbara's bark after all. Charlotte had expected the woman to be mean at first, but she wasn't really. She never smiled, but she didn't yell or swear when Charlotte messed up on a couple cookies. She just told Charlotte what she'd done wrong and left her to do better on the next ones.

A small smile tugged at Charlotte's lips as she stepped out into the sunshine of the hot day. Barbara had even said Charlotte could start decorating cakes tomorrow. She must have done well.

A strong hand grabbed Charlotte's arm, and the cookie went flying.

She tried to jerk away as she looked to see her attacker.

Tommy.

"Hey, baby." His lips pulled into a smile, but there was nothing friendly about it. His green eyes were dark like they always got when he was mad. He yanked her arm as he took her into the alley next to the bakery, pulling past a parked car.

He pushed her up against the wall, his hands squeezing her arms.

The brick scraped her back through her new tank top. Her heart pounded in her ears but not from surprise. She'd known he'd find her. But how would he punish her?

"I missed you, baby." His furious glare said it was another lie. "Thought some joker musta broke in and took my woman. 'Cause for sure she'd never leave me." He put his hand on the back of her head, painfully gripping her hair. "She knows what I'd do to her if she pulled a trick like that. Ain't that right?"

"Tommy, I—"

He jerked her hair. "Ain't that right?" he barked in her face.

She winced at the pain and from the beer stink of his breath.

"What'd I tell you, Charlotte. What'd I say?"

"You'd never let me go," she whispered.

"That's right." The flash of his eyes faded as he grinned. "I ain't never gonna let you go. You're mine forever, baby. You're mine."

She forced herself to meet his gaze. "I know, Tommy. I know.

I wasn't trying to get away. I just..." She licked her lips, trying to think fast. "I had some stuff Momma wanted me to take care of is all."

"Yeah, I know all about your momma. I heard her tellin' you about your old man."

He knew? Charlotte's heart sank to her stomach. This whole time. She didn't have a chance.

"I knew it was a good thing I done listened outside the door when she was sayin' her dyin' words. She always hated me, your momma. Always tryin' to turn you against me." Tommy's eyes narrowed.

"Oh, no, Tommy." She started to shake her head then hid a wince at the pain from his grip on her hair. "It's not like that."

"Harper, Pennsylvania, she said. I remember 'cause I thought it's such a dumb name for a town." His fingers tightened on her arm, digging into the skin. "Didn't think you'd up and go there."

"I was coming right back, Tommy. I was coming right back. I just thought we could use some more money..." She licked her lips. "I thought maybe if I asked real nicely, my old man would want to help us out." She made herself smile and look into Tommy's eyes. "I'd never leave you, baby." She stroked his cheek with the hand that was free. "I wouldn't want to."

It worked. He loosened his hold on her other arm and slowly took his hand away from her hair. "That's more like it." He took a step back and his gaze roved over her. "You look better."

She swallowed against the flash of pain. He used to say she looked hot. Now he wouldn't even say she looked good.

"I seen the nice setup you got goin' here." He hooked his thumbs in the belt loops of his jeans. "I been watchin' you with that guy, shackin' up at his house."

The gross taste of his sick assumption slid up her throat. "He's my father."

Tommy laughed. "You're supposed to be a good liar."

"He is, Tommy." Charlotte crossed her arms. "He's the one Momma told me about."

Tommy's smile drooped when he seemed to see how serious she was. "Lucky for you he's so rich. Must be pretty dumb to let you stay with him. Don't he have a family?"

"Yes." Charlotte looked down at the sandy dirt by her sandals.

"Don't make sense he'd want you around." His words matched her thoughts every day since she'd been there. What didn't make sense probably wasn't true.

He closed the distance between them and put his hand on her waist. "I missed you, baby. I had to go back to snatchin' purses and liftin' wallets to get here." He shook his head. "Hard, stinkin' work all that runnin' and followin' folks everywhere. Things is a whole lot easier with you and the kid. I need you, baby."

There was no flutter in her stomach and no tingling in her toes like the first times he'd looked at her like that. Years with him had taken that away. But she did feel better when he ran his eyes over her face, as if he liked what he saw. He needed her. He was the only person who did.

"Are we going back to Texas now?" Being needed wasn't a bad thing.

He chuckled. "Nah. We're gonna get as much as we can out of this deal with your old man. You got an angle you're workin' on, right?"

"No, I—"

His eyes darkened.

"I mean, I was going to get a payoff from him, but he didn't care about his family knowing about me, so it didn't work out."

The wrinkles on Tommy's forehead deepened. He looked older than when she saw him last. Had she aged him that much when she left?

"Well, I don't got money for a place for you right now

anyhow. You just stay with Daddy-o for a while. Let him pay the rent." His sideways grin reappeared. "But we'll get the dough we need soon. I been checkin' out this here town. It's gonna be a cinch. Even easier than back home. Some of these stores here don't have nothin' for security."

Her heart went to racing again. "Tommy, maybe we shouldn't do it here. We could have a fresh start. No record."

Tommy laughed. "You're so lucky you ain't even got a record."

"I know, but you do. We could just live normal here and never have to worry about cops or—"

"You sayin' you want to stay here all the time? With your old man instead of me?" His eyes darkened again. "I just want a better life for us." He pushed off the wall, spinning away from her then back to face her. "I could've really let you have it, you know. But I thought to myself, and I remembered what a good team we was and all our plans. The life we're gonna build together."

"I know, Tommy. I want that, too."

He went to her again and put both his hands on her waist. "We could get that here. We got it made. Nobody knows us, so we won't even be watched like back home. We can get rich and then slip out of town before anybody even knows what hit 'em."

No, not again. Not here. It wouldn't work.

"Come on, baby. This ain't Dallas. It's just some sleepy little town with a few sorry cops. They won't ever catch us."

Charlotte bit her lip. Gabe could.

Tommy looked at her lips and moved closer, like he was going to kiss her. Maybe after her time away, the magic of those first times he had kissed her eight years ago would return.

A car rolled over gravel as it stopped in front of the bakery.

Tommy pulled away and went to look around the corner of the alley. He let out a low whistle.

Charlotte walked over to see.

Nye sat in her fancy car, parked along the curb.

"She's the daughter of the man I came to see. My father."

Tommy stared at Nye, that sideways grin crawling onto his face. "Sure ain't no family resemblance."

Charlotte pulled back from the corner, smarting like he'd just slapped her.

"Bet she hates you."

"I don't think so." Charlotte didn't hide the defensive edge to the words.

Tommy turned to look at Charlotte. "Just be sure they ain't snowin' you under, baby. You and me are the ones gonna come out on top." He peered out at Nye again. "Man, she's got some hot wheels, too. We're gonna get us some of that. I'll buy you a car like that someday, baby."

"She's probably here to pick me up." Best guess, anyway. "Should I tell her I'm going with you?" At least that would make Nye go away, and Charlotte could stop watching Tommy drool over her.

"What are you, stupid? Go with the hot babe. You gotta make 'em love you." He touched her arm as she started past. "Just like I do, baby."

Charlotte looked for a sign he meant it. There was nothing like what she'd seen in Marcus's eyes. Was that what she should be looking for?

"Don't tell 'em nothin' about me."

Charlotte nodded and started out of the alley.

"And tell her you won't need a ride the next time. You'll take the bus."

Charlotte was still close enough to hear his final instructions, but she knew not to look back in case Nye was watching.

Charlotte's luck was holding.

Nye was looking down at something. A book? Weird, but at least she hadn't seen Charlotte come out of the alley instead of the bakery.

Nye looked up when Charlotte reached the passenger door. She unlocked the doors automatically instead of rolling down the window. Must be there to pick Charlotte up.

Charlotte pulled the door open and got in.

"Hi." Nye smiled perfectly with sparkling white teeth, her blue eyes like the sky and her fine features showcased by her swept back hair.

Tommy was right. No family resemblance here. "I thought Marcus was picking me up. I can take the bus if he's too busy."

"He was going to pick you up, but he called me from the bank to say he'd gotten tied up with something and couldn't get away."

Charlotte looked out the windshield. "He sure goes to the bank a lot."

Nye could drive now. What was she waiting for?

"He works there." Her delicate eyebrows dipped. "Or rather, he used to work there. He's supposed to be retired, but it's more of a partial retirement. They seem to need him at the bank so much still. He was very good at his job. Mom thinks it's good for him to have something to do anyway."

"Oh." Why weren't they moving yet? Tommy was probably about to lose it and just walk out of the alley. He was never long on patience.

"Would you mind using the seatbelt?"

Charlotte barely stopped the groan that fought to come out as she reached for the seatbelt. What was it with these people and their safety concerns? Why did it matter to them what she did or if she was *safe*?

Nye finally put the car in drive and pulled out, using her blinker.

Charlotte turned her face to the window as she rolled her eyes. At least she wouldn't have to worry about getting killed in the car. She was riding with the two safest drivers in the world today.

"I'm actually glad that Dad couldn't pick you up." Nye glanced at Charlotte and flexed her long, elegant fingers on the wheel. "I've wanted a chance to talk to you."

Charlotte braced herself. Was this the stay-away-from-my-dad speech she'd been waiting for?

"It would be nice to get to know each other better."

Charlotte's eyebrows popped up.

Nye gave her one of the beautiful model smiles. "I know that on Sunday I probably did not give the impression that's something I would want."

Charlotte shrugged and looked away, glancing out the window. "It was a shock."

"Yes, it was. But that's no excuse." Nye's voice was steady and firm. "I think I'm doing so well accepting all the twists of God's plan for my life, and then He catches me off guard with something like this—something really unexpected, and I see how far I still have to go."

Another apology? The whole family was crazy.

Nye's reason for apologizing didn't even make sense. Of course, happily believing in some control freak in the sky would be easy for Nye. She'd never had a hard day in her life. She was like a rich princess in a fairytale land. Charlotte might talk like that, too, if she'd been born into the perfect life Nye had.

"I'm truly sorry, Charlotte, for being unkind to you at our brunch on Sunday."

If Nye called that unkind, she really was a Disney princess. Charlotte barely stopped herself from saying her thoughts out loud. "Doesn't matter."

"It does matter. But thank you." Nye switched on the blinker and turned at a light. "How was your first day on the job? I understand you're quite an artist with decorating."

"I just frosted cookies." And kept her mouth shut and her head down. Jobs were the same everywhere. Life was the same everywhere.

Charlotte's stomach tried to force its way up her throat as she sat there, starting to think too much. Her mouth was dry when she tried to swallow. Tommy was here. Nothing had changed. Nothing would ever change. Charlotte stared at her fingers as they started to tremble on the arm rest.

The car stopped. The community center sign stared down at Charlotte through the windshield.

She opened the car door and sighed to herself when Nye got out, too. Did she have to go in? One Sanders woman at a time was hard enough to deal with.

Nye came around the car, her hand resting on her round belly as she smiled at Charlotte. "You know, I think Oriana is right. Having another sister will be fun."

How many hours had she practiced that line?

Charlotte turned away and headed for the door to the building, walking fast enough to put Nye behind her. These people must think Charlotte was dumber than a cactus to believe such garbage. As if Nye and Oriana spent their perfect lives sitting around just dying to have another sister show up. When she was little, Charlotte had longed for a sister, cried for someone she could talk to, someone who would play with her and make the misery of her childhood a little less just by being there. But she had reason to. The perfect Sanders sisters did not.

Charlotte didn't buy it for a second.

She pushed into the door without looking back at Nye. A few steps into the hallway, Phoebe appeared at the end of it, running for Charlotte.

Charlotte's heart took off. What was wrong? Had Tommy gotten to Phoebe?

Then she saw the smile. Phoebe's face stretched with the size of it. Charlotte had never seen a smile so big on her daughter's face before. She couldn't even remember the last time Phoebe had smiled at all.

Phoebe screeched to a stop in front of Charlotte and held up the paper she carried.

Charlotte looked at the pencil drawing on white paper. A woman and a girl, both surprisingly real, stared out from the page.

Phoebe pointed to the little girl. "Me." She pointed to the woman. "And Momma."

Charlotte wouldn't have needed to be told that one. She recognized the sadness in the eyes of the woman, as if looking in a mirror. Had her baby girl really drawn that? She heard a sound past Phoebe and lifted her head to see Gabe walking toward them.

The guy was everywhere, dropping her off at four thirty and now here at twelve-whatever it was.

"Isn't it awesome?" A beaming smile stretched across his face. He looked as proud of Phoebe as...a daddy.

It was awesome. Charlotte hadn't heard Phoebe use a single *and* in her life, and she didn't know Phoebe could draw. Didn't know she could smile anymore either. That she could be happy.

Charlotte cleared her throat. "Did you help her draw the picture?"

"No, ma'am." He shook his head. "Well, I might have given her the paper and pencil, but the idea and the drawing were all hers. We've been having fun here today. Phoebe's been talking up a storm." He looked down at Phoebe and winked. "And she's been showing us her artistic talent."

His gaze met Charlotte's. "Artistic talent must run in the family." He chuckled, a deep sound that warmed Charlotte to her toes.

There was a tug on her lips, as if a smile was trying to work its way onto her face. She quickly looked at Phoebe. The little girl's happiness must be contagious. That was the only possible explanation for a feeling so nice at such a time.

Phoebe studied Charlotte's face, her own more serious again. "Pretty picture?"

"It's beautiful, baby girl." Charlotte gathered Phoebe into a hug. Charlotte risked an upward glance at Gabe.

He watched them, but he wasn't making her as nervous this time. Maybe his relaxed smile and friendliness explained why she felt a little calmer. Or maybe the way Phoebe kept beaming at Gabe did the trick. Phoebe was connecting with him like he wasn't a cop or a dangerous man.

If only Charlotte could forget all that so easily. She could get used to being treated so well and seeing Phoebe happy. Everyone was so friendly and kind here.

Even Nye was getting in on the act, if that's what it was, as she came around Charlotte to *ooh* and *ah* over Phoebe's picture. Charlotte hadn't known people like them existed. Phoebe deserved this kind of life.

But she wasn't going to get it. Not here or anywhere.

Charlotte wanted to grab Phoebe and run, keep running until they were far enough away that they could be free.

Tommy would always find them. And if not Tommy, someone else like him.

Phoebe shared the smile she had for Gabe with Charlotte as she glanced up.

This couldn't be the last time Charlotte would see that smile. She'd do what Tommy wanted to keep him away from Phoebe a little longer. To see her smile as long as she could.

Charlotte looked at the happy off-duty cop. Here's hoping he was as lousy at his job as Tommy thought.

nine

> "If you abide in My word, you are truly My disciples, and you will know the truth, and the truth will set you free."
> – John 8:31b-32

"THE INVESTIGATION IS CONCLUDED, and you've been cleared of any wrongdoing in the stabbing."

Gabe frowned as he watched Lieutenant MacDonald across the desk. Cleared, even though it was his fault.

"You're a good cop, Gabe. Everyone makes mistakes." The lieutenant flashed a smile. "This is your one, so you're not allowed anymore."

Nice attempt at humor, but the situation wasn't funny to Gabe at all. He was getting away scot-free while Jim got sidelined with physical therapy to regain full use of his arm.

"There's just one more thing I wanted to talk to you about." The lieutenant picked up a pen and started fiddling with it. Not a good sign. "Some of the men have reported a change in your behavior on calls since this incident."

Gabe tensed.

The lieutenant held up a calming hand. "Nothing officially. They've just been concerned."

"Concerned about what, specifically?" Gabe tried to keep the defensive note out of his voice but failed. Maybe he should have said he wanted his union rep there for the meeting after all.

"They tell me you've been a little unpredictable. Edgy. You've been coming down heavily on some suspects and civilians. You did get a complaint from a woman you booked last night as well. She said you scared her, made her think you might become violent."

Had he really slipped so far that the lieutenant was going to believe a fabricated complaint from the repeat offender who was even strung-out at the time? Gabe opened his mouth to respond.

"I don't believe you did anything really wrong there." The lieutenant met Gabe's gaze. "Reed and Madison witnessed the arrest and said you did nothing out of line. But this is the first time you've gotten a complaint of this nature from a woman."

And Pete had probably told the lieutenant how Gabe had behaved. No, he hadn't done anything wrong, but he had treated her like a criminal. He had treated her like a dangerous person who had stabbed him in the back and might do it again. Worse, he had felt dislike rising in his throat when he looked at her, and every woman he saw on the job, aside from the female officers.

"Are you all right, Gabe?"

Gabe glanced at the lieutenant, who watched him with concern in his eyes.

The prognosis might be good for Jim, but the outlook for Gabe's career in law enforcement wasn't looking so positive. He was getting emotional, and that made him a very bad, even dangerous, cop. Emotion needed to be left at home for this job. He just couldn't seem to find the middle ground he used to tread.

"I don't know." He probably shouldn't admit that to his lieutenant. But Mac was a friend, too.

"Can you still get the job done?"

Could he? He had no desire to protect or serve when he didn't care about the people anymore, but when he had cared, innocent people got hurt. He even dreaded DV calls now like his fellow officers, though stopping domestic violence was the reason he'd wanted to join the force in the first place. "I'll tell you if I can't."

The lieutenant looked at him for a long moment. "Good enough. For now."

Gabe nodded and went to the door.

"Gabe."

He turned back.

"If you want to talk about it..."

"Thanks." Gabe couldn't exactly tell his lieutenant everything that was going through his head right now, no matter how close they were.

He stepped out into the hallway and closed the office door behind him. Falling for that one woman's injuries and tearful victim act had farther reaching consequences than he would have predicted. Or maybe he'd been headed down this road anyway. He was just so tired of picking up the same offenders all the time, fighting what felt like a losing battle against the same types of awful crimes, of learning he couldn't trust, couldn't care about anyone. Any other job seemed simpler, even inviting at this point.

"All you were guilty of was caring about someone," Cullen had said when Gabe met the church guys for basketball the night before. "You cared about a woman who got beat up. That's not a bad thing. In fact, it's downright Christian."

"It's death to a cop." Gabe's answer had been sharper than he intended.

Cullen had shrugged. "You have to be tough. I get that."

"We have to stay sane. We can't feel for every person and care about everyone we encounter. We just have to focus on getting the job done." Gabe could still feel the frustration that had welled up in his chest as he'd tried to explain. "If we didn't do that, the job would eat away at us until there was nothing left but our depressed souls. The officers who can't do that don't make it."

"You sound like someone who knows."

"Let's just say I'm finding out."

Gabe shook his head. He had to get away from his thoughts before he went crazy.

He rolled on the first call he heard—a bar fight at a sleazy joint in one of their worst areas. He'd been there more times than he cared to remember. Hopefully, there wouldn't be any women involved this time. He couldn't figure them out right now.

Take Charlotte. The thought of her almost made him smile as he got into his squad and drove out of the garage. She hadn't seemed to like him at all the first couple times he saw her, even when he drove her to work, but then she had looked at him very differently when Phoebe showed her the drawing. A little smile had tugged at Charlotte's lips, revealing a hint of dimples in her cheeks.

He had tried to keep watching Phoebe so he wouldn't scare the smile off Charlotte's face, but he had really wanted to just stare. He didn't think he'd ever seen anything so cute as those dimples and the rosy flush that colored her usually pale cheeks.

She'd turned those huge eyes on him, and he'd had to work doubly hard at pretending to focus on Phoebe.

There was something so unusual about Charlotte. He couldn't put his finger on it. She gave off all the vibes of someone who was a bad risk, maybe a loser, but for some reason he wasn't scared away like he should be.

She was the victim in whatever she had experienced, that

much was clear. The evidence was written all over her scared eyes and skittish demeanor. And he knew her history of having no father. The poor woman hadn't had a chance at a better life until now. If her change at CCC that afternoon was any indication, she was going to take advantage of her chance now.

Gabe neared the bar and slowed. Squad G-14 was already there, both officers apparently inside.

Gabe parked and headed into the bar, which looked like it usually did after one of these calls.

Only one chair was left standing upright. The mirror the owner replaced behind the bar after every fight was smashed again. A table toppled. Not the worst mess Gabe had seen there but worse than some.

Madison took the witnesses' statements at one of the upright tables while Pete had the happy task of talking to Frog Junger.

The owner and bartender's baggy face sagged in his usual scowl as he complained to Pete. Frog had a different legal name, but it was so awful that he actually preferred the unflattering nickname.

Gabe crossed the room to the bar to hear Frog's statement.

Pete nodded at Gabe. "Frog here says a cowboy got drunk and started banging on the regulars. He was gone when we got here."

"Of course he was." Frog wiped at his full cheeks. "It takes you a half hour to get here, so what's the point?"

Gabe held in what he'd like to say to that. Just get the job done. "Why a cowboy?"

"He had on cowboy boots and talked funny." Frog's tone whined with the obvious. "Like he was from Texas or something."

Cowboy boots. Like at the garage burglary.

Something to share with the detectives, perhaps, but they probably wouldn't do anything with it. In a city Harper's size, there had to be plenty of people passing through or living there who wore cowboy boots, even if he hadn't seen any.

"So you're a sergeant, right?"

Gabe braced himself for the challenge in Frog's watery eyes. "Yes."

"Maybe you can tell me something. I hardly ever ask you people for help with anything. I'm a good citizen, a responsible business owner, but the one time I call the cops, it takes you forever to get here, and you can't even catch the guy. What good are all my tax dollars to pay you guys when you can't even do what we pay you for?"

Gabe glanced at his watch as Frog continued to rant. It was going to be a long night. At least in seven and a half hours, he'd get to chauffeur a certain very pretty Texan.

CHARLOTTE HOPED Gabe didn't see her shake as she sat in the gray passenger seat of the car and waited for him to close the door. Her knees had to be knocking. She knew for sure her fingers wouldn't stop trembling. That's what came of not breathing all the sleepless night or during the ten minutes it took her to get ready for work.

The reality had hit her somewhere around midnight. She might be staying under a different roof, but Tommy's hold on her was as strong as ever. She couldn't get out. She had to do what he wanted even though she could lose everything she had just found here. Maybe she could have had a family with these crazy Sanders people.

And then there was Gabe.

How could she ride with a cop when she knew what Tommy was going to make her do that very day? Gabe could find out. Didn't cops have special instincts or something? He might know.

She risked a peek out the corner of her eye at his strong, serious face. Why did he have to be a cop? She looked down and tucked her thin hair behind her ear with a shaking hand.

"Is something wrong?"

She held her breath. Had he seen her shaking? Did he know? Oh, why did he have to be a cop? "Why do you do your job?" She could have bitten off her tongue. Stupid question popped out of her mouth before she could stop it.

He shot her a glance with his black eyebrows raised. "You mean law enforcement?"

She cleared her throat. "You're not anything like the cops I know." She shouldn't be telling him that, but she couldn't stop herself. She had to know why he was so different. If he was really as different as he seemed.

"Thank you...I think." He gave her half a smile. "Not all police officers are the same, but I wanted to do this job to make a difference. I was blessed to grow up in a good home in a nice neighborhood, but I still remember when I was very young before my dad walked out." His lips pulled down into a frown as he signaled for a turn. "He used to abuse my mother."

The pause and the muscle that flexed in his jaw showed the pain he didn't put into words. "I wanted to be able to protect innocent people like my mom, the victims like her, from people like my dad. From violence and harm."

Her heart swelled as warmth moved from her chest to her toes and trembling fingers. Tears blurred her vision. Was he for real?

She stared at his strong profile, the fierce emotion in his eyes as he glanced at her, the set of the jaw she already knew could melt into a smile in a heartbeat. Why couldn't she have met a man like him before? Why couldn't a man that good have wanted her? Things would be so different.

He looked at her again and the flash in his eyes softened. "Are you crying?"

She swiped at the tear she hadn't noticed had dropped to her cheek and looked out her window. The *BARB BAKES* sign slid into view, darkened by shadows, as Gabe pulled the car up to the curb.

Charlotte grabbed the door handle. She had to get away fast.

"Wait." His deep voice was as warm as the touch on her wrist.

She turned to see his dark fingers resting on her pale skin. Such a large hand, but gentler than any she had ever known.

"I know you're hurting, Charlotte. You seem afraid of something. I wish..." He paused. "You can tell me what's bothering you."

How wrong he was. He was the last person in the world she could tell the trouble she was in, especially what she was going to have to do today.

"Do you know that man?" He stared past her, his voice turning firm like his dark eyes.

She twisted around.

Tommy. He waited for her in the darkness by the side of the bakery, just outside the alley.

Her chest pinched. Why would he show up there when she was getting dropped off? Momma had always said Tommy was dumb. *I don't need smart,* had been Charlotte's answer. But this was something else.

She bit her lip. She'd have to say something, or Gabe would probably get out of the car, and Tommy would do something even more stupid like get in Gabe's face.

"Yes, I know him." She swallowed. "He's my boyfriend."

Gabe pulled his hand away from her wrist, leaving a cold spot where his fingers had rested.

"Boyfriend? I thought you hadn't been to Harper before."

Charlotte turned to face him. Was that hurt in his eyes? Or was she just dreaming again?

"I hadn't. He followed me here. I didn't know until yesterday."

"He followed you?" His eyes sparked.

Charlotte could imagine the wheels turning in Gabe's head as his suspicions ran wild, probably hitting close to the truth. "I'll be late."

He reached for his door like he was going to get out.

"I'll let myself out." She tried to keep the panic from her voice. Steady. Slow and calm. "It's fine, really."

Good, her voice was so smooth even she'd believe it. "I'd like to talk to him before I go to work. Thanks for the ride."

She got out quickly and stalked over to Tommy. "What are you doing here?" She kept her volume at a whisper. Her stomach rebelled at the familiar stink of booze.

He leaned toward her and flopped his hand on her shoulder. "I gotta talk to you about... 'bout where we're gonna meet."

"For Pete's sake, Tommy," she hissed. "That's a cop in the car."

Tommy grabbed her upper arm, the one away from Gabe's view, and squeezed hard. "You brought a cop? You squealed on me?" His clouded eyes bored into her.

Charlotte's anger faded with the rapid jumping of her heart under that stare. "He's a friend of Marcus. He always drives me to work. That's all." She threw out the explanation and forced a smile in Gabe's direction. Why didn't he just leave?

"You gotta let me go, Tommy, or he might come out here." She tried not to imagine what Tommy would do to her if Gabe got wise to him because of her. Or what Tommy might do to Gabe.

Tommy blinked slowly and gave her arm a shake as if trying to keep himself alert. "You better be on the bus at noon."

She nodded. "I will." She didn't care where. He just needed to get out of there now.

"No foolin'." He squeezed her arm until she winced. He sneered and let go.

Charlotte waved to his back as he left, as if they'd had a happy talk. She waved at Gabe, too, since he still watched her. The glimpse she got of his grim face in the shadowed car was not encouraging.

She knocked on the bakery door and waited for what seemed like a half hour before Barbara finally pulled it open.

Charlotte hurried inside, but Barbara leaned out. "It is so sweet how Gabe always waits for a lady to get safely inside before he leaves." Barbara waved at Gabe, and the sound of his car signaled that he finally left.

Yeah. Real sweet. Maybe he'd wait for her to get safely inside the bars when he put her in jail, too.

ten

> "Real truth is distinguished from mere words, however correct they may be, by what happens of importance—that people are released by it, set free."
> – Dietrich Bonhoeffer

CHARLOTTE'S BELLY wadded into about ten knots as she watched the antiques store across the street.

"What are you waiting for?" Tommy was short on patience even when sober.

"Are you sure about this?" Charlotte bit her lip. "A little shop like that won't have enough money to make it worthwhile."

"How do you know? I'm the one that cased it." Tommy leveled a glare at the store. "The old geezer's got more than we do. Just do your job, and don't try to think."

"Maybe we don't have to do this." She'd give it one more shot. "Why take the risk? We can have a fresh start and go straight. We'd never have to be afraid of getting caught anymore."

"You're the only one who's afraid, baby." Tommy grinned, but his eyes were anything but kind. "You should be more scared of what I'll do if you don't hurry up and get in that store."

She moistened her lips as she stepped on the street, forgetting to even check for traffic until she was halfway across. Not like it mattered. Getting hit by a car might be a good way to end this.

But then Phoebe would be alone. A pain jolted her chest at the thought.

She wiped her palms together, knowing the hot sun had nothing to do with the sweat that coated them. Her stomach curdled but not from hunger. The feelings were the same as that first time when Momma had made her take a pack of cigarettes from a gas station.

Don't make me, Momma, Charlotte had pleaded, again and again. That was the last time she'd cried about taking something and the only time she had messed up. But she always got scared.

She took a deep breath and stepped into the antiques store.

The inside felt hotter than outside. From the dusty, used furniture and cast-off jewelry that cluttered the shop, she'd guess the owner was too poor to have air conditioning. Definitely too poor to have a camera on the cash register, which made the shop perfect for Tommy.

An old man came out from behind a beat-up rocking chair and shuffled toward her. "May I help you?"

"I hope so." She slipped into the role without missing a beat, laying her drawl on good and thick. "I'm lookin' for a gift for my granny. She's turnin' ninety next week, and she so wants a handmade quilt for her birthday. I hear y'all sell those?"

"Yes, we have some very special quilts—handcrafted and each with their own story. Come with me, and I'll show you." He waved a pale hand at her and shuffled slowly toward the back of the store. The guy must be at least ninety himself, the way he could barely walk.

She followed next to him. letting her gaze wander over the old knickknacks so she didn't stare at him too much.

His stooped frame made him shorter even than her, but there was life in the eyes that sparkled from behind his glasses as he started to tell her the story of his quilts. He seemed nice.

She swallowed. Don't think about it. She couldn't be convincing if she thought about the person they were taking money from. It wasn't her fault. She didn't have a choice. She was as much a victim as the old man.

She glanced over her shoulder when the old man wasn't looking and spotted Tommy, darting into the store.

He hadn't waited until they were at the back of the store like he was supposed to, but hopefully the old guy's hearing was bad, too.

Charlotte focused on the old man, looking at him and smiling while he talked. She pretended the quilts were the most beautiful things she'd ever seen and asked him the story of each one. Anything to do her job and not think about Tommy getting the cash drawer open and taking the money from it, leaving this poor old guy to wonder how he'd lost his dough when he finally found the empty drawer.

Charlotte risked a glance to the front of the store when the old man got to the third story.

Tommy had to be done by now. There was no sign of him.

She forced herself to let the owner finish his story, which she could barely hear past the blood pumping in her ears.

"Well, thank you kindly for showin' me your fine quilts." Meet his eyes. Be natural. Be nice. "I'll have to go and have a talk with my husband before buyin'. He always likes to make the decisions with money matters."

Seemed to work. The old guy blinked but then nodded. "That's quite all right. You do that and come on back tomorrow. We're open from eight in the morning to four in the afternoon."

"I'll likely be seein' you then." She smiled and turned away with a wave before she had to think too hard about that sparkle leaving his eyes when he found his empty cash drawer. What if he had a heart attack?

Don't go there. She stopped herself from looking at the cash register to be sure Tommy had closed it as she left the store. The hot sun hit her in the face when she walked out, but she kept going, not looking at anyone or anything but the sidewalk in front of her. She tried to breathe more evenly. She'd be far away by the time the old guy realized what had happened.

At least Tommy hadn't made her bring Phoebe this time. Charlotte didn't have to look to know he had skedaddled with the money. He'd be on his way to spend whatever he managed to get on booze.

She'd like to hope he would save the money, and they really would start the kind of life he had promised he'd give her when they first met. But she'd lived too long to believe in her dreams. She knew her future wasn't good. Didn't matter, as long as she could get something better for Phoebe.

With the thought of Phoebe, Charlotte looked up. Wrong direction for the bus stop. She turned around and headed the other way, trying to think of a believable excuse for why she was late getting Phoebe from the center.

She couldn't very well tell the truth. Nobody would believe she was just trying her best to survive this miserable world and save her baby girl.

It wasn't her fault.

CHARLOTTE WIPED AWAY the drop of sweat that slid down the side of her face as she opened the door of the community center. The day was too hot to walk as fast as she had from the bus stop. The hallway inside was cool, though probably more from the size of the building than air conditioning.

Phoebe didn't run to meet her this time.

Don't panic. Charlotte tried to keep her breathing calm as her heart took off again. She looked into the craft room. Empty.

She picked up her pace as she continued down the hall. She was just on edge. Tommy's store jobs always made her like this. Phoebe was probably fine. She must be in one of these rooms somewhere, having a fun time with Oriana.

Charlotte looked in the kitchen.

Nothing.

Her throat went dry.

A voice came from farther down the hallway, but not as far as the gym. Sure enough, there was another doorway Charlotte hadn't even bothered to look inside when she'd been at the center before. She went toward it.

The voice was a woman's. Sounded like Oriana.

Charlotte reached the open doorway and peeked inside.

Oriana sat on an overstuffed armchair in a space much smaller than the craft room. A bunch of kids sat on the carpeted floor in front of her, most of them watching Oriana.

Phoebe sat closest to Oriana, staring at her face as if there was something terribly wrong with it. Or terribly right? Charlotte couldn't tell.

"But the man who couldn't walk had some very good friends, and they heard about a great teacher who could heal people." Oriana leaned forward in the chair.

"Jesus!" a black boy shouted.

Charlotte's gaze jerked to Oriana. She was telling these kids about Jesus?

Oriana smiled. "Yes, very good, Owen. The teacher they had heard about was Jesus, who was actually much more than just a teacher. He was the Son of God who was there for a very important mission, but we'll learn more about that later. At this point, all the man's friends knew was that they had to get their friend to this Jesus, so he could be healed and walk again."

Charlotte's stomach started to twist as Phoebe's eyes widened.

"The man's friends carried him on a stretcher because he couldn't walk, but when they got to the house where Jesus was, they couldn't even reach Him because there were too many other people there who also wanted to see Jesus and listen to Him teach. So do you know what the friends did?"

The kids shook their heads, except for Phoebe, who still watched Oriana. Phoebe never focused on one thing for that long.

Charlotte would be happy to see the change if Oriana were telling Phoebe anything besides a Bible story.

"They cut a big hole in the roof so they could lower their friend down into the house." Oriana showed the size of the hole with her hands reaching above her head. "When they set the paralyzed man in front of Jesus, they thought Jesus would heal him right away, and he would be able to walk. But Jesus surprised everyone. The Bible says that 'when Jesus saw their faith,' He said to the man who couldn't walk, 'Son, your sins are forgiven.'"

There it was. The same stupid stuff every Christian Charlotte had ever known spouted at her. They always judged, always said she was a terrible person who just needed to ask for forgiveness from some old guy in the sky and then everything would be great. As if that's all it would take for her life to be like the people who tried to feed her those lies.

No wonder they thought that way when their hero, Jesus, did the same thing. Wouldn't even give a paralyzed guy the help he really needed. The man wanted to walk, not follow some religion. He couldn't live the perfect life unless he could walk any more than Charlotte could become all goody-goody unless she was dealt different cards. She'd been born to rotten beginnings, and there was no way out. If God really existed, and He wanted her to be good, He should've given her a life like Nye's and Oriana's.

Phoebe didn't need to hear those lies.

Charlotte stomped into the room and went to Phoebe. She grabbed the little girl's wrist and lifted her to her feet while the other kids started to whisper.

"What's going on?" Oriana's brow furrowed, her voice edged with concern. "Charlotte, is that you?"

"Yes." Charlotte ground her teeth together. How dare Oriana try to make her daughter turn against her.

"Is something wrong?"

"I don't want you telling Phoebe those stories and lies."

Oriana blinked. "I see...Can we talk in the kitchen for a minute?"

Charlotte gave a short nod, then remembered Oriana couldn't see it. "Okay."

"I'll be right back, kids." Oriana mustered a smile. "If you stay here and are very, very good, I'll tell you the end of the story when I get back." She lifted the strap on Sunny's harness, and he stood up next to her chair.

Charlotte gripped Phoebe's hand as they followed Oriana and Sunny to the kitchen.

Mrs. Peters stood at one of the counters, pouring orange juice into paper cups.

"Mrs. Peters, would you mind sitting with the kids for a few minutes?" Oriana's voice was calm, as if she wasn't about to get in a fight with her almost, could've been sister.

"Not at all." Mrs. Peters smiled at Phoebe as she passed by and left the kitchen.

Fiery heat surged inside Charlotte's chest as she waited for Oriana to say something.

"Now what was it about the story that you didn't like, Charlotte?" Her voice was so soft, her gaze so understanding, even though her blind eyes couldn't quite meet Charlotte's.

Charlotte took in a breath. She let it out slowly. Maybe she'd let her temper carry her too far again. "I know you've gone to some trouble to take care of my kid, and I appreciate that. I just don't want her head getting filled up with stories about somebody who's going to come and make everything in life all better if you just say you're sorry for things you couldn't even help."

"Wow. That's saying a lot."

Too much. Charlotte's cheeks burned hot. "I don't want her to believe in something that isn't real. Something that's not going to happen. I don't want her to get disappointed like that."

"What if she wouldn't be disappointed? What if it's real? If *He* is real?"

Charlotte shook her head and squeezed Phoebe's hand. "No, ma'am. That stuff isn't real for folks like us. And I don't want Phoebe looking down her nose at people the way religious folk do."

"I'm so sorry that's been your experience. When Christians are living like they're supposed to, they look up, not down." Oriana bit her lip, then let it go. "Charlotte, I really don't want to argue with you, but I have to be honest."

Charlotte braced herself.

"Telling these kids about Jesus is the greatest thing I can do for them. I learned that the hard way. These kids are hurting and need help. The hope and redemption of Jesus Christ is the best help I can offer them. I couldn't bear to deprive Phoebe of the greatest gift I can give her." Pools shined in Oriana's brown eyes. "Please don't ask me to do that, Charlotte. I've come to love Phoebe so much."

Did she really mean that? The tears were there and the emotion in the voice.

Charlotte could almost believe she did love Phoebe. Either way, Oriana had Charlotte where she wanted her. Charlotte would have to go along with letting Oriana tell Phoebe all the stories she wanted. There wasn't anywhere else safe for Phoebe to stay while Charlotte was at work. She'd have to stomach it for now.

"Okay." Charlotte turned away from the smile bursting across Oriana's face and looked down at Phoebe, who was trying to pull a stain off the front of her dress. She better not pick up any of that religious garbage. Even if it didn't build Phoebe's hopes up too high, it could still teach her to turn on her own mother, judging Charlotte like everyone else. Charlotte could take a lot and keep going but losing her baby girl that way would kill her for sure.

GABE'S TIMING was royally off lately. He would come to CCC just in time to hear Charlotte lay into Oriana for teaching Phoebe about Jesus. Oriana had a great response, as usual. She could win anybody over.

"Do you and Phoebe have to leave right away?"

Guilt started to creep up on Gabe as he listened to Oriana's question. He hadn't meant to eavesdrop. He just couldn't have walked in on the middle of their heated conversation. Should he go in now? Or would they guess he had been listening?

"We need to get lunch." Charlotte's voice didn't sound nearly as pleasant as Oriana's.

Still, that could be his cue.

"We actually tried to feed Phoebe lunch since you were late, but she wouldn't touch it. I guess mac and cheese isn't her favorite?"

Gabe stepped into the room at the end of Oriana's question, hoping he looked like he had come from farther away than just outside the door. "Hello, ladies."

Charlotte jerked around to see him, fear in her eyes again. What had he done to earn such a reaction?

At least Phoebe looked at him with a cute little tilt to her mouth, her blue eyes bright.

"Hi, Gabe." Oriana's friendly welcome didn't soothe his wounds as much as it should have. "Hey, have you eaten lunch yet?"

Gabe couldn't help smiling at Oriana's assertiveness. Was she matchmaking? "No, I haven't. And," he continued before Oriana could take over, "I was about to ask if the lovely Miss Davis would like to join me for a bite." He let his gaze go where it had wanted to all along, to Charlotte's face.

Her hair was a little mussed, maybe from the hair net Barb probably had her wear, and the tousled locks brushed her cheeks in a distracting way.

Her brown eyes widened as she stared at him, the fear battling with something that looked like surprise...or terror? Maybe he'd gone too far with the *lovely Miss Davis* bit. Charming women never did come naturally for him.

"That sounds perfect." Oriana beamed as if her hopes had been realized. "We'd love to have Phoebe eat here, if you want to go to lunch, Charlotte. We can try giving her a hotdog this time."

"I ..." Charlotte swallowed as her gaze dropped to the floor. "I've left her alone long enough."

"Oh, she should come with us. That's what I meant, actually." Gabe's mind formed a plan as he talked. Bingo. He knew where he'd take them. "We can grab a sandwich at Burger John's or wherever you like, and then I want to show Phoebe a special place. Something I bet she's never seen before." He smiled at Phoebe.

The little girl tugged her hand out of Charlotte's and walked over to Gabe.

His heart swelled as she stopped next to him and slipped her tiny hand in his. He swallowed through the tightening of his throat.

Charlotte stared at them with her eyes as huge as if she were seeing a UFO.

"I hope you'll let me buy you lunch. I'd like to pay you both back in some way for scaring Phoebe that first day." The only bargaining chip he could think of. Why did he feel as if more than a sandwich was hanging on Charlotte's answer? "You're not going to make me beg, are you?" He caught her gaze when she glanced up. He grinned.

"Okay." She looked away. Were her cheeks a little pink?

Wishful thinking. But at least one wish had been granted. He was getting to have lunch with the two lovely ladies he couldn't stop thinking about.

When they left the drive-thru of Burger John's ten minutes later, he glanced at Charlotte as she unwrapped her sandwich. "Sorry if this is too casual. I think it'll be worth it when you see where we're going." Why was he second-guessing himself? He never did that.

Charlotte shrugged. "Phoebe likes fries."

Gabe glanced in the rearview mirror. Judging from the way the little girl rapidly stuffed French fries into her mouth as she sat in the backseat, Charlotte was right.

"I hope you don't mind there's a drive to get where we're going. I think you'll like it, though."

She nodded, but the fingers of her free hand squeezed the armrest on the door hard enough to turn white.

Maybe this was a bad idea. He glanced at Phoebe again.

Six French fries stuck out of her small mouth at once as she slowly chewed.

He laughed. "Charlotte, look." He tilted his head toward Phoebe.

Charlotte turned to her daughter. As she faced forward again, she looked at Gabe for a second.

His heart lurched like it had no business doing. She wore the sweetest little bit of a smile he'd ever seen, complete with a hint of dimples like cherries on the top.

Heaven help him. She hadn't even shown any teeth, and he was already a goner.

She's got a boyfriend, lover boy.

The reminder worked. He tried not to think about what he was getting into as they rode the rest of the way in silence. They left downtown behind, cruised through the wealthy outskirts and a suburb before they reached their destination.

"Here we are." Gabe slowed the car for the turn. "Welcome to Reagan County Forest Preserve." He turned the car onto the narrow, paved road that was bordered by tall trees on both sides. He glanced at Charlotte and Phoebe. Would their reaction be the same as his had been the first time?

Phoebe's eyes widened as she stretched toward the window, ducking her head, probably trying to see the tops of the trees.

Charlotte stared out the windshield with her brow furrowed as if she wasn't sure what to think. Maybe she was still nervous about what they were doing here.

They reached the small parking lot that was surrounded and overshadowed by huge trees. Gabe stopped the car and turned to Phoebe. "I bet you've never seen so many trees in your life, huh, Phoebe? Want to get out and look?"

She grabbed the door handle.

"Hang on. We have to get you unbuckled first." Gabe chuckled as he opened his door and went to help Phoebe.

Charlotte got out on her side of the car and watched Gabe unlatch Phoebe's seatbelt.

The little girl took his hand again when she slid off the seat.

Gabe sucked in a deep breath as he led them away from the car and toward one of the paths. "Man, I love the fresh air and beauty out here. I never knew I loved the woods until I came to

Pennsylvania. Hadn't seen them much at all growing up in the Mid-Cities. How about you?"

Charlotte looked up at the trees, her chin raised high. She lowered her gaze, as if she'd just remembered he was there. "No. I never...I've never seen so many trees." Amazement filled her voice the way it had overwhelmed him the first time his church group had brought him there to hike.

Phoebe tugged Gabe's hand, pulling him faster. "Okay, okay." He laughed as he let the sweet girl tug him from tree to tree along the edge of the path. When she reached the bottom of each tree, she tilted her head back as far as she could to see the top.

Charlotte lagged behind, her gaze darting back and forth, as if she thought something dangerous was about to pop out of the shadows.

Shafts of sunlight broke through the trees and touched the path ahead so that it wasn't too dark, but maybe she was afraid of getting lost in the woods. They better not go much farther in.

The next tree Phoebe stopped at, Gabe touched the bark above her head. "Feel that? That's the tree's skin."

Phoebe slowly reached out her tiny hand, moving toward the tree by inches. Her fingers touched the greenish-brown bark. She giggled. At least that's what he thought she did. The tinkle sounded like music, almost as beautiful as her full smile when she looked up at him.

She nearly tipped over backward, her head craned back to see him. He gently steadied her with his hand behind her head, and she giggled again.

He glanced at Charlotte.

She watched Phoebe, her mouth hanging open.

Charlotte must have heard Phoebe laugh before. Why wouldn't she? Gabe didn't like the twisting in his gut that answered the question.

Phoebe turned her head toward Charlotte as she moved her

palm over the rough bark. "Warm." Her quiet little voice was barely above a whisper.

Charlotte moved closer to them while Phoebe watched her own hand moving over the tree.

Phoebe stopped. She looked at Charlotte again, fine lines appearing in the pale skin of her forehead. "It can't run away."

Charlotte bit her lip. Were those tears shining in her eyes?

Phoebe flew to her mother, clinging tight as Charlotte closed her arms around the little girl.

What just happened? What had Phoebe meant? He was clearly missing something.

"Will you take us to Marcus's house, please?" Charlotte's voice was thick with emotion.

"Sure. Is she okay?"

Charlotte either didn't hear him or ignored the question as she picked Phoebe up and started back the way they had come.

The mystery was driving him nuts by the time they got back to the car. He couldn't shake a feeling of guilt, but he didn't even know what he had done.

The silence was deafening as he drove to Harper. He opened his mouth to speak, then shut it. If he could figure out what had happened, maybe he'd know what to say.

Something had happened to Phoebe for sure. She stared out the window with her forehead pressed against the glass, seemingly without blinking, as if hypnotized.

"I'm sorry if I did something wrong." He glanced at Charlotte but could only see the back of her head as she faced the passenger window. "Or maybe I shouldn't have brought Phoebe out there? I hoped it would be a special time."

"It wasn't your fault." She didn't turn her head.

He pressed his lips together. He probably shouldn't ask, but he had to say something. "Phoebe is so special...But I've wondered about her."

Charlotte turned her head forward, and her body stiffened. What was she afraid of?

"She just seems so sad and scared sometimes." Like you, he wanted to add.

"She's tougher than she looks. She'll be fine." Charlotte faced the passenger window, her voice dropping to a murmur. "We just shouldn't have come."

"If this is about your boyfriend, I didn't mean anything by this. I'm not trying to get between you or anything." At least, he didn't think he was. He tightened his grip on the steering wheel. "I just wanted to do something nice for Phoebe."

The words hung in silence.

"I know." Charlotte looked at him with an expression he hadn't seen on her face before—puzzlement, gratefulness. Or was it regret? Anything was better than the fear that had been in her eyes earlier.

"It's probably none of my business, but is he Phoebe's dad? Your boyfriend, I mean?"

Charlotte's cheeks turned red. She nodded and looked away.

"That's good." His sinking heart called him a liar. "Phoebe needs a daddy in her life." He wanted to ask if the boyfriend was a good dad, but he bit his tongue. He'd already asked more than he should. Besides, the sad answer was written all over Charlotte and Phoebe. He didn't have to be a detective to figure out why they had run all the way from Texas to Pennsylvania to find refuge.

It's hard to get free, Momma had told him one of the few times she'd talked about getting beat up by his father.

Gabe squeezed the wheel like it was the neck of Charlotte's boyfriend. The whole point in becoming a police officer was so he could fix situations like this. He hated not being able to fix them all, not being able to shield innocent victims like Charlotte and Phoebe from getting hurt again.

By the time Gabe slowed the car and pulled into the Sanders' driveway, he'd decided he had to try, even if he was sticking his nose where it didn't belong. "Charlotte."

She paused, her hand on the door handle.

"If he doesn't treat you right, you don't have to stay with him. We could help you. Things could be better."

Her lips angled into a humorless smile, but she didn't look at him. "Like Oriana's Jesus? Making everything perfect somehow?" She pointed at the house through the windshield. "See that? For some folks, life is like that. Then there's the rest of us."

She dropped her hand. "Momma always said you play cards with the hand you been dealt. All you can do is try to come out on top." Charlotte pushed into the door and got out.

Her glower as she beat him to getting Phoebe out of the car and marched into the house spoke volumes. She didn't want help from the Dealer any more than from Gabe. But she was wrong. Gabe could help her if she'd just trust him.

Gabe sank behind the wheel and looked at the time. He better hoof it, or he'd be late for work.

He had to find out something about this boyfriend character. He was ninety percent sure the guy was intoxicated that early morning Gabe had seen him, though it'd been too dark to be positive.

Even if he was Phoebe's dad and Charlotte wouldn't admit she needed help, Gabe was not going to sit by while some jerk hurt that little girl or her mother. They didn't deserve that.

eleven

> "And it is now the crystal-clear word of the Bible that those who are enslaved by lies are set free by the truth that comes only from God."
> – Dietrich Bonhoeffer

"I LOVE FAIR FOOD."

Charlotte stared at Nye across the picnic table as she took a large bite of her hot dog.

The supermodel dancer was eating a hot dog. Unbelievable.

"Oh, Nye." Oriana waved her hand in front of her nose. "That smells terrible. I'm glad I don't have to watch you eat it."

Nye smiled around her mouthful as the sounds of carnival rides and games mixed to play a confused tune behind her. "Relish and Hershey's chocolate together are a culinary masterpiece."

"And hot sauce, I suppose. I can smell the hot sauce blended with all that other stuff."

"Icing on the cake."

Oriana snorted. "You're making me wish I'd sat on Charlotte's side of the table. At least I'd be a little farther away from the smell."

"Can I help it if I'm pregnant?"

"Nice try." Oriana rolled her eyes. "I think the cravings excuse wore off a while ago."

Nye raised her eyebrows at Charlotte as she took another big bite.

"I guess everyone has a right to eat whatever they want at the fair." Oriana smiled and popped a fry in her mouth. "Phoebe gets her cotton candy for dinner, and Charlotte gets pimped out grits."

Nye looked at the bit of deep-fried grits left on Charlotte's paper plate. "Dad would so love that."

"Really?" Something about the way Nye said *Dad* made Charlotte's heart feel like someone was squeezing it. That could have been her if their places had been reversed. She could have had Marcus as a real dad and known what he liked and didn't like.

"Yeah, Dad loves grits." Oriana picked up her napkin. "Mom says it's the part of the South he'll never let go."

"What's he like?" The question was out before Charlotte had a chance to think it through. She might as well finish it. "I mean as a dad."

The teasing smiles on the women's faces faded.

"He's wonderful." Nye met Charlotte's gaze with compassion in her eyes. Or was it pity?

Charlotte didn't need any of that.

Oriana nodded. "He's supportive, loving, kind. Understanding when we need it and willing to push us when that's what we need."

"Sounds perfect." And hard to believe.

"Well, he's not quite perfect." A small smile softened Nye's mouth. "But most importantly, he taught us both about Jesus. We've been so blessed to have him for our dad."

Yeah. They were blessed, and Charlotte wasn't. She grabbed her napkin and wiped at the sugary, cotton clumps on Phoebe's face so Nye wouldn't see the anger she was sure must be showing. Charlotte hadn't done anything to deserve that, coming so close to having a great dad, and instead getting only a wretched mother. Either God was really sick, or there was no such thing as God.

"Something you might not know about Dad yet is that he's also a lot of fun." Oriana's eyes sparkled. "He always brought us to the fair when we were kids, and he'd take us on all the rides. I think he loved them even more than we did."

"Poor Dad." Nye's smile broadened. "He's probably crushed that he missed out on this, but I'm glad we're doing a sisters' night out."

Oriana laughed. "If Dad saw us now, he'd say we're wasting time we should be spending on the rides."

"Well, I'm ready if you are." Nye placed her folded napkin on her empty plate.

"Whoa, where'd this sudden adventurous streak come from?" Oriana patted her flat stomach. "It'll take longer before my belly is ready to face anything too exciting, I think."

"Fine." Nye let out an exaggerated sigh and moved her gaze to Phoebe. "What do you think, Phoebe? Should we take it easy on your Aunt Oriana and go on a slow ride?"

Phoebe continued to gulp her pink cotton candy without looking at Nye.

"Aunt Oriana." Oriana smiled. "I like the sound of that."

Charlotte was still trying to figure out what she thought of it. Technically, these women were Phoebe's aunts. Charlotte hadn't gotten that far yet. Just a name, a title, but it meant something. *Aunt* meant family.

Charlotte stared at the two women as Nye stood, taking Oriana's plate. They weren't trying to deny they were related, that they were family with Charlotte and Phoebe. Was it possible they did really want the intruders in their family?

"May I take your plate?"

"What?"

Nye waited on the other side of the table.

"Oh...sure." Charlotte watched Nye walk to the nearest garbage barrel. If Nye and Oriana were still putting on an act, they were the most convincing cons Charlotte had ever met. But why would they want to pretend to like her? The better question was, why would they want misfit family members like Charlotte and Phoebe?

Nye walked back to the table, floating gracefully even with a baby bump. "Okay, which ride should we try first?"

"Phoebe can't go on much." Charlotte wasn't actually sure Phoebe could go on any rides. "She'd get scared."

"She's not the only one." Oriana wrinkled her nose. "I haven't gotten used to the feel of those rides without being able to see. It's freaky not knowing what's coming next."

"Well, Phoebe, why don't you choose?"

Phoebe didn't respond to Nye's question.

Charlotte was about to answer for her when Nye passed behind Oriana to lean across the table in front of Phoebe.

"Phoebe, honey." Nye watched Phoebe until the little girl finally looked up from the small puff of cotton candy left on the paper cone. Nye rewarded her with a dazzling smile. "Which ride do you want to go on? Can you show me?"

Phoebe blinked her blue eyes. Then she stretched out her arm and pointed at the sky behind Nye.

Nye turned around. "The Ferris wheel?" She whirled back to Phoebe. "Good choice, Phoebe. I love the Ferris wheel."

Phoebe returned to licking her cotton candy as the deep-fried grits started to swirl in Charlotte's stomach.

"Now that, I can handle." Oriana wiped her hand across her forehead in an exaggerated acting job.

"I don't think that's a good idea." Charlotte glanced at her little girl. "Phoebe's really scared of heights."

"Oh, that's right." Oriana bit her lip.

"But she picked it." Nye looked at Charlotte. "Do you think she didn't understand?"

Teachers always thought Phoebe didn't understand.

Charlotte knew better. She didn't want Oriana and Nye treating Phoebe as dumb either. "No. She got it."

Charlotte was stuck with this one. She shrugged. "Okay. I guess we can try it."

"If you change your mind, just let us know." Nye met Charlotte's gaze. "We'll have to wait in line for a while, so there's time to think about it."

"I'm ready, guide dog." Oriana shot a teasing grin in Nye's direction.

Nye rolled her eyes. "You're really enjoying this, aren't you?"

"Well..." Oriana pulled her legs out from under the table. "You aren't as soft as Sunny, so that's a disappointment."

Nye laughed as Oriana took hold of her elbow. "I can't say I'm sorry to hear that."

Charlotte held Phoebe's hand as they followed the two sisters. "Which ride do you want to go on, baby girl?" She talked quietly so Nye and Oriana wouldn't hear. "Can you point to the one you want to go on?"

Phoebe pulled her hand out of Charlotte's and pointed to the Ferris wheel, all lit up against the sky that was starting to dim with the setting sun.

"Great." Charlotte's stomach churned at the scene they were in for. What if they were all the way at the top when Phoebe panicked? What if Charlotte couldn't hold her in the seat?

Those questions were still running through Charlotte's head by the time they reached the front of the line, and the teenager running the ride locked them in the seat. He wouldn't let the four of them ride together, and Charlotte told Nye that she and Phoebe would be fine when Nye offered to ride with them.

The grits dropped to the bottom of Charlotte's stomach as the wheel started to rotate upward. They might not be fine at all. She kept her arm firmly around her little girl's bony shoulders. Maybe if Phoebe never looked down, they'd be okay.

Phoebe leaned forward to look as the wheel took them higher.

Charlotte gripped Phoebe's arms as the whole car rocked. "Not so far, baby girl."

Phoebe stared with huge eyes at the ground far below. It didn't make sense, but she wasn't showing any signs of panic yet.

Charlotte made herself breathe. If she stayed calm, Phoebe might, too.

Glancing around as they reached the top, Charlotte couldn't help but notice the beautiful view. Orange and pink streaked the sky around the setting sun. Lights from the city twinkled in the distance. In the other direction, there was a big dark patch. Gabe's forest? If he were with them now, she could ask him.

Her breath caught. Was she wishing Gabe was there? Her belly lurched to her chest as the wheel dropped them much faster this time and swung them back up.

"People?" Phoebe looked over the bar in front of them as they neared the top.

"Yes, baby girl. Those are people down there." They looked like very little people from this high up, but there was enough light yet to make them out. She smiled as she watched couples milling about, most of them with children.

But one man stood alone, staring up at the Ferris wheel, the shape of a cowboy hat on his head.

Her smile fell. Tommy?

Phoebe shrieked.

Charlotte jerked to grab Phoebe as she launched herself too

hard against the back of the seat. Panic surged Charlotte's pulse. "It's okay, baby. Please, baby girl. It's okay."

Phoebe shrieked again and again, struggling and kicking. The car swung forward and back with her movements.

"Phoebe, stop!"

The Ferris wheel slowed. Were they bringing them down? Charlotte managed to pull Phoebe into her arms and squeeze her tight as the wheel lowered them to the platform. Phoebe's shrieking dimmed to a whimper as she cried into Charlotte's chest.

"What's going on?" The teenager's eyebrows touched his hairline. "You can't move the gondola like that."

Charlotte shot daggers at the punk with her eyes. "Get us out of here."

He opened the bar across the car, and Charlotte hefted Phoebe out as quickly as she could. She tried not to notice the stares of the people around her. Looked like Phoebe's screeches had drawn quite a crowd. Charlotte scanned the faces for Tommy as she carried Phoebe away from the wheel. What was he even doing there?

"Charlotte!"

Charlotte turned to see Nye leading Oriana toward them.

"We heard Phoebe. It sounded like she was screaming." Nye put her hand on Phoebe's back when she reached them. "Is she all right?"

"What happened? Was it the height?" Oriana's eyes filled with concern.

Charlotte swallowed. They actually cared. She'd never had anyone else there before. No one who cared. "Yeah. The height." The lie stuck in her throat, where lies usually slid through as naturally as the air she breathed.

"I'm so sorry we went up. We should've listened to you." Oriana's unseeing eyes looked right at Charlotte. "Is there anything we can do? Anything that would make her feel better?"

Making Tommy leave them alone forever. But Charlotte couldn't say that. What would Oriana and Nye think if they knew about him? If they knew what he was making Charlotte do now, the things she had done before? They wouldn't look at her like they were now. There'd be hate in their eyes instead.

She hefted Phoebe a little higher. "Let's just go back to your father's house."

Nye nodded. "Sure. We're so sorry, Charlotte."

Yeah. Everybody was sorry. But sorry didn't change a thing.

CHARLOTTE STEPPED OUTSIDE into the light rain. Probably be pouring soon the way this day had gone. Or technically yesterday, now that it was four in the morning again.

Seemed like the same day to her since she hadn't really slept.

The raindrops glistened on Gabe's dark car in the moonlight. Why was he even there if it was his morning off?

She headed for the car in the driveway as Gabe got out and went to her door.

"Hi." His voice was like the rumble of thunder.

"Thanks," she muttered as she slipped past him. Why was she mad? He was doing her the favor. But she hadn't asked him to.

He sat behind the wheel and backed out onto the street.

"Caroline said you didn't work this morning."

He nodded. "That's right."

"Then why are you here?"

He glanced at her. "You mean picking you up?"

She jerked a nod.

"Would you rather I didn't?"

She opened her mouth. She shut it. She didn't know what she wanted...or what she was doing treating him like this. "I was just wondering." She crossed her arms and looked out the passenger window.

"Because I don't want you riding on a bus alone at this hour."

She sneaked a look at him out the corner of her eyes. Why should he care? He had even less reason than Nye and Oriana. And he had even more reasons to hate her if he ever found out the truth.

"How's Phoebe?"

She jerked her head to see him. "Did you talk to Oriana?"

His eyebrows ducked. "No."

"Nye?"

He turned to look at her. "No. Should I have?"

"You asked about Phoebe."

"Yes, because of yesterday. Because of what happened in the woods."

"Oh." Charlotte stared out the windshield. Her and her big mouth. Why did she let Tommy mess her up so easily? So he showed up at the fair. It shouldn't bother her so much. But he knew it would. Had he known what seeing him would do to Phoebe?

"Did something else happen to Phoebe?"

"She's—"

"Please." He cut her off with a sharp, deep tone. "Don't say she's fine if she isn't." His dark eyes gleamed as he glanced at her. "I want the truth."

No he didn't. No one did. But she'd give him part of it. "She got scared on the Ferris wheel at the fair. That's all."

"Ah, the heights. Is she okay now?"

"She was sleeping when I left." Finally. After two hours of moaning and rocking.

"Good. That's good."

They fell into silence, no sound between them except for the windshield wipers until they reached the bakery.

"Wait a second."

Charlotte froze at Gabe's low-pitched command when she was about to open the car door.

He nodded at something outside. "Wait for them to go by."

A group of young bangers swaggered past the bakery, apparently not bothered by the rain as they laughed and shoved each other around.

Charlotte started to feel very warm while she watched Gabe follow the bangers with a serious gaze. He was so different. Tommy probably would've pushed her out in front of them just to see what would happen.

"Okay." Gabe got out of the car when she did, his gaze roving the street and sidewalk as he went with her to the door of the bakery.

He looked down, and his gaze collided with hers. The raindrops streaked down his face, glistening on his dark skin. "Charlotte...I—"

The door swung open, and Barbara waved Charlotte inside. "Come on in before the whole place gets flooded."

Charlotte looked back to see Gabe give her a small smile. "See you soon."

She sure hoped so.

CHARLOTTE MARCHED to the bar where Tommy had said to meet, sweat dripping into her eyes under the sunlight that burned up any memory of the early morning rain. The heat really wasn't so bad, but her nerves were. And this time, a spark of anger heated her chest, too. She had a bone to pick with Tommy.

She swung open the door of the bar and stopped just inside as she waited for her eyes to adjust to the darkness. Never guess the day was bright and sunny from inside this dump.

She started to be able to make out the bar counter, a pool table, some chairs, and smaller tables—the usual. No trouble finding Tommy. He was always as close to the drinks as possible.

He sat on a bar stool, hunched over a mug of beer, his cowboy hat tilted on his head. He better not be drunk yet. Charlotte did not want to get stuck in some store while he tried to open a cash register when he couldn't even see straight.

She walked over to him. "Tommy."

"Hey, baby." Tommy gave her a sideways grin. He was a little drunk all right, but not too bad. The friendly stage came first with him. "Come on and sit." He patted the stool beside him.

She stayed standing. "Why'd you go to the fair last night?"

"Same reason as anybody. To have some fun." He guffawed and raised his nearly empty mug.

"You don't like fairs."

"How do you know what I like? I do lots of fun things when you're not around, baby." He turned on the stool to look at her, challenge in his eyes. "Wanna hear?"

She tried to block out the images he put in her head. He had still come to get her back. He still needed her. But he'd have to leave Phoebe out of it.

She met his gaze. "You scared Phoebe."

He laughed as he turned back to the bar.

The sound of his cackle scraped Charlotte's nerves.

"Did you do it on purpose?"

He looked at her over his shoulder, his lips curling. "What are you, some perfect momma now or somethin'? We both know that ain't so, don't we?"

He might as well have punched her in the face.

Charlotte squeezed her eyes against the pricking pain and braced herself with one hand on the counter. Why had she ever told him? Why had she trusted him? Loved him?

"'Sides, that kid loves me." He slid off the stool and stood in front of Charlotte. He touched his rough hand to the side of her head. "Just like you, right, baby?" The warning flickered in his eyes.

She swallowed and nodded.

He pulled his hand away and grabbed the beer mug. "What are you hangin' out with those super babes for anyway? Tryin' to make 'em like you?" He chuckled and sipped the last drop of beer.

"That's what I'm supposed to do, isn't it?"

He set the mug down hard and stared at her. "Just don't forget who you belong to."

She hid a shudder under that stare.

He was slipping into the mean stage, but he was sure to still make her hit the next store with him. Maybe if she did it perfectly, he'd go off with the dough and take out his meanness on somebody else.

"I won't, Tommy." She couldn't ever forget.

"You wanted to see me, L.T.?" Gabe stuck his head through the open doorway of the lieutenant's office.

"Gabe. Yes, come on in." The lieutenant took off his reading glasses and laid them on the desk. He gestured to the chair opposite him.

Gabe sat down, starting to wonder if he should be nervous. Sitting down meant a bigger deal than he'd anticipated.

"I suppose you know why you're here?"

"Maybe not."

"It's about those thefts in your district. Two yesterday. Your day off, I know." The lieutenant nodded. "And one more today before you came in. The thieves are getting bolder."

"Yes, sir." Why they were picking only his district, he didn't know. Maybe their transportation was limited. Or their imaginations. "I just came from meeting with Jack and Brian about the thefts."

Gabe's fellow sergeants were just as baffled as he was, but they were doing what they could to beef up coverage for the areas that were being targeted.

"Good. Glad to hear it." The lieutenant leaned his arms on the desk, clasping his hands together. "Unfortunately, the media has gotten a hold of the story."

Gabe squashed the urge to roll his eyes. That explained the call to the lieutenant's office.

"We're getting pressure from the top now, and we've got to wrap this up quickly."

"We're doing our best."

"You increased patrols?"

Gabe nodded. "Yes, more foot patrols, too. And this afternoon we're visiting the small store owners to talk about security."

"The detectives still haven't been able to get any leads, so our best hope right now is to catch them in the act."

"That's what we're aiming for." A spark of determination fired Gabe's words. At least there was one kind of police work he could still get into. This was a straightforward case—no betrayals, no surprises. Just two or more pure criminals who weren't trying to look like innocent victims. "Most of the thefts happen before my shift, but I'm working with Jack on coordinating our efforts in case the suspects hit later in the day than usual."

"With their method, they need the stores to be open to hit."

"Exactly."

"Sounds like you're handling the situation." The lieutenant picked up his glasses. "Ride this one hard and get it wrapped up as quickly as you can. And pass along the message to Jack, will you? I want both day and night patrols taking this seriously."

"Yes, sir." The daytime sergeant was doing all he could, too, but maybe he and Gabe could come up with a way of predicting the thefts better if they put their heads together again. There could be a pattern they hadn't spotted yet.

"Well, you're not catching any bad guys just sitting there." The lieutenant looked at Gabe over his glasses with a straight face.

"No, sir." Gabe rose from the chair with a grin, glad he'd known the lieutenant long enough to recognize his form of teasing.

Gabe headed into the hallway feeling more optimistic than he had in weeks. Catching the bad guys was what good police work was all about. For once, maybe he could do that with this case and know he had accomplished something good. Whoever the smalltime culprits were, they better watch themselves. Sergeant Gabe Kelly had just made busting them his number one priority.

twelve

> "We are all afraid of the truth. And this fear is basically our anxiety in the presence of God. God is the truth and no other. And before Him we fear that He will stand us in the light of truth and expose all our lies."
> – Dietrich Bonhoeffer

CHARLOTTE LEANED into the mirror as she smoothed a stray hair into place. She pulled back and stared at her full-body reflection in the long mirror on the wall. She hadn't looked this good since she was sixteen and figured out how to use makeup. She wished she had some now but borrowing Caroline's didn't seem like a smart idea.

The woman staring at Charlotte in the mirror had a few lines on her face and bags under her eyes that the sixteen-year-old hadn't. Still, sleeping in instead of getting up early for church had helped shrink the bags a little. She'd even spent time fluffing her thin strands with the hair dryer, and the pink sundress she wore made her look thinner and brought color to her cheeks. At least she hoped it did.

Charlotte sighed and turned away from the mirror.

For all she knew, Gabe might not even come to the brunch. Charlotte rested her gaze on Phoebe, who sat on the floor by the bed, drawing pictures on white paper.

Not like Gabe was the reason she had spent so much time getting herself to look nice. She was just tired of feeling dowdy around the supermodel sisters.

The sound of voices in the house sent a tingling feeling through her body. Nerves like that didn't come from competition with Nye and Oriana.

"Come on, Phoebe. Let's go face the music." At least having other people around might distract her from her silly thoughts.

Unless Gabe was already there. The thought sent another shot of nerves through her veins as she took Phoebe's hand and left the bedroom.

She followed the voices to the living room.

"Hi, Charlotte. Hi, Phoebe." Nye was the first among the glamorous couples to greet her, which prompted hellos from Oriana and Cullen, and a nod from Nicanor. How strange to have so many people look at her with smiles on their faces.

No Gabe, though. Charlotte tried not to notice the sinking feeling in her stomach as she let Phoebe go to pet Sunny. Maybe Gabe didn't want to see Charlotte again after she'd been so snippy Saturday morning.

Nye sank onto the sofa. "I'm sorry you weren't feeling well this morning. Are you better now?"

Must be the excuse Caroline gave them for why Charlotte had skipped church. Had she told them Charlotte wouldn't let Caroline take Phoebe? "I guess."

"Working the hours you do must be wearing." Cullen sat on the arm of the sofa and rested his hand behind Nye's back.

Charlotte shrugged.

"I'm going to see if Mom and Dad need any help." Oriana

left harness-free Sunny with Phoebe and went to the kitchen, her arm looped through Nicanor's.

Great. What was Charlotte supposed to talk about alone with the Hollywood couple? She should've stayed in her room.

The front door opened. "Is that Phoebe?" The cheerful rumble flowed into the open living room.

A shiver shot through Charlotte clear down to her toes as Phoebe and Sunny scrambled to their feet. The house must be cold.

Gabe crouched to greet his two admirers with a broad smile.

As if the air conditioner was really Charlotte's problem. She walked closer while Gabe fussed over Phoebe and petted the dog. She didn't know a guy could look that good in dressy black slacks and a blue golf shirt that squeezed the muscles of his huge arms.

He eventually stood, lifting Phoebe in those arms, and his gaze fell on Charlotte. His eyebrows went up.

She started to feel warm all over when his eyes filled with appreciation. How did he do that? She'd never known a man who could admire a lady without a hint of dirtiness. He looked at her face, not gazing downward at everything else that all the guys she knew ever cared about.

Her heart squeezed, almost painful, like when Gabe got Phoebe to giggle that day in the woods—the first giggle she'd heard out of the girl since she was two years old. He was the kind of man Phoebe should've had for her daddy.

"Hi." His white teeth contrasted with his skin as his lips stretched into a slow smile.

Charlotte dropped her gaze. Why had she told Gabe that Tommy was Phoebe's daddy? The lie was days ago, but she still didn't know why she'd...Yes she did. She had suddenly cared what he thought and didn't want him to know she'd been used by more than one guy. She didn't want the concern on his face to turn to disgust.

Momma had to be rolling over in her grave right now to see her girl crushing on a black man. But Momma could relax. Nothing could happen between Charlotte and Gabe. Tommy would never let her go, and Gabe wouldn't want her if he knew the truth about her. She'd see that disgust in his eyes instead of the heart-throbbing smile he gave her now.

"We should go sit down." She couldn't meet his eyes.

"Yes, ma'am." He lowered Phoebe to her feet.

Charlotte reached out her hand and Phoebe took a few steps to grab it. Before Charlotte could move, Phoebe took Gabe's hand with her other one.

Gabe sent Charlotte a devilishly cute smile over Phoebe's head as the little girl pulled them to the dining room.

Caroline stood on the far side of the table, watching them with twinkling eyes as they entered with Phoebe still between them. "What a cute family you make."

Charlotte could've choked. Heat shot up her neck and hit her cheeks. Was Caroline joking? She had to be joking. Charlotte couldn't bring herself to look at anyone to find out, so she let go of Phoebe's hand and grabbed the nearest chair.

The chair slid out faster than she pulled it. Gabe's massive hand gripped the back of it. He was pulling out her chair for her? Charlotte didn't look any higher than his hand as she scooted onto the seat.

"You are all just in time." Caroline smiled like she couldn't be happier with what she was seeing. Wasn't she bothered to see her precious Gabe doing something like that for Charlotte? "I'll fetch everyone else."

Gabe pulled out the next chair over and helped Phoebe onto it before he sat down on the other side of her.

Charlotte breathed a little. At least there was some distance between them, but now they looked even more like a little family.

"Hi, Charlotte, Gabe." Marcus carried a platter of ham into

the dining room and set it on the table. "And my pretty Phoebe, of course." He directed a smile at the little girl who watched him but didn't smile. "Are you feeling better, Charlotte?"

Charlotte looked for an edge in the question, but there wasn't a sign of anything but concern. Marcus and Caroline weren't even upset she had slept in instead of going to church?

She cleared her throat. "Yes."

"Good."

Charlotte watched the smiling faces of the rest of the family trail into the dining room, the husbands seating their wives around piles of colorful food on a table that looked like it belonged on some magazine cover. She was seriously in a fairy-tale land. And the weirdest part was the people who lived there seemed to want her to stay. This couldn't be happening. None of this was possible...was it?

"Let's pray." Marcus bent his head as the rest of the family copied him. "Lord, You are wonderful and mighty, You are awesome in mercy. We thank You for the mercies You have lavished on us. Today, we're especially grateful that You have grown our family by sending us Charlotte and Phoebe. We thank You so much for the blessing they are to us, Lord..."

Charlotte stared at Marcus's bent head as he continued, not hearing another word. She'd heard so many prayers since she got there—Marcus's prayers every night at dinner, Oriana's at the fair, and even the one Marcus had said at that first brunch, the first meal they ate together after Charlotte had shown up and changed their lives.

In every single one of them, they thanked God for Charlotte and Phoebe. Charlotte had thought that stuff had to be an act, especially at first when she knew they didn't even like her. But now...

Charlotte swallowed as a lump clogged her throat.

The lump didn't stop her from eating too much when Marcus finished the prayer, and the brunch went by in a blur.

Momma always told her not to eat so much when she got nervous. Charlotte kept her head down and her mouth full, hoping no one would talk to her.

"So Gabe," Marcus reached for his glass, "I just saw a story on the news last night about a string of thefts at some small businesses downtown."

Charlotte nearly choked on the cooked carrot she was trying to swallow.

"Are you involved with trying to stop those?"

Gabe nodded. "They've all happened in my district, actually."

That was his district? They were only hitting his district? Charlotte shrunk down into the chair.

"Ah, so you're taking the heat for it, I suppose."

Gabe smiled slightly. "Well, there's some pressure for sure."

"It's so bold of the thieves to do it in broad daylight like that, isn't it?" Oriana joined in.

"Maybe," Gabe's tone turned serious, "but not very bright. We'll get them soon if they keep it up. That kind of thief is never content. They'll keep going until they make a mistake, and then we'll catch them."

Charlotte's heart pounded in her ears. Something good had actually happened to her for once—Gabe couldn't easily see her from the other side of Phoebe. Didn't stop the fear from racing through her veins. *Please don't look at me. No one look at me.*

"Seems strange the stores don't have security cameras."

Great, now even Cullen was jumping in. Why did they all care about this so much?

"We're encouraging the victims and other small store owners to install security cameras, but most of them are barely making ends meet as it is and can't afford the extra cost." Gabe had the stores pegged all right. He probably knew that's why Tommy picked them. What else did he know?

"If the stores don't have much money," Oriana's eyebrows pushed together, "are the thieves even getting a lot?"

"Probably not enough for them, which is why they're hitting so many." Gabe talked like he had listened in on Tommy's conversations with Charlotte. "They're small-time jobs, really, but the media loves that sort of curiosity. I'm thankful the thefts have all been nonviolent so far."

Charlotte gripped the wooden edge of the table from underneath while everything in her screamed to run. She had to stay put. Getting up now would be suspicious. But they must be able to hear the pounding of her heart.

"Maybe we should pray for whoever is doing the stealing."

Charlotte's gaze jumped to Oriana.

"They must be pretty desperate."

Was she kidding?

"Could be, but just as likely they'd do the same thing if they had more money." Gabe's rumble ended that idea. "Or they'd do something worse. For some people, crime is the only way they know how to live."

Oriana smiled. "Then I guess we have to show them a better way."

"Some people don't want to know the better way," Gabe's voice was firm.

Oriana's smile faded. "Then we really do need to pray."

Did they know they were talking about Charlotte? They were both dead wrong. She didn't have any other option. There was no better way, even if she wanted one. Prayer sure wasn't going to change that.

"Amen." Marcus set his napkin on the table. Had he just prayed? Or was he just commenting? "I know Oriana and Nicanor have to get going early today. Gabe, are you up for some pool?"

"Actually, I need to talk to Charlotte about something first if you don't mind."

Charlotte couldn't breathe.

Caroline raised her eyebrows at Marcus with a little smile. "Of course. Phoebe can stay with us girls."

If Charlotte wasn't so busy fighting off panic, she'd set Caroline straight. This was no date—it was an interrogation.

Gabe must have found out something— some evidence to tie her to the thefts.

Still clutching the table while her mind raced around like a chicken with its head cut off, Charlotte jumped when she felt her chair move a little.

Gabe stood behind her, apparently about to slide her chair out like all the guys in this crazy family did for some fairytale reason.

She jerked her head forward and stood as he pulled the chair back.

"Would you take a walk outside with me?"

She gave a short nod, not looking up at him.

For some reason, he didn't go out of the dining room.

She finally glanced his way to see him gesture with a hand that she should go first. Seriously? She wished he'd drop the storybook knight act and get to what he really wanted to say. She walked past him and went to the front door, which he, of course, reached past her to open.

The warm air felt like a soft blanket on her bare arms as she stepped onto the path outside.

Gabe walked slowly beside her.

She followed his lead down the shaded path onto the sunlit sidewalk, her heart double-timing their steps.

He cleared his throat. "I was sorry to hear you weren't feeling well this morning."

How many people did Caroline tell that story?

"You look great."

Charlotte glanced up at him.

"I mean, you don't seem ill anymore..." He looked away, then down at her again. "Are you feeling better?"

No. She felt sick for real now. Would he hurry up and get to the questioning? "I was just tired. All the late nights, I guess."

"Yeah, your work schedule is crazy."

"You handle it fine."

He smiled. "I don't have a little girl I have to stay up for when I get home." Now he was trying to charm her. Maybe he was finally giving her the *good cop* routine.

Her swirling stomach couldn't take the wondering anymore. "Was there something you wanted to say to me?"

His eyes darted to her face like she just blew his cover.

She braced herself.

"Yes, there is."

Here it comes.

"I should've said this when I took you to work, but...the conversation went in a different direction." He stopped walking and turned to face her.

She froze.

He knew. He knew she was helping Tommy.

"I wanted to tell you how sorry I am about what happened in the woods on Thursday."

Her gaze jerked up to him.

"I'm still not sure what happened, but I know I messed up somehow." His dark eyes were warm and soft, but sad. "Seems like I keep doing everything wrong with you two."

Was that it? Was that really the only reason he'd brought her out here? She breathed again, warmth filling her chest from more than just relief.

This man was totally unreal. So totally kind.

"No." She met his gaze full on. "You've done everything right."

His eyebrows went up.

"I've never seen Phoebe so happy." She swallowed, hoping to

stop the tears at her eyes. But she had to tell him. "It's because of you."

He ducked his head a little, like he was trying to see her better from his height. "I wish I could do the same thing for you."

Her heart lurched. She'd never seen his eyes so black, so intense. But he couldn't mean what he said. If he did, it was only because he didn't know the truth. He didn't really know her.

She turned away and went ahead of him down the sidewalk.

He caught up in a second, probably in one step of his long legs, and walked next to her. "I'm sorry. Again." He put his hands in the pockets of his slacks. "I know you have a boyfriend already, but it just seems like...like he doesn't make you happy."

She almost bit her lip but stopped herself. Gabe didn't need to see he had hit the mark.

"You came here because of him, didn't you? You were running away."

"Please." The word came out in a whisper. She tried again. "Please, don't ask me about him." Why didn't she just lie? She always lied, just like she always breathed. But she suddenly couldn't. Not to him.

He had loosened the bars of her baby girl's prison and was helping her through. Charlotte desperately wished he could do that for her. But it would be enough if they could free Phoebe.

"Well," Gabe's voice dropped even deeper, "I guess it's none of my business."

She felt his gaze on her as they continued to walk.

"But I'm there if you need help."

She looked up at him, meeting those dark eyes for a second. "Thank you." Her gaze lowered, but she still sensed him beside her—his size, his strength, his manly scent. Tall, dark, and handsome. Isn't that what people said? Add strong, kind, and protective, and that was the man beside her.

Her heart felt like someone was strangling it. Why couldn't he have found her first, before Tommy? Why couldn't he want her, not just to help, but to love? If only this part of the fairytale world could be real.

His huge, strong hand hung by his side as they walked.

She couldn't help it. She slipped her hand into his.

He glanced down at her, a flicker of surprise in his eyes. Then he gently closed his fingers around her hand, which disappeared into the soft warmth of safety.

He might not be able to help Charlotte, but maybe he could set Phoebe free from the prison they were in. If he could do that, Charlotte would do whatever was necessary to make him want to.

She told herself that was all she was doing when she kept her hand in his as they walked for a long while and finally returned to the house.

thirteen

"Since therefore the children share in flesh and blood, He Himself likewise partook of the same things, that through death He might destroy the one who has the power of death, that is, the devil, and deliver all those who through fear of death were subject to lifelong slavery."
— Hebrews 2:14-15

A THUMPING SOUND dragged Charlotte from the deep darkness. She forced her heavy eyelids open as the noise continued. Where was she?

Her brain pushed through a fog, slowly waking enough to make sense of her surroundings. She was in bed. Marcus's house.

Another thump.

Charlotte jerked upright.

A face looked through the window.

Charlotte covered her mouth to stop a scream.

Then she saw the cowboy hat outlined in the darkness. Tommy?

He smacked his hand against the window frame.

She jumped.

He was going to wake the whole house. He had to be drunk to do something so stupid. "Get out here." His voice through the window was muffled, but not enough.

If he was drunk, she had no idea what he might do if she went outside. And she could see the spark in his eyes even in the dark. He was mad.

Should she call the cops? She could say she didn't know him. But what if Gabe came?

Charlotte scrambled out of bed and grabbed the silky robe Caroline had loaned her. She glanced at the clock. *2:14*. At least he'd come before Gabe would be there to pick her up.

What had gotten into her that she was thinking of calling the cops? Tommy would kill her if she pulled a stunt like that. She closed the bedroom door quietly behind her and moved as quickly as she could through the house without running into anything in the dark. Good thing Marcus wasn't sleeping on the sofa anymore.

Charlotte went out the front door and started around the bushes. Tommy had to be at the side of the house to be looking in her room.

A dark figure stepped out of the deepest shadows.

She started.

"Hey, baby." His gaze moved over the short shorts and tank she wore for pajamas.

She pulled the front of her robe closed.

He narrowed his eyes.

"Boy, it's chilly tonight." The air was cool, and she did have goose bumps on her legs. She hoped he'd buy the excuse for her sudden shyness. She didn't want to think about the reason for it herself.

He closed the distance between them and gripped her arm.

"You're different. You been seein' somebody?" His stinking breath heated her face.

She made herself meet his glare. "No. Of course not."

He shook her. Hard. "Little liar." He hissed out the words. "I saw you."

Her heart raced. Saw her when?

Oh no.

"That's right, baby. Think I wouldn't find out?"

She wiped her reaction off her face. "He's just a cop. The friend of my old man's. I have to be nice to him, don't I?"

Tommy's thumbs pressed painfully into her arms. "I seen how nice you was. You was holdin' hands."

She thought fast, keeping her breathing slow and even, her expression real. "He wanted a lot more than that. I made him happy with a little hand holding. I got him right where I want him." She smiled, ignoring the bile rising up her throat.

Tommy's forehead wrinkled, and he blinked.

"I mean it'll help a lot to have a cop in our pockets, right?"

A slow smile crawled across his lips. He chuckled. "Yeah. Could come in real handy."

"I was only thinking of us." She tried to get her voice to purr as she kept her smile on. "How are we doing with the money? Got enough saved up to get our own place?"

He let go of her arms and took a step back, a little off balance but not bad. "No. No, we got to get a lot more."

The relief that slowed her heartbeat had to be from seeing he wasn't too drunk, not from what he said. She still wanted to leave as soon as they could. Didn't she?

"We're gonna hit two stores tomorrow."

Her stomach flipped. "Two? Tommy, are you sure? We're drawing too much attention as it is."

He grinned. "Ain't that somethin'? Never got on TV in Dallas. You and me, we're gonna be celebrities." He hooked his thumbs through his belt loops.

"We've got to at least move to some other area. We're doing them too close together. They're all in one cop's district, or whatever they call it."

His grin dropped. "You mean your cop pal."

More of a statement than a question, but he watched her for an answer.

He must have thought he got it in her silence. He smiled, but his eyes stayed mean. "Well, I think I kinda like that part." He moved close again, his nose almost touching hers as he grabbed her sore arm and stared down into her face. "Don't you forget. I'm watchin' you."

"I..." Her voice came out as a whisper as she tried not to remember the screaming pain the night he'd broken her arm. He might do it again, even if he wasn't as drunk. "I won't forget."

He let go.

She watched until he disappeared into the darkness. Then she breathed. She gently felt her arm where he'd grabbed her. If he made bruises again, she'd have to figure out an excuse. The weather was too hot to wear long sleeves without a reason.

She went back to the front door and gripped the doorknob.

It wouldn't turn.

She tried again.

Locked.

Her mouth went dry. Of all the stupid things. She hadn't thought to check if it was unlocked when she'd flown outside. She was just trying to keep Tommy from waking everyone. Now she would have to wake someone herself. Unless she stayed outside until morning?

She shook her head at her second dumb thought of the night. She couldn't very well be sitting outside in her pajamas when Gabe came to pick her up. She had to get back in.

Marcus kept all the windows locked, including hers, so that option was out. She took in a deep breath. There was no other choice.

She knocked on the door, softly at first.

No response.

She bit her lip and tried a little harder. If she had any luck in the world at all, maybe Marcus would be the one to hear her.

The door opened, and Marcus peered through the crack. "Charlotte?" He opened the door wider. "What are you—" He looked her up and down as if he thought he was dreaming. "You don't have any shoes on."

Charlotte looked down at her bare feet. She hadn't noticed. She'd spent so much of her life going barefoot as a kid, it still felt more normal to her than shoes.

"Are you all right?"

She stared at him. He'd just caught her prowling around his house at night, and he was worried about her?

She nodded and brushed past him.

"What were you doing?"

Ah. There was the suspicion. "I thought I heard a noise."

"So did I. I thought it might be the water pipes again." Marcus's eyebrows knit together. "I'd rather you leave that kind of thing for me to check out. This is a pretty safe neighborhood but probably not as safe as we'd like to think."

She nodded then made herself meet his gaze. *Look like you're up to something, and you're gonna get caught,* Momma's voice said in Charlotte's head.

Marcus gave her a small smile. "I'm glad you're all right. Very brave of you to check on your own like that."

That was her. Pure guts down to her little toe. The lie felt like a rock in her stomach. Or maybe the feeling came from getting so little sleep or from the fear eating her from the inside out. "I better get to bed."

"Oh, of course." Marcus looked at the grandfather clock in the corner. "I'm sorry. Here I am talking when you have to leave in just a little while."

Another apology. These people had to learn not to apologize

so much, or they'd get suckered by every crook out there. Just like they were getting suckered by her.

She turned away and went to her room. There would be no more sleep for her tonight.

GABE GLANCED at Charlotte in the darkness of the car. He wished he could see her more clearly or that she'd at least look at him. He shouldn't have expected anything different when he picked her up this time, but the disappointment that gripped his chest didn't make sense unless he had.

So much for great expectations. Charlotte was quieter and shyer than ever. She had sunk into the seat without a word and looked down at her lap or out the passenger window the whole drive, answering any question Gabe ventured with a short nod or shoulder shrug.

What had Sunday been about then? Why had she taken his hand during their walk?

She had looked so pretty in her sundress. So small, delicate...and scared. But he knew there was toughness under that exterior that kept her and Phoebe alive. She cared so deeply about her little girl. She was such a wonderful mother and beautiful woman.

And he was coming to care for her way too much, especially considering she wasn't a believer. He'd convinced himself yesterday that he only cared about her as a friend. She was a woman in need. How could he not care? He prayed that friendship was really all his feelings were for her. He couldn't have a serious relationship with a non-Christian, no matter how appealing she was.

He could've laughed if he'd been alone. His speculation on having a serious relationship with a woman who looked like she might jump out of the moving car just to get away from him was ironic, to say the least.

Light sprinkles hit the windshield, and Gabe turned on the wipers.

Charlotte jerked when the blades popped up.

His heart softened as he looked at her.

She held herself rigid, frozen, but with as much pent-up energy as a deer poised to bound away at the slightest noise.

Something had spooked her. Was it him? Had his response to her on Sunday put too much pressure on her? Maybe she was afraid of what the boyfriend might do if he knew she had reacted to Gabe like she had.

Or had the boyfriend gotten to her? Done something to her?

Gabe's blood ran hot in his veins. He wanted to ask, wanted to drag the information from her so he could stop the abuse. But he had told her he was there if she needed him, not that he'd hound her until she told him everything. He held in his questions and ended the drive in silence.

He desperately wanted to say something as he opened her car door and waited with her until Barb showed up, but he couldn't think of anything that would stop her trembling or the frightened darting of her gaze. Nothing that would make her feel safe.

If the problem was Gabe, he'd have to give her some space. He should probably start by not going to see Phoebe at CCC that afternoon, so Charlotte wouldn't have to bump into him there. He needed to catch up on sleep and do his laundry anyway. Maybe sleep and a dose of normalcy could fix whatever was wrong with his head...and his heart.

CHARLOTTE TOOK IN A SHAKY BREATH, trying to get calm before she reached the small art store. The second theft in one day and probably the hundredth of her life. She shouldn't be scared, but she still was, just like always.

Tommy was all excited about this store, thinking it was bound to have more cash since it sold expensive jewelry and pictures by artists. All that meant was more pressure for Charlotte.

The air in the store as Charlotte entered was like the inside of a refrigerator. Funny-looking jewelry hung on racks and lay on tables that were close together.

"May I help you?" A black-haired woman with bright red lipstick watched Charlotte from behind a desk near the door.

Great. A woman. Women like this one were harder.

A cash drawer sat on the desk by a computer. Did Tommy know how to handle one of those?

Charlotte's nerves fluttered faster as she looked toward the back of the store where a bunch of pictures hung on the walls. "Yes. I'm lookin' for a real work of art. Somethin' I can hang above my fireplace in our new home. Somethin' people will know I spent some real money to buy, you know?"

The woman raised a plucked eyebrow. "I see. Our more expensive pieces are at the back of the store." She pointed with a two-inch, red fingernail.

"Oh, would you mind showin' me?" Charlotte laid on the drawl, though she wasn't sure it would work on this kind of chick. "I don't know much about art, but I have some friends that do, and I want them to like it."

"I can't leave the desk. You'll find we have a very nice piece by Johnny Edwards. Any art aficionado should appreciate his work."

Art what? Panic surged up Charlotte's throat. "I'd really like it if you could point it out to me and maybe tell me somethin' about the other pieces back there? I want to learn more about art and what makes these pictures good."

"Maybe you can take an art class at the technical college."

The woman flashed a bar of bleached teeth like that would cover the nastiness of her comment.

So much for customer service. Had Charlotte been made? Maybe her clothes gave her away. She was in her old tank top and jeans. She hadn't known Tommy would want to hit a place she had to dress for. Whatever had gone wrong, this woman was not going to go to the back of the store. And Tommy would come in any second. Charlotte had to get out fast.

"I guess I'll be takin' my business elsewhere then." Charlotte drew herself up to her full petite height and tilted her chin like Caroline would.

"You do that." The woman's final shot floated out the door as Charlotte opened it and bumped right into Tommy.

"Excuse me, ma'am." Surprise hit Tommy's green eyes as he looked down at Charlotte. "Are you hurt, ma'am?" Lucky he wasn't drunk yet, or he never would've thought to follow her like he was concerned she was hurt.

They walked past the front of the building and stopped in front of the next one, which stood empty.

"What are you doing out here?" Tommy's eyes shot sparks.

"She wouldn't go." Charlotte kept her voice low, just in case.

"What do you mean, she wouldn't go?"

"I tried everything, but she wouldn't leave the cash drawer. She said she wouldn't."

"I oughta just go in there and rob the chick to her face." Spit flew off Tommy's lips as he started to turn toward the store.

"No! Tommy, don't." Charlotte grabbed the sleeve of his checkered cowboy shirt.

He stopped but shook off her hand. He glared at her.

A new kind of fear churned in her stomach. Why would he say he would rob the place outright? He'd never wanted to do anything like that before. That would be stupid. He'd get them both caught.

"How'd she know we were gonna rob her?" His eyes narrowed.

"What?" Charlotte blinked at him. "She didn't. I think she just didn't like me enough."

"I knew we should've brought the kid."

No. Please, no.

"Always worked best that way. Everybody feels sorry for you with her along."

Charlotte wouldn't do it. She couldn't live with herself if she had to involve Phoebe again.

"You'll have to bring the kid to the store later tonight and get her to cry like the other times."

As if it were that easy. Phoebe only cried because she was so scared of Tommy when he bullied and threatened her before they went in every time. Charlotte had to think of something to put him off. "Not tonight, Tommy. That's my only time to sleep before work. I can't do it then."

"Listen to the princess." Tommy sneered. "You need to stop complainin' and do what you're told."

"They would notice. My old man and his wife. They'd notice if I went somewhere. He's always home from the bank by then."

"Bank?" Tommy stared at her. "Your old man works at a bank?"

Charlotte swallowed. "Yes."

"Why didn't you say so before?" The pleased glint in his eyes scared her almost as much as his mean one.

She had to get his mind off what it was on. "I'll bring Phoebe for the next job tomorrow." She'd even give him that, if he'd stop whatever he was hatching.

But he only muttered, "Yeah," as he turned to cross the street.

She hated that thinking look. The results were never pretty.

fourteen

> "They promise them freedom, but they themselves are slaves of corruption. For whatever overcomes a person, to that he is enslaved."
> – 2 Peter 2:19

GABE SHOULD HAVE BEEN REFRESHED after the extra hours of sleep and his relaxed afternoon, but instead he started his next shift feeling as if he'd already worked half of it. Must have been all the thinking he was doing about Charlotte and how he could help her. Thinking that led nowhere.

Gabe tried to stop his thoughts along those lines as he pulled up to Smarten's Tailor Shop. Things might be looking up. The infamous small business thieves had hit a store during his shift. Or the theft had just been discovered now, but had actually happened hours earlier.

Gabe blew out a breath as he got out of his squad and went into the store. He had told Marcus the thieves were dumb, but their technique was actually pretty sound. Targets were carefully chosen—small stores with no cameras and only one employee or owner working at a time.

"You're too late." The forty-year-old male with glasses scolded Gabe as soon as he set foot in the door. "They were, too." He pointed at Pete and Madison, who were behind the counter examining the cash register.

"Do you know when the theft occurred, sir?" Gabe met the heavyset man's accusing stare.

"No." He glanced away and puttered with a shirt that was folded on the counter.

Gabe tried not to let his irritation show. Some people always needed someone else to blame.

"Want to take a look?" Pete pointed to the cash drawer with his pen.

Gabe went behind the counter as Madison came out to make room. "Same MO?"

Pete nodded. "The owner says he doesn't remember anything suspicious and only noticed the money was gone when he started to close up."

Clever. In stores like this, the thief or thieves were able to get the drawer open without alerting the owner or employee. Took at least two people, one to distract and one to get in the drawer.

Gabe studied the lock and edge of the drawer. No sign of forced entry. Whoever was getting into these drawers was smart enough to do some homework beforehand or was a magician with locks. No prints at the scene, no witnesses, and seemingly no mistakes made. So far.

"I wish I knew who suddenly showed up in our town." Pete jotted down some information in his notepad.

Gabe left the officers to wrap up the call and headed back to the station to tackle the paperwork that awaited him. But his mind was not on office work. Pete's half-joking comment had sparked an idea.

Charlotte's boyfriend had just shown up in Harper.

What's more, there was a cowboy boot print at the scene of a burglary, a bar fight with a cowboy, and then Gabe saw Charlotte's Texas boyfriend drunk the same night as the disturbance.

The hair stood up on the back of Gabe's neck. Maybe he just wanted the dots to connect, but the first of these mysterious daytime thefts occurred the same day the boyfriend had shown up.

Gabe went back in his mind to the night of the garage burglary with the boot print. That incident had happened two nights earlier. He sighed. Maybe he wasn't the same guy. Maybe Charlotte's boyfriend didn't even own cowboy boots. Gabe hadn't been able to see him well in the dark that early morning, though he was wearing a cowboy hat.

Still, it was a lot of maybes and nothing concrete. Sloppy police work. Going all these days without learning anything new about Charlotte's boyfriend was eating at him, especially after seeing how edgy she was again. He couldn't run a check when he had nothing to start with.

All he knew so far was that Charlotte was afraid enough to run as far as she could away from the guy, but even that was partially guesswork.

Gabe made himself breathe and relax the jaw that was starting to hurt from clenching it so hard. He needed to cool down and forget the whole thing. He was losing his objectivity. Or he had already lost it. Here he was, trying to make someone he didn't even know into the mastermind of a string of thefts just because he didn't like the guy.

Gabe's instincts told him Charlotte's loser boyfriend was no good, but, like a good cop, he had to wait for the guy to prove it. Gabe just hoped he'd be there to catch the cowboy when he did, and that Charlotte and Phoebe wouldn't get caught in the middle.

CHARLOTTE LEANED her forehead against the doorframe as she listened to Marcus read. Never got old, even though Charlotte listened outside the door like this every night.

She shouldn't have allowed it for Phoebe's sake. The poor girl would be crushed when they would have to leave, and she wouldn't get a bedtime story from Marcus anymore.

Charlotte didn't know why, but instead of stopping Marcus after that first time, she quickly brushed her teeth each night and hurried back to the bedroom, telling herself he wouldn't keep the daddy act going.

But every night, his voice floated into the hallway as he read another storybook to Phoebe.

Charlotte wasn't looking forward to it for herself or anything. She just didn't want Phoebe to be disappointed.

"The end."

Already? Charlotte sighed and pushed the door farther open as she went into the bedroom.

"Good night, princess." Marcus stood and looked down at Phoebe, lying in the bed. "Sleep tight." He bent over and kissed her forehead. "I love you."

Charlotte's heart stuck in her throat.

Marcus walked toward Charlotte. "Hi," he whispered, like Phoebe was already asleep. "Can I talk to you for a second?"

Her nerves kicked in, tingling at the back of her neck.

"Sure." She looked at Phoebe. "I'll be right back, Phoebe. You just wait in bed."

The little girl watched Charlotte with her blue eyes. No hint of panic or fear. Phoebe had been so much calmer at night lately. Back in Texas, nights were always the worst for her. Something about this fairytale land...

Marcus folded his arms across his chest as Charlotte went into the hallway, closing the door partway. He looked serious.

This couldn't be good. "Now I don't want to scare you by telling you this, but I think you should know."

Okay. Now she was good and scared.

"Mrs. Peters...I think you've met her at Oriana's community center?"

Charlotte jerked a nod.

"Well, she told Oriana that she's seen a man outside the center two different days. The second time she saw him, she asked if she could help him with something, and he wanted to know if Phoebe Davis was there."

Charlotte's mouth went dry.

"Don't worry. She didn't give him an answer. She just asked him why he wanted to know, and he left, saying some rather unkind things, from what I gather. Oriana thought you should know. Do you have any idea who the man might be?"

She could guarantee who he was. She searched Marcus's eyes for a sign he was conning her. Nothing but concern reflected back at her. Gabe must not have told anyone about Tommy. Score another point for the man she could never be with.

She cleared her throat. "No. I don't know who he is." Her stomach started to curdle as she spoke. What was Tommy doing there? What did he want with Phoebe? She swallowed, dropping her gaze as her thoughts raced. He could have been planning all along to make Charlotte bring Phoebe in on the jobs. Or did he just want to remind Charlotte he was in control?

She turned back to the bedroom but paused. She wasn't ready to face Phoebe yet with this panic rising in her chest. She'd been doing everything Tommy asked of her, everything to show she wouldn't try to run away again. Wasn't that enough?

She should have known it wasn't over. He had been too nice about needing to find her and follow her here, like he was always holding back. What if he was still planning something to punish her for what she'd done? Tommy knew Charlotte's weak spot was Phoebe.

The horrible things he could do to her baby girl flashed through Charlotte's mind. She cried out in terror.

Marcus was suddenly there, his arms going around her.

She clung to him, shaking, unable to breathe.

"Shhh." He stroked her hair with his hand.

Charlotte's heartbeat slowed as he held her in the arms she had needed so many times before. Where had he been then?

She pushed away.

"Charlotte, what is it? Are you in danger?"

She'd been in danger since the day she was born without a father. She spun back to glare at him. "You're too late." She stalked into the bedroom and shut the door in his face.

GABE KEPT his gaze moving over the dark road as he drove, but his mind was on his destination. Would Charlotte be less nervous with him now that he had given her some space? He had determined that he wouldn't pressure her at all. He wouldn't do anything to suggest his interest and concern came from anything more than friendship. He didn't want to scare her. He only wanted to help.

But was that really all he wanted? Was friendship enough to explain how much he had missed seeing Phoebe and Charlotte in the afternoon before his shift started? He knew better than to fall for someone who was obviously so resistant to God, not to mention the heavy load of baggage she carried. What if his heart wasn't listening to his head and he was falling for her anyway?

The situation wasn't like at work, where he was misjudging someone based on his feelings. With Charlotte, he knew she was a good person who'd had a rough life up to now. She hadn't had a chance to be anything else or to make something better of her life and Phoebe's. His feelings might be stronger than they should be, but they weren't wrong. Of that he was sure.

Now if he just knew how to get her to trust him, there might be some hope for—

Two other cars at an intersection at three thirty a.m.? Gabe's cop instincts went on alert as a black car passed him on the four-lane road and headed for the intersection that another car was approaching.

The black car accelerated through the intersection, just in time to smash into the side of the crossing red vehicle.

Gabe cringed and pulled over to the side of the road. He grabbed his cell phone and called Dispatch as he watched the cars. The drivers of both vehicles got out, apparently healthy enough to start up an argument right off the bat. Thank the Lord the black car's driver hadn't been exceeding the twenty-five speed limit by very much.

Gabe gave Dispatch the information on autopilot as he thought about the next phone call he'd have to make. He wouldn't be able to pick up Charlotte now, since the two yelling drivers would clearly need a witness.

Maybe it was better this way. He'd give Charlotte more time and space. Wasn't absence supposed to make the heart grow fonder?

Is that what he was hoping for? Gabe ended the call with Dispatch and breathed out a long sigh as he dialed the Sanders' number. Maybe he was the one who needed the time and space.

CHARLOTTE PICKED up her pace as she walked the block from the bus stop to the center. She'd be a sticky, hot mess after hoofing it like this in the sun, but she only had a few minutes to pick up Phoebe and get back for the next bus.

The time Tommy had told Charlotte to meet him after work didn't allow for this back and forth by bus, but Tommy would never believe that if she showed up late.

She just hoped Gabe wasn't at the center with Phoebe today.

He hadn't shown up there yesterday, Oriana had told her. Maybe Charlotte would feel better if he'd driven her to work instead of getting caught up in that accident, if that was really why he hadn't come.

He had been so distant in the car ride the morning before. He had barely said a word. Charlotte knew she had been edgy during the whole drive. She kept thinking Tommy might have been watching them as she got in the car or when they reached the bakery. She kept feeling like he was right there, staring over her shoulder or ready to jump out of the shadows.

Still, Gabe couldn't have known all that. She thought he'd talk to her, maybe calm her with that deep, rumbly voice of his. After their conversation on Sunday and the tender way he had held her hand...she thought he might have been different toward her. For a second, she had even wondered if she'd gone too far on Sunday and given him too much encouragement. But she should have known better. He hadn't even talked to her in the car, let alone tried to hold her hand or something more.

Was he that much of a gentleman or just not interested in her? She wiped a drop of sweat off before it slid into her eye.

Maybe there wasn't an accident this morning. Maybe he thought she might have gotten the wrong message and was avoiding her. His way of letting her down easy.

Charlotte crossed the cracked parking lot, a bitter taste crawling up her throat. He didn't have to go to all that trouble. She hadn't thought for a second he actually liked her.

Charlotte slammed into the door of the center and started down the hallway, bypassing the craft room since she didn't hear any kids' voices in there.

"Oh, it's you."

Charlotte started at the woman's voice.

Mrs. Peters came out of the craft room. "I thought you might have been that man that's been coming around. Did Oriana tell you?"

"Where's Phoebe?"

The old woman blinked like she'd been hit. "In the story room with Oriana." She pointed down the hall.

Charlotte hurried in that direction.

"It's the last door on your left before the gymnasium," Mrs. Peters called.

Busybody. Charlotte reached the room and looked inside. Oriana and a woman Charlotte had never seen before sat on the floor with Phoebe between them, all three of them looking at a book.

"Very good, Phoebe." The strange woman watched Phoebe. "Now can you say the word, *elephant*?"

Charlotte's heartbeat picked up speed. What were they doing?

"Momma." Phoebe scrambled to her feet, and the stranger swung the book away as Phoebe ran to Charlotte.

"Hi, Charlotte." Oriana lifted her head.

Charlotte picked Phoebe up and held her as the little girl grabbed Charlotte's neck in a hug. "You okay, baby girl?" Charlotte glared at the strange woman as she stood along with Oriana.

"You're early today." Oriana smiled like nothing was going on. "Barbara didn't need you to stay as late today?"

"No."

"Well, I'm glad you're here. I want you to meet Kathy Grumer. Kathy, this is Charlotte, Phoebe's mom."

The Kathy woman walked over to Charlotte and put out her hand.

Charlotte pretended she had to heft Phoebe higher in her arms.

Oriana grabbed Sunny's harness strap, and he led her to

Charlotte by the door. "Kathy is a social worker. She comes to help out with the kids here when she can."

A social worker? Charlotte's heart thudded against her chest.

"That's right. I've really enjoyed getting to know Phoebe."

"I didn't say you could talk to my daughter." Charlotte lifted her chin a little, making herself stand her ground when her feet wanted to run.

"I asked if Kathy would spend some time with Phoebe, Charlotte." Oriana's smile started to look shaky. "I noticed Phoebe struggles in some areas, and I thought Kathy might be able to shed some light on the problem."

They were examining Phoebe behind Charlotte's back? How could Oriana do that?

"That's right." Kathy nodded. "Phoebe's speech development is significantly behind, but I'm not sure yet about her cognitive abilities." She turned green eyes on Charlotte. "Has Phoebe ever been diagnosed with any developmental disorders or syndromes?"

It was happening again. They were going to take Phoebe away. No. She wouldn't let them.

Charlotte spun away from their questions and passed through the hallway as fast as she could with Phoebe weighting her arms. Charlotte didn't stop outside. She pushed herself to reach the bus stop.

Phoebe squirmed.

Charlotte tightened her hold. "No, Phoebe. Momma has to carry you. We have to hurry."

What if they followed her? She looked over her shoulder, afraid to stop for even a second.

No one was behind them.

How long had Oriana been wondering about Phoebe? When had she brought in the social worker? Oriana seemed so harmless—the most innocent of the Sanders. But she was the one to betray Charlotte first.

Charlotte's vision blurred. She blinked back the tears as she pushed on.

The sign for the bus stop was just ahead.

What was she going to do? What could she do? If Oriana thought Charlotte wasn't a fit mother, she would tell the other Sanders. The whole family would ask more questions about Phoebe and maybe get answers from the social worker. They'd all want Phoebe taken away.

The bus pulled up and stopped just as Charlotte reached the sign.

She hefted Phoebe up the steps and took the first seat that was free.

Phoebe turned around on Charlotte's lap but didn't get down.

Charlotte held her little girl close. She couldn't run again. She didn't have money. She had nothing.

Tommy was her only hope.

Two stops later, Charlotte lifted Phoebe and carried her off the bus. The girl squirmed as Charlotte looked for Tommy. Charlotte set Phoebe down and held her hand.

"You're late."

Charlotte jerked around to face Tommy.

"Oh, Tommy." The tears she had held back flooded to the surface and spilled onto her cheeks. "They got a social worker to look at Phoebe behind my back. She knows something's wrong with her. They're going to take her away." Charlotte tried to hold in a sob, but it came out strangled instead.

"Please, Tommy." She clutched at the front of his shirt. "You have to get us out of here. Take us somewhere far away. Please."

He stared down at her. "Don't I always take care of things? I'll get us out of here." He gripped her arms, not hard this time, and put her away from him.

Charlotte sniffed, squeezing back more tears. Tommy hated her crying.

"It's gonna take a heap more bread than what we're gettin' this way."

The tears dried up as nerves twisted in her stomach. What was he getting at? "We must have enough by now."

He snorted. "We ain't got nothin'. I've had to live on the little bit I could grab."

He drank it all up. Her little flicker of hope snuffed out. What were they going to do?

"I got a plan for a lot more, but we got to do this job first."

"What plan?"

"Never you mind. You just go into that secondhand store across the street and do your job like I tell you. The kids' clothes are at the back."

Charlotte wiped at the wet tracks on her cheeks.

"Leave it." He grinned. "I'd even believe you the way you look."

If only he'd let her leave Phoebe behind. But she could never leave the girl with Tommy anyway.

Still gripping Phoebe's hand, Charlotte crossed the street and went into the store. The old black lady working there looked near to tears herself when she saw the state Charlotte was in, and she fell in love with Phoebe. Getting the woman to the back of the store was no problem, and she probably couldn't even hear well enough to notice Tommy get in and out with the cash from the drawer.

Charlotte got out of the store as fast as she could and took Phoebe with her to the bar down the street.

Tommy waited outside the door. Maybe even he had enough sense to know Phoebe would attract too much attention if they met inside the bar.

He sure was itching to get inside, though. He shifted and played with his hat, taking it off and putting it back on.

Charlotte stopped in front of him with Phoebe. "Did you get much?"

"No." He scowled. "These puny joints ain't hardly worth it."

"Then what are we going to do? We've got to get out of here." Charlotte swallowed back more tears that tried to push to the surface.

"We're gonna get the cash from your old man."

Charlotte coughed. Had to be a joke. A terrible joke.

Tommy looked around, like making sure no one was listening. "I worked it all out. I'll take you and the kid away in front of people like I'm kidnappin' you. Then we'll make your old man get a million bucks from his bank to get you back."

Charlotte's legs turned to mush, like she might collapse if she didn't sit down. She'd known something bad was coming the minute that thinking look showed up on his face. But he'd never come up with something like this before.

Kidnapping and ransom? Treating Marcus like that?

"No." Charlotte forced the word out of her dry mouth. "We can't do that."

Tommy's eyes darkened.

She had to try something else. "Marcus doesn't like me enough to shell out that kind of dough." The truth stung as she said it.

"He likes you good enough. He's lettin' you stay in his house, ain't he?"

"It wouldn't work, Tommy."

"I'll tell you what you do. You tell your old man about me." He grinned. "Tell him you're scared of me, so he'll believe it's real when I kidnap you."

Tommy wanted Charlotte to tell Marcus the truth? Still wouldn't make a difference anyway. And what if it did? They wouldn't be any better off.

"Tommy," she moistened her lips, "this is a bad idea. We shouldn't do it. Even if he gave us the money, think what would happen if we got caught. We'd all go to prison."

Tommy's eyes narrowed as he stepped close to Charlotte and

stared down at her. "I don't get bad ideas. Where do you think we'd go if they caught us now anyway? Man, you're dumb."

"But this isn't like the other jobs, where no one knows who we are. People would know who we were this time."

"No one knows who I am. Just don't tell them my name, and you'll look as innocent as you always do, baby." His eyes flashed. He was angry, but not drunk angry.

Either way, she couldn't do it. "I can't. Marcus has been really nice to me. I can't do that to him."

"So nice he's gonna take your kid away from you?"

Charlotte's teeth sunk into her lip. Maybe Marcus wouldn't. Maybe just Oriana and Caroline thought that way, and he'd stand up for her.

Tommy grabbed Charlotte's arm and pulled her to the brick wall.

Phoebe started to whimper as she watched.

Tommy's hot breath hit Charlotte's cheeks. His hard gaze burned into hers. "I know what you did. You oughtta be afraid of me."

He gave her a push into the bricks behind her back, then let her go.

Charlotte didn't breathe again until he disappeared inside the bar, but even then, it was difficult to push any air through her tight lungs. Would he really do that? Would he tell to get her to do what he said? Or maybe to give her the punishment he still hadn't dished out?

Charlotte went to Phoebe, and the little girl threw her arms around Charlotte's hips, clinging and whimpering. Charlotte's heart squeezed painfully in her chest as she stroked Phoebe's hair.

Of course, Tommy would do that. He'd do anything to get what he wanted.

She had no choice. Unless she did what he said, she would lose Phoebe for sure.

He might as well take her life and be done with it.

~

"I'M ONLY A VOLUNTEER HERE, you know."

Gabe smiled at the elderly Mazie Washington as she cleaned her eyeglasses with a tissue just like Granny used to. "Yes, ma'am."

"Mrs. Stapleton, the lady who runs this place, is from our church. She does it as a ministry, but she's on vacation for a week. Gets back on Friday." Mrs. Washington put her glasses back on and shook her head. "Seems strange a person would rob a place that's only here to help the hurting people who live in this very neighborhood."

"I just need you to tell me what you remember about the day. Did anyone unusual come in?"

"Are you sure you wouldn't rather talk to Mrs. Stapleton?"

"The detectives will when she returns, but for now I need your eyewitness account."

"Eyewitness?" She craned her neck to look up at Gabe. A sparkle lit her brown eyes as if she liked the sound of the word. "Well, no, I don't remember anything unusual. We didn't have many customers, but that's normal for a Tuesday."

"When did you notice the cash drawer was empty?"

"Not until I went to count it up at closing time." She frowned. "I really should be closing right now."

Lewis tossed an amused grin at Gabe as he came back around the counter from checking the cash drawer.

Gabe hid his own urge to smile as Mrs. Washington watched him with her mouth pressed in a worried line. "I'm sure Mrs. Stapleton won't mind if you have us here a little past closing, ma'am. And we won't take up much more of your time. You said you didn't have many customers. Did you ever leave the cash drawer alone anytime during the day?"

"You're going to have to sit down, young man. Hurts my neck looking up at you."

"Of course." Gabe didn't have to hide his amusement this time as he went to grab the chair behind the counter.

Lewis handed Gabe another one, and he positioned the two wooden chairs to face each other.

"Why don't we both sit down, ma'am?"

"Thank you." Mrs. Washington lowered herself slowly and let out a long sigh. "Your momma sure did right with you, young man."

"Thank you, ma'am. Now, did you—"

"Ever leave the cash register?" The woman might be old, but she was still quick. "Well, it's peculiar you should ask, because I almost never do. Not when there are folks in the store anyhow. But today, I did once. A girl...no, she had to be older than she looked because she had her daughter with her." Mrs. Washington smiled at Gabe. "The mother was a sweet, Southern gal, and my, if you could have seen her your heart might've just broke."

Mrs. Washington's eyes filled with moisture. "You could tell she'd been crying, and her little girl..." She put her hand over her heart. "She was a tiny, delicate little thing—just an angel. Blond hair and big blue eyes."

A cold tingle crawled up the back of Gabe's neck. Couldn't be. "How old would you guess the girl was?"

Mrs. Washington looked over his shoulder, as if trying to remember. "Couldn't have been more than seven. She was about the size of my grandbaby, and she's only six."

Phoebe was ten, but she looked seven. Gabe's heart thudded against his ribs. "What makes you say the woman was Southern?"

"She had a real strong accent."

Maybe it wasn't Charlotte. She didn't have what he'd call a strong accent.

"Did the woman say the girl was her daughter?"

"Yes, she did. Said she had to buy her daughter a new dress for a funeral. Her granny died, poor thing." Mrs. Washington shook her head slowly back and forth. "Come to think of it, that was the only time I left the cash register all day, and I didn't even open the drawer again after that until closing."

Her eyes grew to saucers behind her glasses. "You don't think...a nice young thing like that with a sweet baby girl?"

He didn't want to think it. Why did his cop brain have to even consider the idea? There could be hundreds of women in the city who fit that description, even with blond-haired, blue-eyed daughters. Or maybe Charlotte and Phoebe had come to the store but didn't have anything to do with the missing cash. Maybe they just happened to shop there on the wrong day, and someone had taken the money earlier. But that wouldn't explain the story about the funeral.

"Sergeant?" Lewis nudged Gabe's shoulder.

"Oh, sorry." Gabe scrambled to remember the question Mrs. Washington had asked. "I don't know who took the money for sure, ma'am, but you've been a very big help. The detectives should be here in the next thirty minutes. Officer Lewis will wait with you until they get here."

"All right, but then I'll have to pick up my grandbaby. My daughter works nights on Tuesday."

Gabe nodded. "We'll get you out of here on time, ma'am." He stood. "You have a good evening."

"Take care of yourself, officer. It's awfully comforting to know there are nice young men like you two on our police force." Her loving look included Lewis, who appeared to be barely holding back a laugh behind his smile.

"Thank you, ma'am. Good night." Gabe couldn't get out fast enough. His stomach rebelled against the burger he'd eaten before watch.

Charlotte could not be the thief. She wouldn't do that kind

of thing. And with Phoebe along? The idea was ridiculous. Charlotte loved Phoebe way too much to involve her in anything like that.

Her mother's record flashed in his mind. Charlotte had a family history of theft. Yes, but she had nothing on her own record.

The battle waged in Gabe's head as he got into his squad and sat behind the wheel. Is this what he had come to? Had he learned his lesson so well that he was suspecting Charlotte now? Maybe he had been a cop too long. When the first person he thought of as the perpetrator of serial thefts was the woman he was coming to care for, maybe it was time to walk away.

Had he really just thought that? Quitting the force? Gabe shook his head and shoved the squad in gear. He had no idea what was even a rational thought at this point. He'd never felt so disorganized in his mind, so uncertain what was right and what was true.

He better get himself together, or he'd scare Charlotte as much as he was scaring himself. He just hoped by the time he picked her up for work, he could forget his suspicions or figure out a way to find out if they were true.

God help him if they were.

fifteen

"For you did not receive the spirit of slavery to fall back into fear, but you have received the Spirit of adoption as sons, by whom we cry, 'Abba! Father!'"
— Romans 8:15

CHARLOTTE TOOK IN A BREATH. Here went nothing. "I think I know who the guy was."

Caroline and Marcus glanced at Charlotte across the table, their eyebrows up. They were probably shocked Charlotte was actually talking during supper.

She wouldn't if she didn't have to. "That man you said was looking for Phoebe at the center."

"Oh, yes." Marcus set down his fork. "You know who he is?"

"Yeah." She swallowed and looked away from his gaze. At least this time they'd just think she was scared if she couldn't meet their eyes. "I think it's my boyfriend."

"Your boyfriend?" Disgust already edged Caroline's voice.

Charlotte fiddled with the knife that lay next to her

plate. "He followed me here from Dallas. I didn't know 'til now. I'm...I'm afraid of him. He's...not a nice man sometimes."

"Has he threatened you?"

Heat traveled up Charlotte's neck to her face. She nodded.

"Is he the reason you left Texas and came here?"

"Yes." Charlotte couldn't look at Caroline and see the disapproval there. Or would she be enjoying this?

Marcus stood.

Charlotte glanced up to see him come to the chair next to her.

He sat down and put his hand over hers on the table. "You're safe now, Charlotte. You can stay at the house until he's taken care of. We'll get a restraining order, and you don't have to go to work until that's in place."

Charlotte's heart ached. She'd do anything to believe that confidence in his eyes, the love in his concern, the warm safety of his hand over hers.

She'd do anything but give up Phoebe.

Charlotte shook her head. "I don't want to live in fear." For once, she was telling the truth, but the words felt like the worst lie she had ever told.

Deep lines crossed Marcus's forehead. "Will you at least let us tell Gabe?"

"I think he already knows." Gabe knew a lot more than she'd ever told him, like he knew she was living a nightmare. Or maybe he just knew she was living a lie with the Sanders. Either way, she couldn't tell him about Tommy. She couldn't make herself tell Gabe the truth any more than she could tell him another lie.

"Do you mind if we don't talk about this anymore right now?" Charlotte brought her gaze to Marcus's face. "I'm really tired, and I'll have to get up early again."

Marcus shared a look with his wife that Charlotte couldn't

read. "Sure. You'll be safe with Gabe taking you to work. Will you let me pick you up from there?"

"You have a meeting at the bank, dear."

Marcus glanced at Caroline. "I'll cancel it."

"I'd be happy to pick Charlotte up, too."

Marcus looked at Charlotte. "Would you let one of us pick you up instead of taking the bus?"

Charlotte thought a moment. That shouldn't ruin any of Tommy's terrible plans. She nodded.

Marcus sighed. "Good. I'll be in to read to Phoebe in a few minutes."

Charlotte couldn't bear that, not when she knew what she was about to do to him. "I think we both need to get right to bed tonight. Phoebe's had a hard day." She wasn't the only one.

"Oh." Marcus blinked. "Okay. Have a good rest, then." He stood and went around Charlotte to Phoebe's chair. "Good night, princess." He bent and kissed Phoebe's forehead, then straightened and looked at Charlotte. "I love you both."

Charlotte slid off her chair, avoiding his gaze as she took Phoebe's hand and led the little girl out of the dining room. She had the feeling the memory of the hurt in Marcus's eyes as he'd said he loved her would haunt her for a long time.

Charlotte's cheeks were still hot when she reached the bedroom with Phoebe. Shouldn't telling them the truth have felt good? She'd never been able to tell anyone about Tommy before or the truth about anything else either. But she'd never felt so humiliated in all her life, as if she had just shouted to the world that she was a weak loser, a victim—nothing like Caroline or her daughters, who wouldn't be caught dead in such a mess.

Hours later, Charlotte replayed the conversation over and over again as she lay on the bed next to Phoebe. Charlotte stared at the ceiling, no sleepier than she'd been when she first put her head on the pillow. Sleep was impossible tonight. How could she sleep with her insides tangled in knots?

If only there was another way, if she could convince Tommy to change his mind. Maybe if she told him she didn't need to move, that she didn't need the money.

The idea was no better than the others she'd had while lying there all night. He would still want the money himself now that he knew Marcus worked at the bank.

And Charlotte couldn't stay here anyway, not with Oriana and her social worker wondering about Phoebe.

She sat up and looked at the clock. 4:15. Finally. At least now she could get up and end the laps her thoughts kept running in her mind.

She swung her legs out from under the sheet.

Her feet touched something that felt smoother than the carpeted floor.

A picture Phoebe had drawn lay on the floor under Charlotte's feet. Charlotte picked it up. The picture was of Jesus with a bright sun or some kind of light above Him. Phoebe had shown the picture to Charlotte a couple of days ago at the center where Phoebe had drawn and colored it. An adult hand had written *Jesus Saves!* across the bottom of the paper.

If only He were real and could help Charlotte somehow. She sure could use it.

If He was real, He'd probably just tell her she was an awful mother and sinner, and she needed to be better and get her sins forgiven. Some help that would be right now.

She dropped the picture to the floor and slid it under the bed. A face on a page, some guy in an old make-believe story, couldn't do a thing in this world, in this nightmare that never ended.

She went to the dresser to pull out a tank top but stopped. She turned around and went to the closet instead. If this was going to be her last day seeing these people, at least she could leave them remembering her at her best. She took out the pink sundress from the closet and slipped it over her head. Shouldn't matter if she showed up at work in a dress. Barbara always made Charlotte put an apron or white shirt over what she wore anyway.

When Charlotte looked in the mirror, the dress didn't seem as pretty as she had remembered. Maybe because the room was so dark. The pink layer of light material around the outside of the dress barely showed as the dark cloth underneath made the whole thing look different.

Whatever. The dress would still look better than her usual sloppy T-shirt and jeans. Even she knew that much.

She quietly went to the bed and kissed Phoebe's smooth forehead. Charlotte almost wished Phoebe would wake up and need her, but the little girl slept peacefully.

Charlotte went to the door and turned back for one last look at the room.

Home? Phoebe's question that first night echoed in Charlotte's head.

When we find one, we won't have to be scared anymore.

Charlotte bit her lip as tears pricked her eyes. This place had been as close to home as they were ever going to get.

She left the room and made her way to the front door, trying to memorize every piece of furniture, every picture on the wall, every rug, and every conversation she'd had there.

Caroline waited at the door with the thermos. "Are you sure you want to go?" Those elegant eyebrows dipped. "I'll worry about you."

Charlotte took the thermos as she looked at Caroline's lovely face. Concern in her eyes and voice. Charlotte could almost believe Caroline meant it. "Thanks."

Caroline touched Charlotte's arm. "I'll be praying for you, sweetie."

Sweetie. Caroline only called her daughters that. Charlotte managed a nod, not daring to talk with the lump in her throat as she went out the door.

Her heart dropped even further when Gabe didn't react to how she looked. He just opened the door for her as always, but his mouth was pressed in a grim line. It shouldn't matter. Wasn't like she had worn the dress just for him.

He was deadly quiet during the drive, but he looked like he had a war going on in his head. His jaw clenched and unclenched while his fingers matched the same pattern on the steering wheel. A couple times, he took a breath like he was about to say something, but he'd stay quiet instead, barely looking at her.

What had him so bothered? Had he found out something? Or had Oriana talked to him about Phoebe?

Charlotte kept her questions to herself. She didn't want to know the answers. The ride was not what she would have dreamed of for her last time with Gabe. When she had started hoping for dreams, she didn't know.

Gabe pulled the car over in front of the bakery, and Charlotte reached for the door handle, hoping to beat him to it.

He stopped her with his hand on her arm, like he'd done once before, but his touch was firmer this time.

She glanced at his face. She couldn't read the expression there or in the darkness of his eyes.

"I know you're in trouble." His deep voice seemed to shake the car.

Her breath caught. Did he know everything?

"I can't stand to see you get in any deeper, Charlotte. I'm afraid of what might happen to you and Phoebe or…" He dropped off, leaving her to fill in what he was thinking.

Or what she might do. Is that what he was going to say? Had he found her out?

She saw what was in his eyes—pain. That look, she knew well. Had she caused it? Without thinking, she gently touched his cheek.

His eyes softened, filling with something else. Something

she could imagine was love. This moment, she wanted to remember forever.

But she had to answer him. She couldn't say it would be okay or that she was fine. She couldn't lie to him again.

She did the only thing she could do. She pulled away and got out of the car.

"Charlotte." His low rumble caught her before she reached the bakery.

She looked back.

He stood on the other side of the car. Even in the darkness, there was no missing the gleam of intensity in his eyes. "Please. Let me help you."

She tried to swallow but couldn't.

Barbara opened the door.

Charlotte looked at Gabe one last time, his gaze burning a hole in her heart. "No one can." She quickly turned and passed Barbara to get inside.

Gabe didn't follow.

WHY WAS HE HERE? Despite his better judgment, Gabe found himself driving into the lot at CCC. He had tried to get some sleep after dropping Charlotte off at the bakery, but the image of her face—pained, lost, and scared—was all he saw every time he closed his eyes.

What he was going to say to her in person, he had no idea. He had royally bombed his opportunity to talk to her on the way to the bakery, but everything he thought of to say sounded either too suspicious or too pathetic. The idea she might be somehow involved in the thefts wouldn't leave him alone, but when he'd seen her again, he couldn't possibly believe it.

Why did she have to wear that dress? She had looked so

achingly pretty and fragile. He would've rather stabbed himself than imply he thought she was a criminal.

So here he was for round two. He got out of his car and headed to the door of the building. He glanced up at the gray sky and the blackening clouds that rapidly moved in overhead, as if rushing to reflect his mood. He reached for the door just as it swung open.

"Oh, hi." Nye came out with a smile.

"Hi." Gabe took a step back as Oriana with Sunny, Charlotte, and Phoebe filed out behind her.

"Hi, Gabe." Oriana turned her head in his direction with a smile bright enough to sub for the hiding sun. "You're just in time. We're trying to get the donations out of Nye's car before the rain hits."

"Why am I always in time for work?" Gabe couldn't have said where he found the humor to tease, but he had to think about something other than the pain in his chest from the way Charlotte avoided looking at him. She was so unpredictable. She wore that dress and touched his cheek, but then the next moment, she acted as scared as if he was about to arrest her.

He could've kicked himself for even letting his mind go there. No one was going to arrest her, least of all him.

He grabbed crates from Nye's open trunk, stacking three in his arms.

"Wow." Nye eyed his tower of crates. "At this rate, you won't need us at all."

"Is Gabe showing off again?" Oriana's laugh was drowned out by the roaring engine of an RV as the vehicle raced into the parking lot.

The brakes screeched as the RV swerved in front of Nye's car and stopped way too close.

Gabe set the crates on the pavement.

"Whoa. What was that?" No one answered Oriana as the

driver, a male, wearing sunglasses and a baseball cap over shoulder-length dark blond hair, jumped down out of the RV.

Not sure why, Gabe reached under his shirt for his concealed weapon.

"Hold it, cop." The driver appeared around the front of the RV, pointing a full-sized semi-auto, probably a Glock, right at Gabe. "I know you got a gun in your belt. You cops always carry guns."

The man's Texas twang made Gabe's skin crawl. The boyfriend.

Charlotte stood frozen in place, staring at her boyfriend with huge eyes. Nobody could fake shock that well. She hadn't known about this.

"Nye? What's going on?"

Out of the corner of his eye, Gabe saw Nye touch Oriana's hand and whisper to her.

"Take out your gun real slow and drop it on the ground. Charlotte, get over here. Bring the kid." The boyfriend kept his weapon aimed at Gabe while Charlotte and Phoebe moved closer. As soon as Charlotte was within arms' length, the boyfriend grabbed her and held the gun to her head, his arm wrapped around her neck.

"Tommy!" Charlotte pulled at the guy's arm.

Gabe's heart stopped.

Sunny started barking.

Gabe's gut seared like someone had stabbed him as he stared at Charlotte's face, the terror of her eyes as she looked at him, pleading for him to save her. He slowly took out his gun, his fingers itching to pull the trigger, to do anything to get Charlotte away from the madman.

But the boyfriend kept the barrel pressed against Charlotte's head.

There was nothing Gabe could do. He set his weapon on the pavement.

Something wet touched his arm. A raindrop. More followed the first as he waited for the creep's next move.

"Back away from it." The boyfriend's eyes were rabid, unstable. He was enjoying his moment of power.

Gabe took two steps back.

"Don't play me, cop. Get away from it."

"Okay." Gabe kept his voice calm as he backed farther away.

"That's enough. Stay there. You two," the boyfriend glanced at Nye and Oriana, "get in." He nodded toward the RV.

Nye looked at Gabe.

He couldn't tell her to go, but if she didn't, this dude looked like he was ready to pull the trigger.

Nye turned her gaze to Charlotte. "Okay. Please don't hurt Charlotte."

Thank the Lord for Nye's unflappable calm. She might just save their lives. Nye held Oriana's hand as the two of them started walking to the RV. Sunny stepped in front of Oriana, blocking her with his body as he continued to bark at the boyfriend.

Gabe's stomach lurched.

"Get the dog out of the way, or it's dead." The boyfriend waved the gun at Sunny before pressing it against Charlotte's head again. "And tell it to shut up."

Oriana dropped Sunny's harness and put her hand on his head. "Sunny," Gabe had never heard Oriana's voice so firm, "that's enough."

Sunny stopped barking.

"Stay with Gabe." Oriana grasped Nye's elbow. "Stay."

Nye started to lead Oriana away.

Sunny stepped in front of her again.

The boyfriend swung the gun at Sunny.

"No, please." Nye's voice made him pause. "Please, don't hurt her dog. Gabe, can you hold Sunny?"

"Slowly, cop." The boyfriend pressed the barrel into Charlotte's head while he watched Gabe walk over to Sunny.

When Gabe reached Oriana and Nye, he took Sunny's harness. Should he push Nye and Oriana behind him and take whatever the boyfriend wanted to give him?

"Don't think about it." The boyfriend shoved the gun into Charlotte's head, making her wince.

Gabe ground his teeth together. If he could just get his hands on the guy.

He gripped Sunny's harness, holding him back while Nye led Oriana to the RV. Sunny barked and lunged against the harness as Nye opened the side door, and the two women went inside.

The boyfriend sneered at Gabe. "Stay right where you are, and don't try to follow, or all these chicks are dead."

"Phoebe." Charlotte reached out her hand, and Phoebe took it.

The boyfriend backed around the RV, holding the gun on Charlotte the whole way until he was on the other side of the vehicle.

Gabe watched through the passenger window as Charlotte and Phoebe got in with the boyfriend's gun pointed at them. He still couldn't do a thing.

The boyfriend cackled just before he shut the driver's door. He turned the RV around and drove out of the parking lot, picking up speed.

The second they were out of sight, Gabe whipped out his phone and called Dispatch as he tried to lure the still-barking Sunny into the building. He pulled Sunny by the harness as gently as he could and got him inside the door while he told Dispatch what had just happened.

"License plate of suspect vehicle: Victor Nora Ida five four five," Gabe said into the phone as he grabbed his gun off the ground and ran to his car. "I'm in pursuit of the suspect."

He jumped in the car and screeched out of the lot, putting

his phone on speaker and laying it beside him. The boyfriend had a lead, but Gabe would have to hang back anyway to be sure he didn't push the jerk into shooting.

He spotted the RV just ahead and forced himself to breathe and stay back. He couldn't remember the last time he had to remind himself to breathe. This was no normal, on-the-job scenario. Two of those women were like sisters to him, one was an innocent little girl he'd come to care for, and the other... Judging from the way he felt right now, Charlotte had his heart.

"Two twenty-four," the woman's voice at Dispatch pierced through Gabe's thoughts, "Victor Nora Ida five four five reported stolen. Registered to Frank Jefferson, 104 Winston Street." No surprise there.

The sprinkling transitioned into heavy rain as Gabe followed the RV, managing to track all the turns it made as he reported the street names to Dispatch.

"Officers en route to your location," the woman said.

They couldn't get there soon enough. Lightning flashed beyond the RV. About five seconds later, thunder rumbled, shaking the ground. They might be in for a bad one, which would make the search harder if Gabe lost the RV.

He clenched his jaw. He wasn't going to.

The RV crossed the train tracks a few cars in front of Gabe. The track signal lights started flashing red.

No way. Everything in Gabe screamed for him to surge past the other cars and race across the tracks in front of the train. He pressed the gas pedal down and pulled around the first car, weaving back into the lane only to see the barrier lower in front of the tracks.

Gabe slammed his brakes and stopped behind the two cars left between him and the train that chugged past the barrier. *Really, Lord?*

The boyfriend was getting away with those helpless women,

and Gabe was powerless to stop it. What would the jerk do to them if he got them somewhere alone and unprotected?

Gabe closed his eyes against the possibilities that raced through his mind, the contents of his stomach surging up his throat. He grabbed his phone. "Two twenty-four. I've lost the suspect." He threw the phone to the floor. He was a cop. He should be calm, in control, devising a plan to free the hostages.

But all he wanted to do was yell at the top of his lungs and make that guy pay.

sixteen

"For freedom Christ has set us free; stand firm therefore, and do not submit again to a yoke of slavery."
– Galatians 5:1

THE NIGHTMARE JUST GOT WORSE. Charlotte bit her lip as she looked into the back of the RV where Nye and Oriana sat on the floor, clutching each other's hands.

Nye's other hand rested on her stomach while Oriana tilted her head as if listening to every sound she could. A pregnant woman and a blind one. What was Tommy thinking?

Phoebe sat on Charlotte's lap and clung to her while hard rain pelted the RV roof like it was a flimsy piece of tin.

Tommy wore a smirk as he drove to whatever unknown place he was taking them. "The storm is perfect. It'll slow the cops down if they try to find us." He glanced at her. "Where'd you get the dress?"

"What were you thinking?"

Tommy ignored her.

"Nye and Oriana?" She lowered her voice. "That was never part of the plan. And where'd you get that gun?" Her gaze dropped to the weapon he still gripped in his hand.

"I figured you were right, baby. Your old man might not give me anything for just you. So I got us some insurance." He laughed.

"You held a gun on them, Tommy. And you put it to my head."

"I had to make it look good. That cop was gonna shoot me if I didn't have the gun."

"How are we supposed to get away now?"

"When your old man pays up, we hand 'em over." Irritation laced his voice.

"Except me and Phoebe?"

"Yeah."

Phoebe crawled off Charlotte's lap and went to the back, shrinking onto the floor by Oriana, who put her arm around the little girl. Phoebe always tried to hide when she heard anger in their voices. Now that would be her only future. Either that or a mother in jail. How could Tommy be so stupid? He'd probably even stolen their getaway vehicle. "Where'd you get the RV?"

He glared at her. "What's with all the questions? You begged me to get you outta there, and that's what I'm doin'. You should be thankin' me."

"I didn't want it like this, Tommy."

"Just shut up!"

A bitter liquid climbed up her throat as she blinked at him. Why had she ever thought she loved him?

Everything about him repulsed her—the long, dirty blond hair that brushed his shoulders, the three-day old beard, the stained cowboy hat he had put back on as soon as they were on their way. He looked every bit of the twenty years of extra age he had on her. Wrinkles lined his face, his eyes were watery, and his nose was almost always red. She used to think he was tall and strong, but he looked so short and puny next to Gabe.

Gabe. He thought she was in danger. She could still see the anguish that had twisted his handsome features when Tommy put the gun to her head.

Her racing heart had calmed when she saw Gabe look at her like that. He cared that she might get hurt. He cared about her. For a second, nothing else had mattered.

But now Gabe was gone. Even he hadn't been able to do a thing to stop Tommy.

Charlotte was right all along. No one could free her...or Phoebe. And now Nye and Oriana were sucked into the prison. They didn't deserve that.

She looked back at the two women. Phoebe scrunched into Oriana's side, trembling like she always did when Tommy yelled.

Nye watched Charlotte with her eyebrows raised, and Oriana's mouth tipped into a grim frown Charlotte had never seen on her face.

Heat crept up Charlotte's cheeks. They had heard.

She jerked to face the huge windshield, but she could feel Nye's accusing stare at her back. It wasn't Charlotte's fault. She didn't want any of this.

"Hey, blondie."

The knot in Charlotte's stomach twisted.

Tommy looked in the rearview mirror, probably at Nye. "Blondie, I'm talkin' to you."

Charlotte glanced back to see Nye tilt her chin. "Are you addressing me?"

Tommy guffawed. "Ooh-hoo, we got a princess on board, baby. Yeah, I'm addressin' you, princess. You got a phone?"

Nye pursed her lips together for a moment. "Yes."

"I want you to call your daddy."

Her blue eyes jerked to Charlotte's face.

A pain shot through Charlotte's gut. She couldn't help Nye.

She couldn't even help herself. Tommy would get his way like always.

"I said, call your daddy." The hard edge to Tommy's voice meant he was getting mad. "Don't make me tell you again." At least he wasn't drunk. Yet.

Charlotte gave Nye a small nod, trying to send a warning with her eyes. Nye might be brave enough to stand up to Tommy, but all of them would suffer if she did.

Nye sighed and took the phone out of her purse.

"That's better." Tommy watched through the mirror. "Now you're only gonna say what I tell you to say. Tell him if he wants to see y'all alive, he's gotta give me a million bucks...in cash."

Nye's startled gaze went to Tommy's reflection this time.

"That's right, sister. Tell him I want it at sunrise tomorrow mornin'. I'll tell him where when I call back."

"That's ridiculous."

Charlotte stopped breathing at Nye's words. Nye's eyes flashed, but Charlotte knew her anger was no match for Tommy's.

"Our father doesn't have that kind of money. He couldn't get it even if he wanted to."

Tommy jerked his head around to give Nye a sneer. "You think I ain't smart enough to do my homework?"

The RV swerved into the other lane.

"Tommy!" Charlotte put her hands on the dash as a car heading toward them blared its horn.

Tommy looked forward and jerked the RV back into the right lane. "Your old man works at a bank. Charlotte here told me."

Charlotte swallowed, not looking back. She could imagine their glares just fine.

"Working at a bank doesn't give him that kind of access." Nye didn't sound intimidated at all. "And he's retired, regardless. Any clearance he did have there is gone now."

Tommy gave a low whistle. "Remind me not to play poker

with you, babe." His goofy smile dropped, and his eyes darkened. He lifted the gun off his lap and waved it in the air. "Now make that phone call."

Nye glared at the phone as she selected the number.

"Hold it." Tommy looked in the mirror.

Nye paused.

"Show me so I can see you're dialin' the right person."

Nye quickly pressed a few extra buttons.

Charlotte's heart picked up speed. Nye had been trying to call someone else. The police? If Tommy noticed...

Nye held up the phone to where Tommy could see the screen in the mirror.

"Good job, princess." Tommy grinned, looking happier than Charlotte had ever seen him. "Make the call."

Nye put the phone to her ear, her hand not even shaking. "Hi, Dad."

A bit of Marcus's voice came through as he responded but not enough to make out the words.

"Well..." Nye moistened her lips. "We've been kidnapped." Her voice was calm and steady as she repeated what Tommy had told her. There was a pause while Marcus said something. "I love you, too." Some emotion finally shook Nye's voice with the last words.

"That's enough," Tommy barked. "Hang up."

Nye set down the phone.

"I said, hang it up."

Nye picked up the phone and pressed a button, holding the phone up to let Tommy see the screen.

"You're a troublemaker, princess." Tommy's volume lowered, but his eyes pierced the mirror. "I'm gonna have Charlotte hold the gun on you 'til we get there if you keep up that kind of stuff."

Nye looked at Charlotte with an unreadable expression.

At least that hurt less than an angry or disappointed one.

Oriana's lips moved as she sat with her arm wrapped around Phoebe. Was she praying? Poor Oriana. She hadn't realized it yet. They weren't in fairytale land anymore. Prayers were worth the same as curses and chants here in the real world—nothing.

"Take their phones, baby." Tommy kept watching the women in the back.

Charlotte swallowed. "Tommy, I—"

"What's wrong with you?" His dark eyes hit her like his yelling voice. "You're givin' me lip with everythin' I say. Just get back there and take their phones!"

Charlotte got up and went to Oriana first.

"I left mine at the center." Oriana's voice sounded dry. Was she scared?

"Sure you did." Tommy watched them in the mirror. "She's lyin'."

"No, she isn't." Nye glared at Tommy. "She keeps it in her purse, which she left inside when we went out to unload the donations from my car."

"Donations." Tommy grinned again. "That's a hoot."

"Isn't it?" Sarcasm dripped from Nye's words as she handed her phone to Charlotte. "Where are you taking us?" Nye looked right at Charlotte like she was the one doing all this.

"That's for me to know, princess." Tommy checked the side mirrors. He never did that. Was he looking for tails?

Charlotte's heart lifted as she returned to the front seat. Was Gabe following them?

She frowned. What was she thinking? That wouldn't be a good thing. She had to get away, now more than ever. If Tommy got caught, so would she. There was nothing to do but make Tommy's stupid plan work and hope they all got out alive.

A sign for the Reagan County Forest Preserve passed the window. Of course. Charlotte should have recognized the route.

"Leave the phone here and get back there with the others." Was he talking to her?

He glanced at her.

Charlotte stared at him. "What's wrong?"

"Don't know, baby. All I know is you're askin' too many questions." He jerked his thumb over his shoulder.

"Get back there and don't peek."

The knot in Charlotte's stomach sank like a rock as she went to the back where the windows were covered with curtains. She sat on the little bench that lined the wall opposite the one Nye and Oriana leaned against.

Tommy didn't trust her anymore. She'd better start focusing on her and Phoebe's survival…and no one else. The way Tommy was looking at her now, she'd be lucky to get that much.

A CRACK of thunder shook the foundations of the police station as Gabe finished giving his description of the boyfriend Charlotte had called Tommy. "A little broader in the chin." Gabe pointed at the computer screen, and Caleb Wentworth made the adjustment to the composite.

"Sergeant," Officer Janice Greer spoke from behind Gabe. "You wanted to know when Mr. Sanders arrived." Gabe turned to see Marcus and Nicanor.

Marcus's eyes were red but dry as he put out his hand to shake Gabe's. "Gabe. I'm so thankful you're here."

A lot of good that had done the women taken hostage. Gabe kept his thoughts to himself and put his hand on Marcus's shoulder. "I'm sorry, Marcus." Gabe didn't know how he got the words out through his tightened throat.

"Nicanor." Gabe nodded at Oriana's silent husband, who looked more stoic than ever. Gabe would've expected blazing mad, like the time he'd caught Nicanor outside Dez's apartment, ready to pummel whoever he got his hands on. This time, Nicanor just returned the nod, his hands casually resting in his pockets as if he was there for anything but a kidnapping investigation.

"He wants one million dollars, Gabe." Marcus's voice choked.

"Yes, sir." Gabe's gut twisted at the pain in Marcus's eyes.

"I don't have that kind of money. He must be some kind of madman."

"Maybe he thinks you'll get it from the bank." A tall woman in an FBI raid jacket stepped into the room, followed by two men in FBI gear. "Agent Foster, FBI Special Agent in Charge. I understand you are semi-retired from T & G Bank, Mr. Sanders." She held out her hand to Marcus.

He shook her hand, but his widening eyes looked like they'd seen a ghost. "You mean he thinks I'll steal the money?"

"It's done all the time on TV."

Gabe shot the agent a look. Humor hardly seemed like the best call at a time like this.

"My apologies." She either read his expression or Marcus's stunned silence. "I don't mean to be glib. What I mean is our kidnapper doesn't strike me as being bright enough to come up with his own ideas, so he's probably getting them from TV or movies. Happens a lot."

She turned dark brown eyes on Gabe. "You must be Sergeant Kelly. I understand you were there when the hostages were taken?"

Heat surged up his neck. "Yes."

There was no judgment in the snappy gaze that she jerked to the composite artist. "I want to know immediately what results you get with that."

She looked at Nicanor. "And you are?"

"Husband of one of the hostages," Gabe answered. They were wasting time.

"I understand two of them are married." Foster squinted at

them all like she was staring at the real culprits. "Where's the other husband?"

"He's driving my wife here." Marcus's voice was weaker than normal. "Nicanor and I were having our Bible study together when Nye, my daughter, called."

"Bible study." Foster raised her eyebrows. "All three of the hostages are your daughters, correct? But one from a previous relationship?"

"Should we get back to the search, Agent Foster?" Gabe barely hid his irritation. She had no business interrogating Marcus as if he had something to do with the kidnapping. "We've got men covering the northeast section of the city where the RV disappeared, and they're searching the outskirts, as well."

"I think we can get a little farther than the outskirts." She gave him a smug smile. At least it looked that way to him, but maybe he was being sensitive. "But I'll discuss that further with your chief. For now, I'm just here to speak with the father..." She arched one black eyebrow. "And the officer who let the suspect get away."

Nope, he wasn't being sensitive. Gabe made himself breathe. Getting mad wouldn't help anything. Control of the search may be taken away from him, but the more people out there looking, the better.

Foster returned her gaze to Marcus. "Have you received any instructions about the drop site yet?"

"No." Marcus's eyebrows knit together. "Agent Foster, I can't possibly get that kind of money by morning."

She gave a brisk nod. "You won't have to, sir. I want you to go with these agents." She stepped to the side, her long black ponytail swishing against her back as she angled her head toward the men who'd stood behind her. "They'll get your phone set up for tracking and recording the next call."

Another clap of thunder rocked the building. A siren sounded from someplace nearby.

"Sergeant Kelly." Greer appeared in the doorway. "We've had to temporarily suspend the search."

"What?" There'd better be a good reason.

"Yes, sir. A tornado touched down outside the city, and it's headed our way."

seventeen

"But God chose what is foolish in the world to shame the wise; God chose what is weak in the world to shame the strong; God chose what is low and despised in the world, even things that are not, to bring to nothing things that are, so that no human being might boast in the presence of God."
– 1 Corinthians 1:27-29

THE PARKED RV shook with another crash of thunder.

Charlotte held her arms around Phoebe as the little girl burrowed into her chest and whimpered.

Tommy laughed. "Maybe this'll keep the cops inside. Probably afraid they'll melt." He raised a beer can into the air like toasting someone who wasn't there and put the drink to his mouth. He shook the can with a grunt when nothing came out.

Charlotte winced as he threw it to the floor right next to Oriana, who jumped.

He got up from the bench seat Charlotte was sitting on and went farther back in the RV. Probably looking for more booze. "None of you dames move. I still got the gun." He cackled as he waved the gun toward them. He had made sure he could see them by leaving a flashlight on the floor between the front seats, pointed in their direction.

Charlotte's stomach churned, her nerves so on edge she might throw up. Tommy wasn't stumbling around yet or slurring his words too badly, but he was headed there. A drunk Tommy with a gun was something she hoped she'd never live to see.

He cackled again.

Might be the last thing she would see.

Lightning flashed so brightly it seemed to blast through the walls of the RV, completely surrounding them. Thunder cracked at the same time. The wind picked up, swirling loudly outside the RV.

The wall Charlotte leaned against started to push into her. Was that possible?

Tommy stumbled, falling against the side of the RV.

The whole RV rocked in the wind.

"I don't think we're safe here," Nye shouted to Tommy, who pushed himself off the wall and planted his feet wider apart so he could take a swig from his new beer can. "The storm sounds really bad."

Tommy snorted. "Don't tell me the princess is scared."

"We were under a tornado watch for this evening. Could be we're getting one."

The RV rocked again as the wind blew harder.

Phoebe shrieked.

"We should at least get Phoebe to safety somewhere." Oriana turned flashing eyes toward Tommy as she yelled above the noise of the storm. "An RV is the worst place to be in a tornado."

"What do ya know? The blind girl can talk. Thought you were one of those deaf and dumb idiots." He snickered.

Great. When he started sounding stupider than normal, he

was getting tanked.

"Oh, I can talk all right." Anger edged Oriana's voice. So there was something that could make her mad. "I've just been saving my words for talking to God."

"Hey, thanks. I reckon that must be why we're gettin' this storm right about now. 'Cause your God wants you to stay with me."

Tommy was right. If God was real, He was lousy to treat Nye and Oriana like this. Everything was working out perfect for Tommy.

"I like your God, lady." Tommy saluted her with his beer can.

A blast of wind tilted the RV farther.

Phoebe screamed by Charlotte's ear.

"Tommy!" A surge of fear drove Charlotte's shout. "They're right. We have to get out of here."

Phoebe's fingers dug into Charlotte's back as she squeezed tighter.

"See?" Tommy lowered the can away from his mouth. "You're against me again. Sidin' with your new sisters, huh? Think that'll make you like 'em?" He pointed at Nye and Oriana with the can. "Any fool can see you'll never be like 'em."

For a second, Charlotte was glad the RV was so dark. The flashlight hopefully wasn't bright enough to let Nye see the hot flush that filled Charlotte's cheeks as she dropped her gaze to the dirty brown carpet by her feet.

"Well, Tommy."

Charlotte jerked her gaze to Oriana. She better not say anything to get Tommy more riled. Nye and Oriana didn't know him like Charlotte did. They didn't know what he was capable of.

"Since you like my God so much, then you won't mind if I tell Phoebe a story about Him." Oriana pulled her legs under her and scooted toward Phoebe, kneeling in front of the girl.

"Knock yourself out," Tommy said into the beer can.

"Phoebe...Phoebe, honey. Do you want to hear a story?"

The girl kept whimpering into Charlotte's chest.

"Well, I'll tell you anyway." Oriana readjusted to sit cross-legged in front of Phoebe. "This story is about Jesus and a terrible storm, and like the others I told you, it really happened."

Charlotte glanced at Tommy as Oriana began the story. He opened another can of beer and watched Oriana while he drank.

"The storm that Jesus was in was much worse than this one because He and His disciples were on a boat out on the water. The disciples were so afraid when a great, strong wind came up and blew the waves high around their boat. The whole boat rocked just like this camper."

Phoebe pulled her nose out of Charlotte's chest, and the whimpering stopped.

"The disciples were very afraid, but do you know what Jesus was doing? He was sleeping."

Phoebe turned her head and stared at Oriana.

Jesus was sleeping? What kind of dumb story was she telling?

"The disciples woke Jesus and begged Him to save them from sure death in the storm. But Jesus said to them, 'Why are you afraid, O you of little faith?'"

Of course. Like it was their fault they were in a storm...that they were afraid to die in it.

Oriana leaned forward. "Then do you know what happened?"

Phoebe's mouth hung open.

"Jesus told the sea and the wind to stop, and they did."

At least Jesus did something in that story. But He still just had to put down the people on the boat first for stuff that wasn't their fault. No wonder Christians had been so nasty to Charlotte her whole life.

The story did get Phoebe to stop whimpering. She sat

forward on Charlotte's lap, looking at Oriana like she wanted something more.

"Thanks for picking that story, Oriana." Nye's lips relaxed, almost into a smile. "I needed that."

"So did I." Oriana smiled toward Nye then turned to Phoebe. "How about a song?" Oriana took a deep breath and started to sing, "Blessed assurance, Jesus is mine—" A beer can flew over Oriana's head and crashed against the back of the driver's seat.

"Shut up." Even in the dim light, Tommy's eyes flashed. "You don't think I know what you're doin', blind girl? Any cops are out there, they'll hear you a mile off. Cut the Sunday school lesson and keep quiet."

Oriana shifted back to sit next to Nye. Their smiles were gone, but their features were relaxed with a calm that hadn't been there before.

Maybe Charlotte was just imagining things.

She jumped when something loud and sharp hit the RV, the roof, the sides, the windows.

"Hail." Nye must have said it for Oriana's sake, but she looked right at Charlotte. Her lips curved into a small smile.

She couldn't mean to smile. Not nicely. Maybe Nye was having fun watching Charlotte get good and scared.

The hail clattered into the flimsy roof and walls around them like it was going to break through and tear them to pieces. The way things were panning out, that might be the easier way to go.

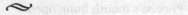

WHAT WAS GOING ON? If Gabe didn't know better, he'd say God didn't want them to save the women and little Phoebe. He couldn't actually believe that, but another tornado had touched down and was headed for Harper, keeping the search for the hostages from being effective if not stalling it altogether.

Gabe stared out the second-story window of the station at the trees that bent in the wind, leaves ripping off the branches and flying through the air.

What had any of those women done to deserve such a fate? And Phoebe was so young and innocent. She couldn't have done anything wrong at all. Gabe should have protected them. That's why he wore the badge. Charlotte and Phoebe had come into his life needing help, and he'd see that they got it. He'd let them down when that jerk took them away, but no way was he going to let Tommy keep them prisoner.

"You shouldn't be so close to the window, you know."

Gabe turned around to see Marcus standing farther back, his arms folded across his chest.

"I should be out there right now."

"It's a tornado, Gabe. Even a man your size would be in trouble."

Behind Marcus, Cullen and Nicanor sat on chairs on either side of Caroline, their heads lowered in prayer.

Gabe looked at Marcus. "I'm sorry."

He sighed and shook his head. "It wasn't your fault."

It was, but Marcus was apparently more forgiving than Gabe. "I've seen some parents of missing people through the years. You're calm enough to be a cop."

Marcus lowered his arms. "Do I look calm?" He held out his hands. They were trembling. "I think the acid might eat through my esophagus soon but hopefully not before this is all over."

"Are you worried about all of them?" Now where had that come from?

Marcus's widened eyes betrayed as much surprise as Gabe felt.

Gabe's nervous energy must have flowed into the part of his brain that was supposed to stop him from saying everything he was thinking.

"You mean Charlotte?"

"I'm sorry. I didn't mean to—"

"No. I deserve that. I didn't do right by her. But, Gabe, you should know I love her just as much as I love Nye and Oriana. Charlotte is my daughter, and I thank the Lord for bringing her to me."

Gabe nodded and checked the weather out the window. The wind still raged as pellets of hail started to bounce off the large panes of glass.

"That makes two of us, doesn't it?"

Gabe shot Marcus a glance. "Two of us?"

"Who love Charlotte."

Gabe's throat went dry. He wouldn't go quite that far, to say he loved her. Or was he already that far?

Marcus chuckled. "My wife was right again."

"I won't do anything about it, sir. She's not a believer, and—"

Marcus held up his hand. "Say no more. I respect you even more for your Christian maturity. I believe Charlotte will come around. With all of us in her life, how could she not?" A small smile curved his mouth. "I'm just glad to know there's a man like you who sees her worth." He looked out the window. "Should the situation ever come about, Gabe, I'd be pleased to know you were there to take care of my daughter and to love her."

"Thank you, sir." Gabe didn't know what else to say. Had he just admitted to loving Charlotte? Loving her enough to make her father think he wanted to marry her? Was it true?

His gut still twisted because he couldn't get out there and search. He was always anxious to find hostages and defend the helpless, but these feelings were new. He was nervous this time, edgy. Had been from that awful moment he'd watched Tommy drag Charlotte away. A cop didn't feel like he was being cut in two when he saw just anyone with a gun to their head.

Warmth started in his queasy belly and flowed out to his

fingertips with the realization. He loved her. How strange the Lord should bring a woman he could love into his life this way. She needed him so much, needed his protection and love. She needed the Lord, too, and Gabe would keep at her until she saw that. Shouldn't take long once she was out of the only kind of life she'd known. She'd been held back so long, stomped down and kept in a prison by Tommy and whoever else had probably used and abused her during her life. Time Charlotte got set free.

"Sergeant Kelly?" Officer Greer stopped farther back from the window, her dark gaze grim.

Gabe's insides clenched. "Any news?"

"The FBI identified your composite of the kidnapper. Thomas F. Wilcox. He has a prison record. Assault and burglary."

Great. No surprise the guy was a felon, but Gabe would've preferred embezzlement or fraud over assault.

Greer still stood there.

"Something else?"

She nodded. "Yes, sir. I thought you'd like to know what I just told Special Agent Foster. The last victim of the store thefts, the one you spoke with, has identified Charlotte Davis as the woman who distracted her while the theft may have taken place."

Gabe didn't hear if she said anything else. He'd forgotten he had given the detectives Charlotte's picture. Oriana had sent him one of Charlotte and Phoebe on his phone, and he had handed it over when he got suspicious. He just had to be a good cop.

"Gabe?" Marcus's voice pushed through the thickness of Gabe's tormenting thoughts. "What does that mean?"

Gabe opened his mouth. Nothing came out. He tried again. "It means she's an accomplice...in the thefts."

"Oh, my."

Allegedly, possibly...the careful terms they were supposed to use weren't necessary. Gabe's gut had known the whole time. Or was it his gut that had told him she was an innocent victim? That she was a helpless woman, battered and bruised, who needed his protection? He suspected her the first day he met her. Why hadn't he listened to his suspicions?

Gabe walked away from the window, out of the room, and into the hallway. He'd thought he couldn't sink any farther than letting Jim get stabbed because he trusted a woman. This felt even worse.

He hadn't just been duped into helping someone this time. He had actually fallen in love with the woman who was conning him. He'd fallen in love with a lying, thieving criminal. He'd throw up if it wouldn't add to his humiliation.

"Sergeant Kelly. Good."

Gabe blinked to clear his vision.

Agent Foster marched toward him. "The tornado touched down a quarter mile from here and cleared out. I want you out on the streets with Agent Fenworth five minutes ago. He'll brief you on your search sector."

The moment Gabe had been waiting for. Nye, Oriana, and Phoebe were still counting on him. He had to remind himself of that over and over as he went to look for Fenworth. If Gabe only thought of Charlotte, he might not set foot out of the station.

eighteen

"Fear not, for I have redeemed you;
I have called you by name, you are mine."
– Isaiah 43:1b

CHARLOTTE'S EYES POPPED OPEN.

Everything was quiet. No hail pelted the walls, and the RV was still.

Phoebe lay on the floor, nestled beside Charlotte.

Then what had woken Charlotte up?

A moan.

Charlotte sat up, and a beam of light hit her face. "Tommy." She put up her hands to block the bright flashlight that Tommy shined on her from the bench.

"Mornin', sleepyhead."

"What was that noise?"

Tommy set the flashlight down, leaving it on to shine over them all. He nodded toward Nye.

She was still propped up against the wall but squeezed her

eyes shut as she puffed out a long breath, her hand on her round belly.

No. Oh, no. Charlotte's stomach lurched. Nye couldn't be having the baby. Not now.

"Breathe, Nye. Just breathe," Oriana coached, her voice as calm as Nye's usually was. "It'll be okay."

"No, it won't." Charlotte looked at Tommy. "She's having the baby, Tommy."

"What baby?" He snickered. Or was it a hiccup? He stood to his feet, slowly, swaying a little, the gun swinging in his hand.

The rock in the pit of Charlotte's gut rolled over. Had he been drinking all night? "What time is it?"

"Almost sunrise, baby." He lifted another beer can to his mouth. How many had he brought? "Pay time. If daddy does what daddies do." He giggled, a sickening sound for a grown man to make.

Nye sucked in a breath and grimaced.

"Tommy, you have to let them go."

"If daddy pays up."

"No. Now. You have to let them go now." Charlotte got to her feet, ignoring the stiffness in her back and legs. She pointed at Nye. "She needs a doctor, Tommy."

"I need money."

"Tommy, stop! This isn't a joke."

"You had your kid without a doc."

Charlotte looked at Nye, her perfect features scrunched in pain. "I wasn't kidnapped. They didn't do anything to deserve this." She looked at Tommy. "You're letting them go now. This is wrong."

Tommy busted out with a loud laugh. "Wrong?" He coughed, probably choking on beer. "Like you know what wrong is." He took a step toward her, shoving the beer can into her face. "Long as I known you, you never admitted to doin' nothin' wrong. You always get away with everythin'."

He waved the gun at her as he swung his head to sneer at Nye and Oriana. "She's a better thief than I am. Started when she was a little kid." He lowered the beer can to show the height of a child. "Stole things for her old lady. She's hit more places than I have."

He swung his head back to Charlotte, his smile replaced with a glare. "But you got away with all of it. Never had to do time like me. Never had to pay."

Charlotte's cheeks burned. Why did he have to say all this? Now, in front of Nye and Oriana? "That wasn't my fault."

His eyes darkened. "It ain't never your fault, is it, baby?"

She held her breath as he stared at her. She knew that look too well.

"You want your sisters to like you? Why don't you tell 'em what you did? Tell 'em how you wanted me to do this."

Charlotte closed her eyes. "Stop it, Tommy."

"Tell 'em how you begged to go with me so they wouldn't take your kid away from you."

Charlotte's gaze went to Nye and Oriana. They were pale. Shocked. Hurt?

"How about what you did to Phoebe? Think they'd like you if you told 'em that?" He looked at the women. "I'll tell 'em, and we'll see."

"Shut up!" Charlotte threw herself at Tommy with a scream. Rage fired her limbs as she tried to scratch his face.

He grabbed her neck and slammed her back against the wall.

"Charlotte!" Oriana reached toward the sounds of the fight.

Phoebe shrieked.

"Leave her alone!" Nye sat up, wincing.

Tommy squeezed his hand around Charlotte's neck, pushing her into the rough wall.

She couldn't breathe. He was going to kill her.

Hate shot from his eyes into hers.

She weakly clutched at his hands.

"Tommy. Dad will only pay for all of us." Nye's voice was weaker than before. "You hurt her, you lose the money."

Tommy's grip loosened.

Air filled Charlotte's lungs as she pulled away. She put her hand on her throbbing neck.

Tommy pointed the gun at Nye. "You better be tellin' the truth, princess."

Nye closed her eyes, leaning back against the wall with a grimace.

Phoebe whimpered as she clung to Oriana.

Tommy stalked to Phoebe and grabbed her arm, yanking the girl to her feet.

Pain shot straight to Charlotte's heart. "Tommy! What are you doing?" *Please, not Phoebe. Not Phoebe.*

"I'm takin' her with me. Everybody loves Phoebe. Your old man won't try nothin' with her there. And y'all won't try nothin' either."

"Please, Tommy. Don't take her." Charlotte stumbled toward him. "Take me instead. I'm sorry. I won't fight you anymore. I'm so sorry." She choked on a sob. "Please, just leave Phoebe here. I'll go with you."

"Shut up!" He pointed the gun at Phoebe.

Charlotte froze.

"Those two ain't goin' nowhere." He looked at pregnant Nye and blind Oriana with a sneer, then glared at Charlotte. "Do I gotta tie you up?"

Charlotte shook her head.

"No. You won't try to come after me. You'll be a good girl like always, especially since you know what'll happen to your precious Phoebe if you don't." He looked at Charlotte's feet. "Just in case you get brave again, take off your shoes."

Phoebe's whimpering stung like acid in Charlotte's wound. "Tommy, don't do this. I'll do whatever you want."

"Take off your shoes!" He jerked Phoebe's arm as he yelled.

"Okay. I'm taking them off." Charlotte held up a hand as she slipped her feet out of the sandals. "Just please don't hurt her."

"That's up to you, baby. Now get over there with your sisters."

Charlotte went to stand next to Nye, who was still lying on the floor.

"I wouldn't get too close." A drunk grin twisted Tommy's mouth as he shoved the gun in the waistband of his jeans and picked up the sandals. "They might tear you to pieces now they know the kind of trash you are."

Charlotte could try to make a move now, with the gun in his pants. But he still had Phoebe. He could break her neck with one quick jerk. He could kill them all that easily.

He grabbed the flashlight and shook the whimpering Phoebe as he took her to the door. "Shut up, kid."

"Phoebe, try not to cry, sweetie. Momma will be with you soon."

Phoebe looked back as Tommy pulled her through the door. Tears streaked her pale cheeks.

Charlotte's heart seared like a thousand knives were cutting it to shreds. She ran to the door and looked out into the little clearing. "Don't be scared, Phoebe! Momma will get you!"

Tommy chucked the sandals as far as he could into the dark trees then pointed the gun at Charlotte. "Get back in there and shut up!"

Charlotte backed inside, watching her daughter disappear into the black forest along with the beam from the flashlight. Streams of tears ran down Charlotte's face, but they didn't soften the unbearable tearing of her heart.

He should've shot her. Anything not to feel this.

A hand touched Charlotte's shoulder.

Oriana stood behind her, moisture spilling over onto her cheeks. "I'm sorry, Charlotte." *She* was sorry?

Charlotte tried to look past her at Nye in the RV, but it was too dark to see.

"Did he take the flashlight?"

Charlotte couldn't get out any words to answer Oriana.

"Yes." Nye's strained voice came from the darkness.

"Just a second." Oriana reached into the pocket of her shorts. Then a small light flicked on.

"You have a flashlight?" Nye gasped through a smile.

"I usually keep it in my purse for the kids in case the power goes out at the center again, but Owen had just used it, so I had it in my pocket."

Oriana gently squeezed Charlotte's shoulder. "The Lord will take care of Phoebe. He's holding her in His hands right this minute."

Charlotte shrugged away from Oriana's touch. "Just like He's holding you?" She spewed out the words. "I'm done being held by people who hurt like that."

"Sounds familiar." Nye looked at Charlotte with soft eyes. "We've learned the hard way to trust God's plan instead of our own. His way is always the best way."

Charlotte crossed her arms over her throbbing chest. "Easy for you to say. You both have perfect lives. Perfect parents, perfect guys." Tears pushed out of Charlotte's eyes again.

Nye sucked in a quick breath and grimaced.

"Nye?" Oriana went to her sister and knelt beside her, taking Nye's hand. Oriana stroked Nye's forehead until the contraction went away.

Nye smiled through the sweat that made droplets on her face. "How do you feel about delivering a baby?"

Oriana laughed softly. "How do you feel about having your blind little sister deliver your baby?"

Nye took in a deep breath. "I think God's getting very creative with our lives."

"What's wrong with you two?" Charlotte stared at them,

lowering her arms. "You should be scared. You should be screaming and panicking." Charlotte dropped her gaze to the brown floor. "You should be angry."

"And the peace of God, which transcends all understanding, will guard your hearts and your minds in Christ Jesus."

Nye nodded at Oriana's words.

Was that a quote?

"It's like Nye said." Oriana tilted her head up toward Charlotte. "God has given us peace. He's promised that everything will turn out for the good of those He calls to be His children. We know we can trust what He's doing. Today and forever."

"You can have that peace, too, Charlotte." Nye tried to lean forward but stopped. "Whatever you've done or haven't done."

There it was. The blame. So they had been listening to Tommy.

"Everyone has done wrong things." Oriana smoothed the sweat from Nye's brow. "But no wrong is too big for God to forgive and save you from a life of sin. Jesus died to pay for all your sins, just like He paid for ours."

Nye looked at Charlotte. "You can be free, Charlotte."

Charlotte bit her lip. They sure wouldn't have had much to pay for, what with their fairytale lives setting them up for success. They didn't know what they were talking about. Couldn't they see how trapped she was?

"Oh my." Nye squeezed Oriana's hand as she crunched forward with a small grunt, like she was trying to be ladylike even now.

"Charlotte, we need help." Oriana bit her lip, too. "Do you think you can try to get some?"

What if Tommy saw her and hurt Phoebe? But Nye could die. The baby could die if Charlotte didn't go.

And Phoebe was alone with Tommy right now. Charlotte's stomach knotted. She had to go.

She went to the door.

"Charlotte, wait." Oriana's voice stopped her. "Take the flashlight."

Charlotte shook her head, then remembered Oriana couldn't see her. "Nye might need it. To see the baby." She turned to go.

"Charlotte," Oriana spoke again, "you should know, no matter what happens, we love you very much."

Charlotte looked back.

Nye nodded and smiled. "Like a sister."

Charlotte stared at them for a second, more tears burning her eyes. This wasn't real. Couldn't be. But what kind of dream had Tommy taking Phoebe away with a gun? That was the stuff of her nightmares.

Charlotte stepped down from the RV, her bare feet pressing into rough sticks and grass. The forest in front of her was like a black wall. She followed the direction she had seen Tommy take Phoebe until they had disappeared from view.

She stopped. Which way did they go after that? She looked for a sign. A footprint, broken sticks, anything. It was too dark to make anything out.

A scream came from the RV. Nye.

Charlotte's heart thumped against her chest as she put one foot in front of the other. She tried not to think about what she was stepping on, the squishy things and the sharp painful ones. Everything was wet. She stepped into a puddle, her foot sinking into mud as water splashed her bare leg.

She kept going, pushing through the darkness. Shouldn't her eyes adjust so she could see more? All the good it would do her. She had no idea where she was going.

Phoebe was alone and scared ahead. Nye was in pain behind, but Charlotte couldn't do a thing to help either of them.

She'd already lost any sense of where she was. She could be going in circles. She splashed into a puddle again. Was it the same one?

A sob pushed up her throat. "I didn't ask for this! I didn't want any of it. I never had a choice." As if there was a point in yelling at the darkness above her.

You can be free, Charlotte. Nye's words reached Charlotte's ears.

Yeah, right. Charlotte made herself keep trudging forward. At least she hoped it was forward. "If You really save, Jesus, then why don't You help now?"

She blinked up at the branches that twisted above her like the arms of a monster. "I know You won't want to help me, but how about Nye, huh? You like her. Or how about Phoebe? She's just a little girl. She never did anything to deserve—" Another sob choked off the words as she bumped into a tree trunk, the bark scraping her arm. Neither had Charlotte. Nobody deserved to hurt as much as her heart did right now.

Charlotte pushed away from the tree. Jesus wasn't going to give her any help, that was for sure. Charlotte was Phoebe's only hope. She had to keep going, even if it was only to some horrible end to this nightmare.

nineteen

> *"I have blotted out your transgressions like a cloud
> and your sins like mist;
> return to Me, for I have redeemed you."*
> – Isaiah 44:22

"YOU'LL LEAVE for the Forest Preserve in ten minutes."

Gabe nodded, though Agent Foster likely didn't feel a need for his agreement. The tall woman disappeared quickly up the staircase without another glance.

Gabe tugged at the neck of the body armor under his shirt as he waited on the bench in the front lobby of the station. He'd never sat there in his life. Made him feel like a civilian, sitting there in street clothes. Maybe he should take the armor off. A shot in the chest might be just what he needed. Might knock some sense into his thick skull and the heart that so easily fell for a woman like Charlotte.

"Don't do anything rash." The accented voice came from above him.

Gabe looked up to see Nicanor watching him. When had he come down the stairs?

"You said to me once, 'Don't do anything rash.'"

"When you were trying to catch Dez." Gabe nodded. "I remember. But believe me, I won't."

Nicanor must be thinking Gabe still cared about Charlotte too much. That his judgment would be clouded. "I'll watch out for Oriana and Nye."

"Charlotte can take care of herself?" Nicanor's blue eyes pinned Gabe's wandering gaze.

"Yeah, I guess so." Gabe looked past Nicanor. "Is Marcus on his way? We're supposed to meet the car out front here."

"Sometimes the rash thing is not caring too much. It's caring too little."

Gabe met Nicanor's gaze, irritation sparking in his chest. Like this was any of Nicanor's business. "Trust me. That's not my problem."

"I don't pretend to know you or people who are like you. I just know sinners."

What was that supposed to mean?

"We're hard to love."

Heat flushed Gabe's face, whether from anger or embarrassment he wasn't sure. "She conned me into believing she was a victim. She played me when I should've known better than to trust her. I should never have..." Gabe blew out a sigh.

"Loved her?" Nicanor slipped his hands into his pockets. "I know what it is to be loved when you don't deserve it."

Gabe looked away. Nicanor meant Oriana and Nye. The way they had forgiven Nicanor and loved him. This was different.

"Don't you?" Nicanor turned and walked away as if he hadn't just punched Gabe in the gut.

Maybe that's what the Lord just did. Gabe leaned forward as the full realization of his massive arrogance nearly choked him. He called himself a Christian, but he had denied his own Savior.

As if Gabe were so much better than everyone else that he didn't even need to be redeemed.

Dear Lord, forgive me. Gabe pressed his fist against his mouth. His own thoughts and words echoed in his mind.

Save the kid so he could grow up to be an addict or a banger?

I'm not sure how to tell who the innocent people are anymore.

For all have sinned and fall short of the glory of God. The verse Momma had him memorize when he was a kid stopped the chain of his own stupid words. Nobody was innocent. Least of all Gabe himself.

Just get 'em off the streets and make the city safer for the innocent, Pete had said. Gabe had thought he was right then. But if that's what they were trying to do, they were fighting a losing battle from the start.

Don't feel for them. Just get the job done. Gabe had told Cullen that anything else was death to a cop, but he was wrong. Not caring was the real death, for Gabe and for the people who needed life. Gabe hadn't even told Charlotte about Jesus, because he was too busy trying to figure out if she was innocent or not, if he was better than her or not, if he should care or not.

Gabe swallowed. He'd never told anyone about Christ in his fifteen years as a cop, though he'd seen people in the worst kind of pain. Counseling people was not a part of tactics and procedures. Getting the job done was first priority at all times.

He rubbed his hands over his face. Maybe that was why he hadn't been able to get the job done right—he was missing the real job, the reason God put him in the lives of those hurting people at their hardest moments.

He turned and sank to his knees in front of the bench. Time to add God and Gospel to his procedures and tactics, starting with some repentance of his own.

"Mind if we join you?" Marcus stood behind him, along with Cullen and Nicanor.

Gabe cleared his throat, but emotion still clogged his voice. "Not at all."

Marcus knelt on one side of Gabe, while Cullen knelt on the other, with Nicanor next to him.

"Marcus." Gabe met the red-rimmed eyes of the man who had been like his father until he'd pushed him away. "I'm sorry I treated you differently after we found out about Charlotte."

Marcus put his hand on Gabe's shoulder. "Forgive us our trespasses as we forgive those who trespass against us." He smiled. "All is forgiven. Now let's pray and go get my daughters."

Gabe almost could have smiled. "Amen."

How long had she been here? Charlotte's legs felt like rubber, and her feet throbbed like they'd been cut a hundred times.

The forest was still dark, and she was still lost. So much for asking Jesus for help. Not like she'd thought for a second it would work. He thought she was a loser like everyone else, even though He hadn't given her any choice. Like that cripple who just wanted to walk, and Jesus told him his sins were forgiven instead.

Charlotte snorted, but it turned into a cough. Her feet were so cold and wet. She'd probably catch the flu...if she lived that long. She stopped, holding herself up with one hand against a tree trunk.

She'd take help from just about anybody right now, even some judge in the sky.

She squinted. Was that light?

A small bit of yellow peeked through two trees ahead. Or was it just a speck of something else?

She pushed away from the tree and trudged ahead. The dot

got bigger. Then there were more and more spots through the trees until she reached something that looked like a path. Her heart surged.

The wide path was like the one she had walked on with Gabe and Phoebe. Leaves covered it now, probably tossed by the stormy winds.

Charlotte stepped onto the path, the leaves like a cushion for her feet. She looked up to see where the path led.

Light.

She scrunched her eyes until they adjusted to the light that glowed from somewhere beyond where she could see. The light pushed against the tree limbs that bent over the top of the path, like the yellow glow might be able to force the dark branches to open and let Charlotte out. She walked on the path toward the brightness. Must be sunrise.

Sunrise. Tommy had said that was the meeting time with Marcus.

Charlotte started to run down the path, wincing at the shooting pain in her feet. Tommy and Marcus would have to meet at the edge of the woods somewhere. She might be almost there.

"I told you to come alone, old man." Tommy's voice blew to Charlotte on the wind.

He was close. That meant Phoebe was close.

"I'm just a friend."

Gabe? Her heart leaped at the rumble she'd know anywhere. She slowed to a walk, moving toward their voices. Maybe she could sneak up on Tommy and get Phoebe away from him.

"Drop your gun, cop." Tommy's white T-shirt and jeans flashed between the trees.

Charlotte left the path and moved in that direction, stones and branches again digging into her cuts.

"I don't have one," Gabe answered. "See?"

She paused at the edge of the clearing, and her heart stopped.

Tommy held his gun against Phoebe's head. "Whatever. Just give me the money."

"You have to let my daughters go first, Tommy." Marcus stepped forward, holding a briefcase in his hand. "Then you'll get your money."

"Stay where you are." Tommy gave Phoebe a shake.

Charlotte pulled back farther behind a tree while everything in her cried out to save her baby girl. She couldn't do anything with that gun so close.

"Okay. I'm sorry, I didn't mean to move." Marcus's voice was calm, patient. "But the only way you'll get that money is to let my daughters go."

Tommy shook his head. "You must really think I'm stupid. What's gonna keep me from gettin' shot if I let them go?"

"Take me instead." Was Marcus serious?

"You're kiddin'." Tommy didn't believe him either.

"Do I look like I'm joking?" Marcus stared at Tommy. "I want you to let my daughters go and take me instead."

"All of 'em or just the pretty ones?"

"What do you mean?"

"Charlotte goes wherever I go. That's what I mean."

Her stomach curdled at Tommy's words.

"You have to let Charlotte go to get the money."

Tommy laughed, making her skin crawl. "You crazy? Man, that girl pulled the wool over your eyes, didn't she? Don't you know she's a no-good liar and a thief? She's been robbin' every one of them stores with me."

Charlotte closed her eyes. Not again. Not in front of the only men who'd ever treated her like she was worth something.

"We know that, Tommy. I still want her back." Marcus's words filled Charlotte's heart. Could it be true?

"Bet you didn't know she made her own kid retarded."

No.

Tommy cackled. "That's right. She used to get drunk every night, and she kept right on drinkin' even when she got herself knocked up. That's why the girl here's so stupid. 'Cause her momma fried her brain. I'm the only one who'd have a tramp that'd do a thing like that."

Charlotte sank to the wet ground behind the tree, her chest pressing into her like a huge log had fallen on it. She couldn't breathe.

They all knew. It was over.

She had lost everything. Even if she got Phoebe away from Tommy somehow, the others would take Phoebe from her.

And they would be right.

Charlotte bit down on her hand to stop the gasp that came to the surface. The truth seared her heart. She had destroyed her baby girl. She'd made Phoebe the way she was and made her life miserable ever since. Charlotte didn't deserve Phoebe. She never had. All Charlotte deserved was what she had now—a certain future of violent death at Tommy's hands or the slow death of imprisonment.

You can be free.

Charlotte's gut twisted. If Nye and Oriana had heard what Charlotte had done to Phoebe, even they would know their God couldn't—wouldn't—save her. Charlotte felt the damning of her own soul burning a hole inside her.

"This is your last chance, old man. Hand over the money now."

"Momma!" Phoebe's shriek reached whatever part of Charlotte was still alive.

She scrambled to her feet. Phoebe shouldn't pay for Charlotte's wrongs anymore.

"Tommy!" Charlotte stumbled out from behind the trees as Tommy backed up a little and turned, probably trying to see all the people at once. "Please don't hurt her. You're right. It's all my fault. I've done terrible things."

"Stay where you are."

Charlotte stopped walking. From this closer distance, she could see the fear on Tommy's face. She'd never seen him look scared before. "If you're going to kill someone, kill me. I deserve it."

"You have to let them all go, Tommy." Marcus didn't give up. "Take me in their place." He would still do that?

Charlotte searched Marcus's face for the hate, the judgment. Neither one was there.

"They're my daughters."

She knew that must be love in Marcus's eyes when he looked at her. "Let them go, Tommy."

"Forget it, old man." Tommy glared at Marcus.

"I'm a much better ransom. Many rich people in the area, including at the bank, know me and would pay handsomely to have me returned."

Tommy's eyebrows knit together. He was thinking again. Never pretty.

"But if you don't take me and you harm Phoebe or one of my daughters, you won't get anything but prison."

"All right, old man. You win."

Charlotte's heartbeat raced like mad. Tommy never said that.

"I'll take you instead."

"You've made the right decision." Marcus started to walk toward Tommy.

"Wa—" Charlotte's warning stuck in her throat as Tommy fired. At Marcus.

"Daddy!" Charlotte screamed as she lunged for his falling body. She hit a wall instead.

Gabe's hard arm blocked her, holding her back as Phoebe ran to them.

Charlotte stopped struggling and stared.

Marcus and Tommy lay on the ground.

No. This couldn't be happening.

Men in camouflage came out from the trees and went over to Marcus and Tommy.

"No." Charlotte squirmed out from behind Gabe's arm.

"Charlotte, wait."

She didn't listen to his warning as she ran to Marcus.

The camouflaged cop or whatever he was who crouched by Marcus stood and let her brush past him. Charlotte dropped to the ground beside Marcus's still body.

Blood seeped through his shirt sleeve.

"Daddy?"

He moaned and opened his eyes.

Charlotte breathed again.

He smiled at her. "You're safe."

She sniffed. "You're hurt."

"Just my arm." He tried to sit up. "Is Tommy—"

Charlotte gently pushed Marcus back down. "You'll hurt yourself."

"Tommy is dead." Gabe appeared, towering over Charlotte and Marcus with Phoebe in his arms. "I'm sorry, Charlotte."

She looked over to where more of those camo-covered cops hovered over Tommy's body. Was it true? Was she free now?

She looked up at her baby girl in Gabe's arms. The tracks where tears had fallen on her white cheeks were still there. Charlotte had done that to her.

The weight of the many people she had hurt, the harm she had caused, still crushed her heart. No, she wasn't free.

Her gaze went to Gabe. She recognized what she saw in his eyes as he gave her that big smile. Love. Even though she didn't deserve it. Could it be possible?

She frowned as she stood. "I want to talk to you about that help you told me I needed." She bit her lip as she squinted up at

Gabe. "But first we've got to get back to Nye and Oriana. Nye's having the baby."

"What?" Marcus tried to sit up but grimaced.

"You stay where you are." Gabe's rumble wasn't to be messed with. "Bentley, call for additional EMS for female in labor."

The guy hovering over Marcus nodded and muttered into his radio.

"Can you tell us where they are?" Gabe stepped around Marcus to stand next to Charlotte, scattering her senses.

She pointed to where she had come from. "I think the path over there should take us back. I couldn't find it at first, but Tommy must have used it when he drove us into the woods."

"Got that, Bentley?"

The camo guy nodded again and said more stuff into the radio.

Three of the camouflaged people who were by Tommy took off jogging for the path.

Charlotte glanced at Gabe. "I'd like to go, too, just to make sure they find them okay."

"After you." He held out his hand in front of her like she was a queen.

As they walked toward the path, her mind drifted to that first story she had heard Oriana tell Phoebe, the one that had made her so mad. Charlotte glanced up at Gabe. "I get it now."

He raised his eyebrows as he looked down at her.

"About Jesus, I mean. He told that cripple his sins were forgiven instead of helping him walk because Jesus knew that was what the guy really needed. Wasn't it?"

"Yes."

The sin was the prison.

Charlotte looked ahead and swallowed. "I want to be free."

Gabe's forehead wrinkled. "From Tommy?"

"No." Charlotte shook her head and took in a shaky breath.

"From living like this. From all the bad stuff I've done." Charlotte glanced up at Gabe. "Nye said Jesus could make me free...I think I'd like that."

"I think He just did." Gabe smiled at her. "And you know, in that story with the cripple, Jesus forgives his sins and then heals him so he can get up and walk."

Phoebe leaned down from Gabe, and Charlotte took the girl in her arms with a smile that sprang from the warmth growing inside her. "You were right, baby girl," Charlotte whispered in her daughter's ear. "Jesus does save."

epilogue

> *"E'er since, by faith, I saw the stream*
> *Thy flowing wounds supply,*
> *Redeeming love has been my theme,*
> *And shall be till I die."*
> – William Cowper, "Praise for the Fountain Opened"

THE BARRED gate slid to the side with a bang, and Charlotte followed the policewoman into the open room, the last one before the doors outside.

Charlotte hadn't been this nervous since she'd stood in front of the judge for her sentence.

Father in heaven, please give me courage. Charlotte scanned the waiting people, sitting on chairs and standing around. Maybe Marcus had come? She wasn't sure anyone else had forgiven her. Except for Phoebe. Hadn't someone at least brought Phoebe?

"Ma'am." The policewoman's voice brought Charlotte's gaze to the desk where the officer waited. "Your personal belongings."

Charlotte went to the desk. Twenty-five cents and a candy wrapper. Not much of a personal life.

"You're free to go, ma'am." The policewoman nodded at her.

Go where? Charlotte thought Marcus, at least, would have remembered the date she was getting out.

Maybe even Gabe. He had visited her so regularly during the six months she was inside. But now that she was being released, a convict with a record, she couldn't expect him to have anything more to do with her. He was a cop, after all. Having a relationship with her could mess up his career. She wouldn't want that.

Charlotte shoved the quarter into her jeans pocket and headed for the glass doors. Broke and completely alone. Not much of a start to a new life.

The sunlight outside beckoned her, a reminder of the light she had inside her now. Well, not completely alone.

You have a plan in this, too, Father. Just like the plan He had to save her in the forest all those months ago. *Just no tornadoes this time, please?* She smiled as she pushed through the door.

The cold air smacked her in the face. She stopped to zip up the light jacket she had brought with her when the weather had been much warmer. Hopefully there was a bus stop close by.

She looked down at the cement steps of the staircase as she started—

"Surprise!"

Charlotte nearly jumped out of her skin at the chorus of voices that shouted at her elbow.

Just to the right of the stairs, a crowd of faces smiled at her. Nye? And Oriana, Caroline, Nicanor, Cullen…Marcus. They came.

"Steady there." Gabe's rumble came from her other side as he gently grasped her arm, suddenly standing next to her on the stairs. "You look like you're about to fall over."

She tilted her head up to see his warm eyes and beautiful smile.

He held her baby girl in his arms. A tingly rush of warmth shot right to her toes at the sight. "I think I just might."

"Momma!" Phoebe leaned down.

Charlotte caught her daughter and squeezed her tight, tears pushing to the surface.

Phoebe squirmed and twisted around to point. "Look!"

Behind the Sanders, people Charlotte didn't recognize held up a sign with huge letters: WELCOME HOME, CHARLOTTE!

Could it be possible? After all she had done to them?

They all smiled up at her.

"Welcome home, honey." Marcus nodded to her, his eyes glistening with unshed tears.

"Welcome home, sweetie." Caroline dabbed her eyes with a tissue as she smiled.

Oriana beamed one of her sunshine smiles. "Welcome home, sis. We missed you."

"Welcome home, Charlotte." Nye held her baby, all bundled up in a snow suit and blanket. "Little Caroline Charlotte missed you, too."

They'd given the baby her name? Charlotte thought her heart might burst. Could a person die from happiness? That was never a question she thought she'd have to wonder.

"Welcome home, Charlotte." The people behind Charlotte's new family waved as they repeated the words.

"The folks from church wanted to welcome you home, too." Gabe beamed at Charlotte. "You're part of a real big family now."

She peered up at him. "Does that mean you and me are family, too?"

His smile slowly faded.

She held her breath. Had she gone too far?

"I'd like to be." His voice dropped even deeper than normal. He looked at the folks holding the sign. "Go ahead."

They flipped the sign over and a new message stared at her: WILL YOU MARRY ME?

Her heart stopped. She finally turned her head to Gabe, who wore the biggest grin she'd ever seen.

"You look so cute when your mouth hangs open like that." His brown eyes twinkled.

She took in a breath, closing her mouth and opening it again. She wasn't sure whether to be mad, happy, or just fall into a puddle of tears.

"I was afraid if I asked you in private, you'd turn me down." Gabe dropped down on one knee, somehow managing to balance on the stair that way. "With all your family here, you can't possibly say no."

Her pulse raced. She couldn't think with that handsome face so close to hers. "But, Gabe, you're a police officer. I'm a—"

"Shh." He put a large finger gently on her lips. "Let's just say we're both sinners, saved by God's grace." Love filled his eyes as he looked deep into hers. "I know I don't deserve you or Phoebe, but if you let me, I will do my very best to be the kind of husband and father that shows you God's love every day. Charlotte Davis, I love you, and I love Phoebe as my own." He touched Phoebe's dangling hand. "Will you marry me?"

"Yes!" Phoebe shouted, a smile brightening her face as she watched Gabe.

Gabe and Charlotte laughed, along with the audience Charlotte had forgotten was there.

Gabe met Charlotte's gaze.

She nodded and smiled. "Yes, from me, too."

Whoops and hollers broke out from the family behind her, but they couldn't tear Charlotte's gaze from Gabe's eyes and the huge smile that spread across his face.

"Don't freeze her to death before the wedding!" someone shouted.

"Are you cold?" A twinkle lit Gabe's eyes.

"A little." Charlotte bit her lip.

He stood with a grin and suddenly scooped her up, Phoebe and all, into his strong arms.

Phoebe squealed and giggled as the crowd cheered.

"Better?" Gabe looked down into Charlotte's face, his own only inches from hers.

Warmth filled her body, rushing to her cheeks. She nodded.

"Good." He carried them down the stairs and across the parking lot as if they weighed nothing.

"Where are you taking us?"

"Home." He turned around so Charlotte could see Marcus, her sisters, and the rest of her family following close behind. "We're all taking you home."

"Home?" Phoebe looked at Charlotte, her little eyebrows raised.

"Yes, baby girl." Charlotte smiled. They didn't have to be scared anymore. They were free. "We're finally home."

Turn the Page for a Special Sneak Peek of
GUARDIANS UNLEASHED, BOOK 1

HIDDEN DANGER

AVAILABLE NOW

hidden danger
CHAPTER ONE

CORA ISAKSSON'S pulse jerked with her arm when Jana tugged hard to the right. The golden retriever never pulled on her leash unless she caught scent of one of two things—narcotics or a human in need of rescue.

Jana tugged toward a black suitcase parked upright next to a man in the baggage claim of Minneapolis International Airport.

"Get that dog away from my luggage." The middle-aged, heavyset man had a smudge of dark hairs on his head and a long, sagging mustache that shaped his mouth into a severe frown.

Cora's mind raced. She and Jana were off the clock, finished logging in their hours searching for narcotics at Departures. The usual TSA officer who accompanied her had left, and Cora had handed in her radio for the day.

But Jana sat next to the man's suitcase and aimed her big brown eyes up at Cora.

She'd found drugs.

Cora swallowed. She glanced past the scattered crowds of people, her gaze finding the nearest glass exit doors.

A security guard, Frank O'Donnell, stood by the exit, talking to a woman with suitcases piled in a precarious stack.

Cora should be able to get help from Frank if the traveler didn't cooperate.

"I said, get it away from me." The man's voice lowered as he grabbed the long handle of his suitcase and started walking. Toward the exit.

"Sir, wait." Cora grabbed a handful of treats from her pocket on autopilot and gave them to Jana as she hurried after the escaping passenger.

A younger man stepped into the mustached man's path, halting him abruptly.

They appeared to exchange some words, then glared at Cora as she approached with Jana.

The golden smelled the suitcase, her feathered tail swishing with excitement.

"Sir, I'm afraid you're going to have to stay and allow your suitcase to be searched." Cora's voice trembled slightly as trepidation coursed through her veins. Confronting a suspect without backup from an officer was risky, but she couldn't let him go. "This is a narcotics detection K-9, and she has identified there may be illegal narcotics in your suitcase."

"I don't care what you or your dog think. You can't stop me from leaving." The man nodded to his companion, and they turned to leave again.

"No." Cora's heart thudded against her ribs, as if an instinctive warning of self-preservation. But she darted in front of the two men, using Jana's wagging body to help block them. "I'm sorry, but you can't leave." She started to turn toward Frank.

Someone grabbed her arm and yanked her backward.

Cora gasped.

"Don't you dare." The younger man leveled the threat in a low growl. He stood just behind her to one side, his body an uncomfortable inch or two away from hers. He squeezed her arm as he leaned in, an odor that suggested he hadn't bathed in a while assaulting her nostrils.

"Feel this?" He pressed something hard into her back through her jacket.

She held her breath. She'd never had a gun poking her before, but somehow, she knew without a doubt what it was. *Father, please help me.*

"You're gonna walk out of here with us like everything is normal. Got it?"

"Díaz, what are you doing?" The mustached man's gruff words returned a burst of oxygen to Cora's lungs. Would he help her?

"What does it look like?"

"We can't afford to kidnap someone right now."

"Maybe you can't." Díaz's grip on her arm cut tighter. "I can't go back to prison. We're getting out of here."

The older man cursed, making Cora wince.

Díaz dug the gun into her spine. "I'm gonna put this in my pocket, but my finger will be on the trigger the whole time. You talk or make a wrong move, and that security guard dies. And whatever other people I can take out before I go down. Got it?"

She moistened her lips as she darted her gaze around the baggage claim. There must be something she could do.

"Got it?" He jerked her arm. "Or I can start shooting right now."

"No." The word popped from her mouth with air she didn't know she had. "Don't hurt anyone. I'll go."

"Move." He released her arm, allowing blood and circulation to return with a surge of pain.

She walked toward the exit, Jana following at her side with her tail swishing as if it were the normal day it had been moments ago. *Please, Father. Don't let anyone get hurt. Show me what to do.*

If only she had made more headway with her proposal to the

airport that metal detectors be installed at the baggage claim entrance. Most airports didn't have any such security measures in their arrivals area but Cora had been concerned about the vulnerability that created. And now a man had brought a gun in, just as she'd feared could happen someday.

Frank smiled as she neared.

The two men walked a few paces behind her.

Blood rushed in her ears. Should she run? Make a dash for the shuttle service counter near the doors and shout a warning to Frank?

Jana bumped lightly into Cora's leg as they walked.

No. Jana could get hurt. Frank could get shot. Anyone here could become a victim of her self-preservation.

She pasted on a smile and waved at Frank. "Have a good afternoon." Did her voice sound normal? It might have held a hint of the trembling that was now more constant than her breathing as fear took control of her body.

"You, too, Cora." Frank turned his head away as she passed through the doors.

Thank you, Lord. She must not have shown the growing terror that threatened to buckle her knees.

What would happen outside on the sidewalk? There were so many people. More than indoors but spread farther apart.

"Get in." Díaz cinched her arm in his grip again, standing too close. "Brown car."

She tried to swallow but coughed instead as frigid, January air broke into her lungs.

"Move." He pushed her forward, toward the empty brown four-door that waited by the curb. Waiting to take her. Where?

Jana nudged Cora's gloved hand with her nose.

Cora looked down at the beautiful golden's face, her hopeful gaze directed up at Cora. What would happen to Jana?

Never get in. Phoenix Gray's words blared through Cora's mind. How many times had Cora's employer told her this was where she was to draw the line? If anyone ever attempted to abduct her, she should do whatever it took to avoid getting into a vehicle. As the owner and founder of Phoenix K-9 Security and Detection Agency, Phoenix should know.

The mustached man opened the front passenger door and slipped inside as if he couldn't get away fast enough.

Díaz yanked open the back door. He started to push her inside.

She stiffened and pulled back.

Giggles.

She jerked her head to the left.

Three children hugged a suited man who kneeled on the sidewalk. He was likely their father, probably returned from a business trip.

"They'll be the first I'll shoot. Get in."

She couldn't risk that Díaz meant what he said. She turned back to Jana and the kidnapper's car. "In."

The golden jumped in easily at the command, as calm and steady as always.

Cora sat beside Jana on the backseat, her fingers shaking as she stroked the dog's fur. Thank the Lord Jana didn't have an ounce of guardian instinct, as her co-worker Bristol liked to joke. If she did, the men might have hurt her in their effort to kidnap Cora.

Or maybe...perhaps, Jana knew something Cora didn't. That there was nothing to fear.

As Díaz jerked the car into gear and pulled away from the curb, Cora's pulse pounded in her ears.

The remainder of Phoenix's repeated warning about abductions seared her thoughts.

If you get in, you're dead.

The greatest threat to this K-9 team is the one they don't see coming.

BUY NOW at HiddenDangerBook.com

Want to be the first to know when you can get Jerusha's next books?
Subscribe to Jerusha's newsletter at
www.FearWarriorSuspense.com
and get a free romantic suspense story to read while you wait!

She never invites visitors. But visitors sometimes invite themselves.

When a winter storm brings more than snow, May Denver is forced to flee from her home and fight for her life. Can she trust an unwanted neighbor and risk her greatest fear in order to survive?

GRAB THIS ROMANTIC SUSPENSE STORY FOR FREE WHEN YOU SIGN UP FOR JERUSHA'S NEWSLETTER
www.FearWarriorSuspense.com

about jerusha

Jerusha Agen imagines danger around every corner, but knows God is there, too. So naturally, she writes romantic suspense infused with the hope of salvation in Jesus Christ.

Jerusha loves to hang out with her big furry dogs and little furry cats, often while reading or watching movies.

Find more of Jerusha's thrilling, fear-fighting stories at www.JerushaAgen.com.

facebook.com/JerushaAgenAuthor
instagram.com/jerushaagen

also by jerusha agen

SISTERS REDEEMED SERIES

If You Dance with Me

If You Light My Way

If You Rescue Me

GUARDIANS UNLEASHED SERIES

Rising Danger (Prequel)

Hidden Danger

Covert Danger (2022)

Unseen Danger (2023)

Falling Danger (2023)

Untitled Book Five (2024)